PRAISE FOR THE NOVELS OF

Christina Lauren

"What a joyful, warm, touching book! I laughed so hard I cried more than once, I felt the embrace of Olive's huge, loving, complicated, hilarious family, and my heart soared at the ending. This is the book to read if you want to smile so hard your face hurts."

—Jasmine Guillory, *New York Times* bestselling author of *The Wedding Party*, on *The Unhoneymooners*

"Readers will laugh out loud. . . . Perfect for fans of Jasmine Guillory and Sally Thorne."

—*Booklist* on *The Unhoneymooners*

"Witty and downright hilarious, with just the right amount of heart, *The Unhoneymooners* is a perfect feel-good romantic comedy. Prepare to laugh and smile from cover to cover."

—Helen Hoang, author of *The Bride Test*, on *The Unhoneymooners*

"With a then-and-now plot similar to Lauren's *Love and Other Words*, the writing duo's latest has a youthful voice that may be a good fit for fans of new adult romances."

—*Library Journal* on *Twice in a Blue Moon*

"[The] story . . . is worth the wait, and the rich family backstories add sweetness . . . [with] a twist that offers readers something unexpected and new."

—*Kirkus Reviews* on *Twice in a Blue Moon*

"Readers inclined toward narratives of forgiveness will appreciate this story of learning to leave the past in the past."

—*Publishers Weekly* on *Twice in a Blue Moon*

"This is a messy and sexy look at digital dating that feels fresh and exciting."

—*Publishers Weekly* on *My Favorite Half-Night Stand* (starred review)

"You can never go wrong with a Christina Lauren novel. . . . A delectable, moving take on modern dating reminding us all that when it comes to intoxicating, sexy, playful romance that has its finger on the pulse of contemporary love, this duo always swipes right."

—*Entertainment Weekly* on *My Favorite Half-Night Stand*

"The story skips along . . . propelled by rom-com momentum and charm."

—*The New York Times Book Review* on *Josh and Hazel's Guide to Not Dating*

"With exuberant humor and unforgettable characters, this romantic comedy is a standout."

—*Kirkus Reviews* on *Josh and Hazel's Guide to Not Dating* (starred review)

"From Lauren's wit to her love of wordplay and literature to swoony love scenes to heroines who learn to set aside their own self-doubts . . . Lauren writes of the bittersweet pangs of love and loss with piercing clarity."

—*Entertainment Weekly* on
Love and Other Words

"A triumph . . . a true joy from start to finish."

—Kristin Harmel, internationally bestselling
author of *The Room on Rue Amélie,* on
Love and Other Words

"Lauren's stand-alone brims with authentic characters and a captivating plot."

—*Publishers Weekly* on *Roomies* (starred review)

"Delightful."

—*People* on *Roomies*

"At turns hilarious and gut-wrenching, this is a tremendously fun slow burn."

—*The Washington Post* on *Dating You / Hating You*
(A Best Romance of 2017 selection)

"Christina Lauren hilariously depicts modern dating."

—*Us Weekly* on *Dating You / Hating You*

ALSO BY
Christina Lauren

Dating You / Hating You
Roomies
Love and Other Words
Josh and Hazel's Guide to Not Dating
My Favorite Half-Night Stand
The Unhoneymooners
Twice in a Blue Moon

THE BEAUTIFUL SERIES

Beautiful Bastard
Beautiful Stranger
Beautiful Bitch
Beautiful Bombshell
Beautiful Player
Beautiful Beginning
Beautiful Beloved
Beautiful Secret
Beautiful Boss
Beautiful

THE WILD SEASONS SERIES

Sweet Filthy Boy
Dirty Rowdy Thing
Dark Wild Night
Wicked Sexy Liar

YOUNG ADULT

The House
Sublime
Autoboyography

THE *honey*-DON'T LIST

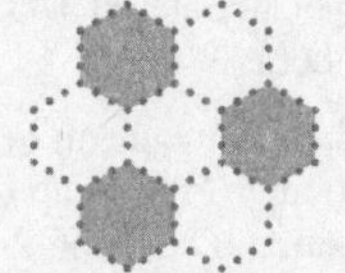

CHRISTINA LAUREN

GALLERY BOOKS
New York London Toronto Sydney New Delhi

Gallery Books
An Imprint of Simon & Schuster, Inc.
1230 Avenue of the Americas
New York, NY 10020

This book is a work of fiction. Any references to historical events, real people, or real places are used fictitiously. Other names, characters, places, and events are products of the author's imagination, and any resemblance to actual events or places or persons, living or dead, is entirely coincidental.

First Gallery Books trade paperback edition March 2020

Interior design by Lexy Alemao

Manufactured in the United States of America

10 9 8 7 6 5 4 3 2 1

Library of Congress Cataloging in Publication Data

Names: Lauren, Christina, author.
Title: The honey-don't list / Christina Lauren.
Other titles: Honey-do not list
Description: First Gallery Books trade paperback edition. |
New York : Gallery Books, 2020.
Identifiers: LCCN 2019035443 (print) | LCCN 2019035444 (ebook) |
ISBN 9781982123918 (paperback) | ISBN 9781982123932 (ebook)
Subjects: GSAFD: Love stories.
Classification: LCC PS3612.A9442273 H66 2020 (print) |
LCC PS3612.A9442273 (ebook) | DDC 813/.6—dc23
LC record available at https://lccn.loc.gov/2019035443
LC ebook record available at https://lccn.loc.gov/2019035444

ISBN 978-1-9821-2391-8
ISBN 978-1-9821-2393-2 (ebook)

To the people working tirelessly behind the scenes,
this one is for you.

Partial transcript of interview with James McCann, July 14

Officer Martin: Can you state your name, date of birth, and occupation for the record?

James McCann: James Westman McCann, August 27, 1990. Director of engineering for Comb+Honey Renovations.

Officer Martin: I have a note here that you're an assistant to Russell "Rusty" Tripp?

JM: I occasionally help with assistant duties when our workload is overwhelming, but I was hired by Mr. Tripp to be the primary consultant for engineering and structural design. Can you please write that part down?

Officer Martin: It will all go on record, don't worry. And where were you on July 13?

JM: I was with Melissa and Rusty here in Laramie, Wyoming.

Officer Martin: You're referring to Russell's wife, Melissa?

JM: Correct.

Officer Martin: Was anyone else there?

JM: Melissa's assistant, Carey Duncan.

Officer Martin: Did you have any sense, before the night in question, that things would get out of hand?

JM: I think we all knew that by this point their marriage was on a pretty shaky foundation—no pun intended—but none of us expected it to get this bad.

Partial transcript of interview with Carey Duncan, July 14

Officer Ali: Can you state your full name, date of birth, and occupation for the record?

Carey Duncan: Like, *full* full name?

Officer Ali: Please.

CD: Fine. Carey Fern Duncan. March 1, 1994, executive assistant to Melissa Tripp.

Officer Ali: And where were you the night of July 13?

Carey: I was in Laramie, Wyoming, with the Tripps.

Officer Ali: Can you state for the record who the Tripps are?

CD: Sure. Melissa and Rusty Tripp are the co-owners of Comb+Honey. But most people know them from their books or TV.

Officer Ali: Rusty would be Russell Tripp?

CD: Yeah, sorry. Melly—*Melissa*—only calls him Russell when she's pissed.

Officer Ali: Can you list who else was present at the scene?

CD: It was me, Rusty and Melly, obviously, and James McCann.

Officer Ali: Was James McCann also employed by the Tripps?

CD: Don't you have all this information already?

Officer Ali: Please just answer the question, Ms. Duncan.

CD: Do I . . . ? Do I need a lawyer?

Officer Ali: That depends. Have you done something that requires a lawyer?

CD: Ever?

Officer Ali: In relation to the events that occurred on July 13 of this year.

CD: Oh. No. I wasn't—it wasn't me. You all know that, right?

Officer Ali: This isn't a courtroom and you aren't under arrest, Ms. Duncan. You aren't obligated to answer any of these questions. I'm just trying to get a sense of the night's timeline.

CD: James, Rusty, and I had just gotten back from the Hotsy Totsy bar. James and I went to get Rusty. It was sort of a mess, and Melly was *pissed*, and—

Officer Ali: I think we're getting ahead of ourselves. We need to go back a little further.

CD: How far back do you want me to go?

Officer Ali: How about the beginning?

CD: I started working for Melly when I was sixteen. I'm not sure you want me to go that far back.

Officer Ali: Let's begin with the end of their first television show, *New Spaces.*

CD: Yeah. Okay. That's a good place to start.

Carey

When I was little, my family had a hen named Dorothy. My dad called her Dotty for short. She was a Blue Laced Red Wyandotte—fairly fancy chicken for our neck of the woods. Her terra-cotta feathers were tipped with blue, and so unusual in color they didn't look like they were real. Dorothy stood out against the dusty background of our small Wyoming farm and was always the center of attention in the yard. She was prettier than the other hens, she was definitely noisier, and despite lower-than-normal fertility rates among the breed, she laid twice as many eggs. It's not that the other hens weren't perfectly good chickens; it's that Dorothy was that much better.

She was also sort of a bully.

I'm always reminded of Dorothy when I look at Melissa Tripp. I realize how that sounds—comparing my boss to a chicken—but it's the image that pops into my head every time I see Melly holding court, like she is right now at the party. Dorothy would strut around the coop, head high, pecking at everything she could reach and daring the other hens to come at her. Like her, Melly sweeps around the room, comfortable knowing every eye is on her, daring someone else to take center stage.

"Can I have everyone's attention, please?" The crowd quiets as Melissa holds a Waterford champagne flute aloft, her bright blue eyes glistening with unshed tears. Melly drinks only when there's no getting around it, and most don't realize that there's sparkling cider in that glass, not champagne.

"Alcohol is nothing but empty calories and can make you messy," she once told me. "I have zero time for either." With a Tiffany bracelet dangling from her tiny wrist, she'd taken the glass of rosé from my hand and given me a judgmental once-over. "As long as you work for me, Carey, neither do you."

Turns out, she's not wrong. With Melly and her husband Rusty's current home renovation show, *New Spaces*, officially wrapping today, their newest book releasing in two days, and the super-secret, as-yet-unannounced new streaming show launching in a matter of days, I've hardly had time to sleep, let alone get my drink on. But for the love of God, a night with no work, my DVR, and a couple of beers would be divine.

Sadly, as you've probably guessed, there's sparkling cider in my champagne flute, too.

Melly's pink lips curve into a bittersweet smile as she surveys the quieting crowd now watching her expectantly. Hand pressed to her heart, she makes sure to look at each member of the television crew in turn. "Sixty-five episodes, three holiday specials, countless promo clips, and one very large going-away party. We couldn't have done any of this without each and every one of you."

Another round of solemn eye contact, a pause. A resigned nod that makes her sleek platinum hair fall gracefully around her shoulders.

"Five seasons!" When she thrusts her glass forward in the air in cheers, her wedding ring catches the overhead set lights and casts stars across the walls.

Hearing it really does blow my mind. We're standing in the set where we've shot five seasons of the show, and it all went by in a blip—probably because I didn't sleep for most of it—and now it's ending. I met Melissa Tripp when I was sixteen, on the verge of dropping out of high school and needing to make some money because my parents didn't have any to spare. The Tripps had recently opened their home décor store, Comb+Honey, in Jackson, Wyoming, and posted a HELP WANTED sign in the window. Although the local Hardee's hired, on principle, any high schooler from our area who wanted a job, the idea of working as a fry cook between Mitch "Sticky Hands" Saxton and John "Toothless" McGinnis wasn't tempting. So I walked inside the upscale store and applied.

I'm still not sure what I was thinking or what she saw in me. I was in my *good* cutoffs, and my fingers were still smudged with charcoal from sketching under the bleachers instead of attending my last two classes of the day. I smelled like sunblock and my hair was bleached to a fine, pale crisp, but I was hired.

For the first few months, I helped customers whenever Melly was busy, and eventually ran the register. Once I got that down, she let me start managing custom orders and invoices. When Melly learned more about my love for art, she pushed me to play around and dress up the window displays—on two conditions: it couldn't interfere with my regular duties, and I had to finish high school.

Melissa and Rusty were sweet as pie back then: parents to two kids, struggling to get their business off the ground, and head over heels for each other. They treated me like their third kid, and celebrated my remaining high school victories when my own parents slacked on the job. Mom and Dad had always been better at yelling at me and my brothers for being ungrateful than they were at earning our respect. Suddenly the Tripps were there, showing up to my art shows, driving me to dentist appointments, and even helping me buy my first car. I would have happily given them my right arm if they asked for it.

But that was ten years and a lifetime ago. Comb+Honey isn't just a home redesign store anymore; it's a booming corporation with ten storefronts and a host of exclusive product lines with a dozen retail partnerships. The Tripp kids are in their twenties, and Melly has new boobs, lashes, and teeth. Rusty has been outfitted as the fashion icon carpenter dad in Dior jeans and Burberry blazers. The world knows them as affectionate, playful, cooperative, and innovative.

And fun: their seven million Instagram followers are treated less to glossy promotional shots and more to video clips of Rusty pulling pranks on the *New Spaces* cast and crew, Melly visiting an estate sale and happening upon the perfect addition to a remodel, and photos of Melly and Rusty being adorable or adorably exasperated with each other. Fan favorites are the GIFs of Rusty being Rusty:

dropping a hammer on his foot, clumsily spilling a bottle of Coke onto one of Melly's famous honey-do lists, messing up his intro again and again to the great amusement of the entire crew. People love Melly for being polished and patient. They love Rusty for being goofy and approachable. And they love them as a couple for being the two perfect halves of a whole.

You wouldn't know from scrolling through their idyllic Instagram feed that Melly and Rusty aren't quite as sweet on each other anymore. Looking back, I'm not really sure when they decided their marriage mattered less than their brand. It chipped away slowly. A bit of sarcasm here. An argument there. Slowly their worst sides seemed to take over: Melly is a neurotic perfectionist who never sleeps. Rusty is impulsive and easily distracted by whatever—or whoever—is around him. Luckily, only their inner circle sees this downward tilt because the Tripps still manage to put on an impressively convincing show for the public.

Like now. Rusty stands at her side, nodding and clapping at the more sentimental points in her toast. It's an after-party, so the blazer is gone and he's wearing one of his custom Broncos jerseys. *He can let loose! He's a fun dad and relatable!*

He's forty-five now, and while viewers still swoon over the strong jaw and quarterback build, they love even more the way he looks at his wife. Rusty looks at Melly like they're celebrating their first anniversary this year, not their twenty-sixth. It's the way she rolls her eyes at his jokes but then blushes, totally endearing. When they're like this, it's easy to see why their on-screen chemistry made them instant favorites on *New Spaces*. They were relatively unknown when the show started, but they—and their infectious love—immediately eclipsed the popularity of their costars, including the show's former-Miss-America host, Stephanie, and the expert, Dan—a younger, hipper home remodeling icon who'd had his own show for years.

The Tripps' outwardly enviable marriage is why Ford Motor Company used Melly and Rusty in a truck commercial. It's why they have merchandise lines at Target and Walmart, emblazoned with their bright, blissful smiles; why their two home design books have both been longtime bestsellers, and why their soon-to-be-published book on marriage is already at the top of the sales charts and hasn't even been released yet.

And, of course, Melly is an enormous stress case over the upcoming announcement of their new solo show, *Home Sweet Home*. We're all overwhelmed, trying to strike while the iron's hot, but what else can we do but work our hardest?

"Some people might say what we do is *just decorating*." Melly is apparently not finished addressing the crowd, because she pulls attention back to where she stands at the front of the room. The table behind her is filled with empty champagne bottles and the remnants of a stunning six-tier petal-pink cake.

"They say it's *just home remodel*," she continues. "Just design." Her high, sugary voice works well for TV because it matches her bubbly personality, white-blond hair, and animated expressions. But off set—and especially when she's displeased and on a tear—that voice becomes cartoonish and piercingly loud. "But it's always been our motto that the home reflects the person. Build the home you want, be flexible, and life will be a Tripp! Thank you for helping us share our philosophy! We love you all. Here's to the next chapter!"

A chorus of cheers echoes through the group. Everyone drains their glasses and disperses to offer congratulations. *Now* the toast is over—never mind that the cast of *New Spaces* is composed of four independently famous individuals, and Melly has just monopolized the moment and ended with her own personal slogan, making it clear that no one else is going to speak in acknowledgment of what they've all accomplished together.

I glance over to gauge the reaction of Stephanie Flores, the aforementioned former Miss America, social media darling, and host of *New Spaces*. She seems to be keeping her eyes from rolling with great effort. Renovation god Dan Eiler is huddled with a producer, speaking in hushed, angry tones and jutting his chin toward the front of the room, where Melly just stood. Publicly, the show is ending so that everyone can pursue other new adventures—like the Tripps starting *Home Sweet Home*—but honestly I think it's ending because no one can stand in Melly's ever-growing shadow anymore. She may wear a size two and need sky-high heels to reach the top shelf in her own stockroom, but she is the alpha dog, and she will never let you forget it.

I see Rusty tug at Melly's hand and nod toward the door. I don't need to be a lip reader to know that she's reminding him that this is their party—they have guests. Never mind that this entire room full of people essentially works for the

Tripps, and a party with your boss isn't really a party. I don't think anyone would be all that disappointed if Melly and Rusty called it a night.

Setting my drink on the tray of a passing waiter, I check my watch and wince when I see that it's almost eleven. Melly catches my eye across the room and looks around us in commiserating horror. *What a mess*, her expression groans. I scream through a smile; this mess is not her problem. Whether or not Rusty and Melly decide to stay, I am nowhere close to getting out of here. Sure, we have waiters circulating food, but in a half hour they'll get to toss their aprons into the back of a catering van and head home. I'll be left cleaning up.

I do the mental math. If I can get the place cleaned by one, I might be able to catch a few hours of sleep before our nine o'clock meeting. Netflix execs are actually flying to Jackson freaking Hole first thing tomorrow for a face-to-face, and the day after that, the Tripps leave for their book launch in Los Angeles and *I* get an entire week of living in my pajamas and not answering text messages in the middle of the night. I have to remind myself that this is mile twenty-five of the marathon; if I can just make it two more days, I can crash. But I'm running on tired legs: Before even prepping the wrap party today, we shot the remaining scenes for the two final *New Spaces* episodes—one with a family remodeling their craftsman home to welcome their first baby, and a five-season retrospective to close out the show. A normal day with Melissa Tripp is exhausting. Today was completely debilitating, and it's not over yet.

I exhale slowly, calmly, surveying the damage to the room, and decide one way to let people know they should start heading home is to begin cleaning up.

A few minutes later, a shadow appears at my side. I can sense by its tense, annoyed presence exactly who it is. "Did you see where Rusty went?"

I look up at James McCann: tall, lanky, always exuding superiority.

"I'm not in charge of Rusty," I say. "He's yours."

He stares for an annoyed beat, but I know it's only partially meant for me. I'm an assistant and have been for the entirety of my adult life. By contrast, James—a nerdy engineering type—wasn't hired to work as Rusty's right-hand man, but that's exactly how his job has panned out. Midnight beer runs, dry-cleaning duty, sports ticket procurement, and daily coffee retrieval. Not what he bargained for at all.

"We have an early meeting with the Netflix folks tomorrow," he tells me, as if it hasn't been a topic of conversation—the date all but branded onto my brain—for weeks. As if we aren't all sweating bullets about how the new show is going to fare with audiences and what that will mean for the company.

"I remember, James." I slide a cluster of empty beer cans into a recycling bin.

"In fairness, you never write anything down or log in to the shared calendar. I thought I'd check in." Unfortunately he misses my eye roll when he blinks down to his watch and then out over the room, tense again. "Don't you think we should be wrapping this up?"

This question could only come from someone who works for Rusty, a boss who is used to being bossed around.

Anyone who works for Melissa Tripp would know that trying to shepherd her out of a party in her honor is like trying to get a cat to tap-dance.

"Probably," I say.

I carefully drop a few empty champagne bottles into the recycling bin before shaking out my hands. It's been a long day, and the left one is starting to act up. At this point, massage doesn't really help, but I try to casually rub out my fingers before moving on.

"I don't know why you're following me when he's over there," I say, and motion toward the front of the room, where Melly gave their speech.

"Over where?"

I groan in frustration and turn to show him. But my irritated smugness dissipates when I find only Melly near the remains of the frilly pink cake. I don't see Rusty anywhere. "Have you texted him?"

James gives me a blank stare through the perfectly unsmudged lenses of his glasses. From this close, it's impossible to miss that he has really pretty eyes. But, like many men, he ruins the effect by speaking. "Don't you think I'd do that before asking you?"

"Just checking," I say.

His brows come together in irritation, which makes his glasses slide down his nose. "I texted him. He's not answering."

"Maybe he's in the bathroom." I step around him, tired of being in charge of everyone every second of the day.

"He'd definitely answer if he was in the bathroom," James says, following close behind. "He takes his phone everywhere so he can check sports scores."

James is obviously a smart man—Lord knows he reminds me all the time—but like my dad used to say, sometimes I wonder if he's only got one oar in the water. Is he incapable of walking around a set and finding a six-foot-four grown man by himself? I'm about to blow up and ask him, but when I look up I'm surprised by the desperation in his eyes. The dread and suspicion there make my stomach sink.

I pass my gaze around the room—to the back corner where some of the set designers are opening fresh beers, to the small seating area where Dan is now pretending to enjoy chatting with Melly. In the crowd of nearly seventy people, I don't see Rusty, either.

"You don't want to go searching, do you?" I ask quietly, on instinct.

James shakes his head slowly, and we share an extended beat of eye contact. It's not that I immediately suspect anything, but like I said, Rusty can be impulsive. Who knows what kind of trouble he could be getting into?

"Maybe he's out getting high with some of the camera guys," I say.

Another shake of his head. "He doesn't like to smoke, and he tried edibles a few weeks ago and said he'd never do that again."

"Maybe he left?" I say.

"Without telling us?"

I exhale a shaky breath, growing a little uneasy myself. "I swear to God, if he's cheating on his diet . . ." On Rusty's current honey-do list is Melly's instruction that he lose a few pounds before the new show is announced. According to her, he looks puffy on-screen. If he's hiding somewhere with cake in his lap I'll never hear the end of it.

For the most part James and I have kept to our own schedules since he joined Comb+Honey two months ago. It's not that I dislike him, exactly, but the way he writes off my job as disposable and frivolous and treats me like I'm only intelligent enough for remedial assistant activities—unless he needs help performing one himself, of course—really pisses me off. But I don't want to pretend the Tripps' world would be an easy one to walk into and immediately comprehend, either. Even I sometimes have no idea what's going on with them. Rusty and Melly pay well and make it possible for me to keep the health coverage I need, but their relationship is obviously complicated.

"Okay," I finally say. "Let's go find him."

With a grimace, James follows me out of the main room and down the hall that leads to the warehouse. The air conditioner seems abnormally loud in the small space, loud enough to drown out James's clunky footsteps on the industrial carpet behind me. Along the way there are five doors, each closed. One is an A/V room, the next is a janitor closet. After that there's a greenroom for visiting guests, a small crew lounge, and the editing studio. Trying to imagine what we'll find inside any of these tonight makes me queasy.

The A/V room is dark and empty. The door hinge squeaks into the quiet room.

The janitor closet is locked, and too small to be useful as a hiding place for a grown man.

The greenroom is empty; the crew lounge, too.

The soundproof editing booth is last, and the door is locked.

I'm not sure why I'm nervous as I pull my key ring off my belt and find the right key, focusing to keep my right hand still as I carefully slide it into the lock.

We both hold our breaths as the knob slowly turns.

The sound hits us first—deep groans, skin slapping against skin—followed by the briefest flash of thrusting white butt cheeks, swinging testicles, and a bright red floral dress pushed up over a woman's shoulders, her dark hair really all that is visible of her. It takes a couple of grunts and thrusts before my brain connects the dots and melts. Unspotted, I carefully pull the door shut again.

Rusty was definitely not eating cake.

I slowly turn around. James is still staring past me at the now-closed door, unblinking, mouth open.

"That was *Rusty*," he whispers.

I give Captain Obvious a nod. "Yes."

They have a TV show and a book coming out. A book on *relationships*. Rusty—and his thrusting butt—has impeccable timing. "And *Stephanie*," James adds.

I hoped I was the only one who realized that, but no such luck. I exhale slowly, already trying to mentally Tetris my way out of what I just saw. Moments like this make me realize why professional distance is a good thing. I've done holidays with the Tripps and watched as they grew from owners of a single store to rulers of an empire. Literally no part of my life isn't somehow tied up and overlapped with theirs.

"Yes, James, with Stephanie." I press the heels of my hands to my eyes, trying to figure out what the correct response is here.

When I look back at him, James is staring at me, his eyes round with shock. *"But he's MARRIE—"*

I clap a shaking hand over his mouth. "Shut up, oh my God!" I look up and down the hall to make sure no one has witnessed what we've witnessed. "Shhhhhhhh!"

I pull him with me around the corner toward the warehouse. A vent blows overhead, hopefully masking our voices. "You have got to keep your cool about this!" I haven't even figured out how *I* feel; I cannot deal with James freaking out on top of it.

"Carey, he's *cheating on his wife*!"

I stare at him for an astonished beat. Did we not both just witness Rusty and his swinging balls? I visibly shudder. "I got that."

"But . . ." James trails off, bewildered. "Doesn't that bother you?"

"Of course it bothers me," I tell him calmly, trying to not feel frustrated that this newbie, of all people, is telling me how to react to a couple I've known my entire adult life. Defensiveness bubbles to the surface. "But I've worked for them for a long time, and I learned years ago that some things are not my business."

Marriages have ups and downs, Melly told me once. *I need you to focus on the work, not what's happening between me and Russ.*

I'd grown up watching my dad come home stumbling drunk and reeking of perfume, only to see him and Mom happily canoodling on the couch two days later, enough times to know Melly was right. The lines are blurry in this job, but I do my best to let the Tripps' marriage be their marriage, and their business be my business.

From his expression, I gather James is not on board with Operation Look the Other Way. And his horror triggers an uncomfortable dissolving sensation in my stomach. I'm mad and sad and frankly horrified by what we just saw, but I can't help but feel embarrassed and slightly protective, too. I shove my hands into my pockets.

"They're about to release their book on relationships," he says, voice high and tight. "Their book *of marital advice*."

I shift on my feet. "I know."

"And launch a new show that's based almost entirely on their brand!" he says, struggling to keep his voice down. "That brand being their blissful marriage!"

I work to hide my irritation. To be honest, I don't see James often because, whether he likes it or not, so far he's good at his job and keeps Rusty in line. So much so, in fact, that I didn't realize Rusty was having another affair.

I narrow my eyes. "You're sure you didn't know about this? You were awfully reluctant to go looking for him."

James flushes. "I thought I'd catch him eating a *sandwich*, Carey, not"—he points behind him, back to the room—"*that*."

I deflate. "Yeah, me too." I close my eyes, take a deep breath, and then look around the empty hallway. "We can't let anyone else down here."

"You're not going to tell her," he guesses, frowning. "Are you?"

Defensiveness is my default: "Melly made it clear a number of years ago that she wants me and all assistants to stay out of her private life. That includes you."

I can see by the way his chest rises that his first instinct is to correct me—yet again—that he is not an assistant, but self-preservation wins out. "This could all blow up in our faces," he tells me. "You get that, right?"

"What do you want me to do?"

He takes another deep breath. "I think we need to tell Melissa."

"You also thought we should go find him, and you can see how well that turned out."

He gives me a long stare.

"I am not telling Melly that we saw her husband plowing their cohost." I laugh. "*Hell* no."

Talking to them about this would be like talking to my parents, but multiplied by the Also My Employer factor of awkward. James probably doesn't realize that my relationship with the Tripps isn't just employer-employee. How would he? We barely interact.

But I can't be the one to rat out Rusty. My dad died when I was seventeen. He'd been noticing some swelling in his legs and feet but brushed it off as a hazard of working on his feet all day, climbing up and down ladders and sometimes having to work on his knees. He put off seeing a doctor until it was too late. Years of smoking had left him with stage-four lung cancer, and he died within just a couple of months. Rusty tried not to be obvious about stepping in, but he's always been there when I needed him. Not to mention he distracts Melly when she goes off on one of her tirades, and he gives me free rein in his shop whenever I have time. I really don't want to do this.

James looks at me, silently disappointed. "Carey."

"Maybe she already knows?" I ask hopefully.

"If she knows," he begins, "then she needs to tell him to be more discreet. It could have been anyone walking into that room, and someone with less loyalty and a cell phone camera could have blown up their entire livelihood, and ours, with a single tweet."

It's physically painful to admit that he's right. Freaking Rusty.

"Fine," I say, but decide to give myself a temporary reprieve. "We'll check in with her tomorrow after the meeting."

"*Check in* with her?"

"God, why are you like this? We'll *tell* her after the meeting. Are you happy?"

He wearily pushes a hand through his hair. "Not even a little bit."

We both jump at a voice coming out of the quiet hall. "Tell who what after the meeting?"

It's Robyn, the Tripps' publicist: a tightly coiled, neurotic busybody.

"Nothing." I wave her away with false ease.

"Come on," she says, face pinched. "You're down here hiding when you should be getting things organized and packed up out there." She looks between us. "Clearly something is going on."

I resent the reminder that I need to be cleaning up after all these people and mentally give Robyn the finger. "James and I were saying that we need to talk to Melly tomorrow. I'll let her know—"

"Why does James need to talk to her?" Robyn asks, too astute for her own good. Melly has never needed James for anything that didn't need to be opened or reached on a high shelf. "Is it a big deal?"

I give a breezy "No" just as James utters an emphatic "*Yes*."

I turn to glare at him. He glares back at me.

"Robyn should know," he says quietly, and in my head I'm grabbing my hair at the roots, yelling, *Goddammit, James, be cool!*

But Robyn seems to be picking up what we're putting down. She chews her lip, worrying for a reason now. "We'll do it tonight."

I let out an incredulous laugh. "It's already been a really long day, and I still need to clean up once everyone goes."

Now would be a great time for one or both of them to offer to help, but the silence is thunderous.

Robyn sighs deeply and checks her watch. "Netflix is at nine. I'll grab Melissa and meet you both in the office in an hour."

An hour means that I'll have to hustle my ass off here and then book it over to the Comb+Honey offices across town. Awesome.

Robyn turns to leave, and I glare again at James, who gives me a triumphant smile. "We're doing the right thing," he says.

"We now have a work meeting at midnight."

"It's the right thing," he repeats.

One hour. He's lucky that doesn't leave me enough time to make a James McCann voodoo doll.

Partial transcript of interview with Carey Duncan, July 14

Officer Ali: Ms. Duncan, have you ever seen Melissa Tripp angry before?

Carey Duncan: Is that a serious question?

Officer Ali: Am I to take that as a yes?

CD: She's my boss. Of course I've seen her angry.

Officer Ali: Can you elaborate?

CD: How long do you have?

Officer Ali: Ms. Duncan. Please answer the question to the best of your ability.

CD: Melly is a perfectionist. She's ambitious and impatient, but she's also insecure. It's a bad combination.

Officer Ali: Would you say she has a temper?

CD: Yes.

Officer Ali: I see. What about toward Mr. Tripp? Have you ever seen her angry with him?

CD: They've been married for twenty-six years. So, yeah.

Officer Ali: Carey, can you talk about the first time to your knowledge that Rusty Tripp had an affair?

CD: Well, it was the year after I started. So 2011, I think, with his old assistant, Marianne. It was just the two of us in the store—Melly and me—but then her friend Susan came running in like a cat on fire. She grabbed Melly and took her into the back and closed the door, and pretty soon Rusty showed up, totally freaked out, and went in after them. I'm guessing Susan caught Rusty doing something. If you know what I mean. Susan left, and maybe a minute went by before all hell broke loose.

Officer Ali: You're saying Mrs. Tripp was upset.

CD: "Upset"? That's a nice way to put it. They came out of the office yelling at each other, and Melly just lost it. Started calling him a liar, a cheat—lots of names. Then she started throwing stuff, at him, around the store. Melly is really big on appearances and coming off very prim and proper and family-oriented. She never swears—it's actually sort of a rule that anybody who works for her shouldn't, either. But wow, she can.

Officer Ali: Was Mr. Tripp injured?

CD: No, not that I can remember. I'm sure you've seen Melly. She's tiny and couldn't hit the broad side of a barn with a shovel.

Officer Ali: And what happened then?

CD: It was pretty awkward, so I went home.

Officer Ali: I mean more generally. What happened afterward between Mr. and Mrs. Tripp?

CD: They must have worked it out because he was there the next day, all bright and shiny like nothing had happened.

Officer Ali: The next day? Didn't that seem odd to you?

CD: I mean, I was seventeen and my parents used to fight constantly, so not really. Plus, things were really starting to take off for the Tripps, and Melly would never have let something like that get in the way of what she wanted. She told Rusty that if he ever did it again she'd leave and take him for everything he had, and got back to work. He's always been really flirty. That's probably how we ended up with James, eventually.

Officer Ali: Maybe you can clear that up for me. I show that James graduated from Vassar and MIT, but he works as Mr. Tripp's assistant?

CD: Rusty is what my grandma used to call a tomcat's kitten: a giant flirt but relatively harmless. Melly just doesn't like women working for him, plain and simple. The assistant position happened to be open at the same time that Rusty was looking for an engineer for the show. James was there interviewing for the engineering job, but when Melissa saw him sitting outside Rusty's office, she hired him on the spot. Told Rusty he could do both jobs, probably because Melly doesn't know much about either engineering *or* being someone's assistant. On paper James is the primary structural something something. But he still picks up the dry-cleaning, just like I do. Heaven forbid you call him an assistant, though. "I'm an engineer. Smart words, smart words, blah blah."

Officer Ari: So, back to Mrs. Tripp and the incident between Melissa and Rusty at the store. Was this when *New Spaces* was filming? Or earlier?

CD: Oh, like way earlier. This was just after the *Wyoming Tribune* did an article on Comb+Honey—the original design store in Jackson. The window displays got a lot of local attention, and the general aesthetic was getting really popular in town. Rusty's original woodworking pieces were selling like crazy. After the *Trib* article, there was a feature in the lifestyle section of the *LA Times*, and that caught the attention of HGTV. So, in 2014 Melly and Rusty were cast on *New Spaces*, with Stephanie and Dan. In hindsight, I think that's when Rusty got bored, and Melly's ambition got the best of her. The cracks started showing again. At least to me.

James

It's 1:11 a.m.

I'm not going to look at the clock for five minutes.

I'm not going to look at the clock for five minutes.

I'm not going to—

1:13 a.m.

Goddammit.

We were supposed to meet here over an hour ago, and Melissa and Robyn still haven't appeared. It feels like we've been waiting for a year. Ignoring Carey's occasional glares in my direction, I shift on the long leather couch in Melissa and Rusty's office and let my head hang over the aesthetically pleasing but completely uncomfortable low armrest. From this angle, the open staircase in the corner looks like it's on the ceiling, and the idea of that—of creating something so counterintuitive and wild—sends a hot burst of adrenaline into my blood.

I look at the clock again. 1:15 a.m.

I groan, rubbing my eyes with the heels of my hands. "Okay," I finally admit. "You were right."

Carey is quiet in response. Knowing she's worked for the Tripps since long before I came around, I can't help but wonder whether she's ever heard those three words together before.

"I'm torn between wanting to get this conversation over with," Carey finally says from the other side of the room, "and wanting to postpone it forever."

"Our Netflix meeting is at—"

"Nine," she interrupts, and I hear the edge of irritation return to her voice. "Trust me, James, it would be impossible to forget."

It may seem strange that tonight is probably the first time Carey and I have been alone in a room together since I took this job, but it isn't, really. The Tripps aren't usually in the same place at the same time unless they're filming. Which means that Carey and I are rarely in the same place at the same time, either.

I look over at her again. It's not like there's a lot more to do while we're waiting for Melissa to arrive and for the most awkward conversation of the century to begin. My brain was too chaotic earlier to really take her in.

Carey is taller than I think I realized, with dark blond hair that, right now, is messily piled on her head. Her eyes are green, blue, something like that. My guess is she's aware that people aren't looking at her in this job because she usually dresses casually, but she must have dressed down even more sometime between cleaning up the warehouse and coming in to the office. She's wearing gray sweats, untied sneakers, and a sweatshirt with the words NAMA-STAY IN

BED. She's also a fidgeter. We might not have spent a lot of time together, but it's one of the first things I noticed. Her hands are always moving or clenched into fists. I'm not sure if it's some kind of nervous tic, or what exactly, but she sits on them a lot or keeps them hidden under the table. And I could be wrong, but I don't think she likes being touched. She shrinks against a wall when I pass too close or takes a step back if we both reach for something at the same time. I don't take it personally—we all have our stuff—and do my best to respect that and not do anything that might make her uncomfortable.

She also has some of the oddest sayings. At the end of our first meeting together she stood up and said she had to hit the bushes. It was only later that I realized she meant she had to use the restroom, and I still don't understand why she didn't just say that.

Right now she's messing with one of the bookcases, frowning at the way it won't rotate the full one-eighty to display the books on the other side of the shelf. It's a classic Tripp design—made to best utilize whatever limited space is available. Carey checks a few of the bearings and finds a stuck pin, fiddles with it for a moment before it resets, and then lets out a quiet, satisfied "There" when the shelf glides easily again.

"Exactly how long have you worked for Melissa?" I ask her. She bends to inspect another shelf, a small furrow of her forehead the only indication that she's heard me.

"About ten years."

I feel my eyes go wide. "How old are you?"

She hesitates. "Twenty-six."

Wow. Wow. Wow.

I study her again. She's fresh-faced and so innocently unsophisticated she seems more like a new intern and not the person in charge of nearly every logistical detail of the Tripps' schedule.

Is this the only job she's ever had? I'm the new guy and am still piecing everyone together, but I've been here long enough to know that Melissa and Carey's relationship is not healthy. Ten years together, though, would certainly explain how Carey anticipates all of Melissa's needs before even Melissa is aware of them, and how Melissa can't or won't do anything without Carey at her side.

"Have you always been her assistant?"

"No, I started as a cashier in their first store," she says. "I've done pretty much every job there. When things took off, I just stayed with them." She glances over and seems suddenly aware of my attention. I blink away. She moves to the opposite side of the bookcase. "What did you do before you came here?"

I'm saved from having to answer this when the doorknob turns, and both Carey and I turn to see Rusty walk in ahead of Melissa and Robyn—a willowy, nervous bird of a woman.

"Jim, Carey!" he bellows in greeting. His smile is as loose from inebriation as Melissa's is tight from irritation.

"James," I correct in response, almost like a script I have no choice but to follow. Of the great many things that seem to bring Russell Tripp joy in this world, near the top has to be calling me any variation of Jim. Even better is calling

Carey and me "Jim Carrey," like it's the world's cleverest joke.

He laughs, slapping my shoulder as he passes. "You know I'm kidding, Jimbo!"

Lowering himself into a chair across from me, he winks. Rusty Tripp is hard to despise, despite his best efforts—swinging testicles and all—and given his jovial mood, it's clear he has no idea that we saw him . . . or what's about to go down.

Melissa glides across the room like a vampire, slipping her heels off and tucking them into a cubby in a sleek black bench near the window. She gives a pointed look to Rusty's feet, propped on the delicate suede ottoman. Without the benefit of the added height, Melissa is minuscule and suddenly looks very, very tired. But one glance at the fiery glint in her eyes and I know that anyone who suggests this is—

"You look exhausted, Mel." Robyn frowns in concern.

Rusty, Carey, and I—in unison—suck in our breath and hold it.

If I've learned one thing in the last two months, it's that Melissa Tripp does not like being called Mel; nor does she appreciate any suggestion that she is tired, sad, worried, no longer in her twenties, or in any other way human.

"I am *fine*, Robyn," she hisses, and gracefully sits down in the chair beside Rusty. I'm aware if a camera were near she would reach over and casually link her fingers with his. As it is, with only the five of us in the chilly, dark room, she hasn't even looked at his face yet.

"So what's up, guys?" Rusty asks, glancing from me to Carey as she takes a seat on the couch at my side.

Per usual, Robyn paces in the background, tapping at her phone.

Carey looks at me. I look at her. When we requested this quick conversation, we were both expecting Melissa to come alone. It is infinitely more awkward with Rusty here, and almost impossible to imagine having this conversation with Robyn's nervous energy further cloying the space.

"We really just wanted a word with Melly," Carey explains carefully.

Melissa's eyes narrow, but despite her being close to forty-five, not a single line creases her face. "Both of you?" she asks.

I clear my throat. I don't usually talk to Melissa. "It's personal."

"Are you two fucking?" She's glaring at Carey when she guns this question at us, so she misses the way I nearly swallow my tongue.

"No." Carey's jaw clenches as she and Melissa engage in a silent stare-down, and I internally urge her to not break eye contact, not break eye contact, not bre—

Carey looks down at the rug.

"Then just spit it out," Melissa says, and waves a tired hand as if to suggest that we're the reason she's still up, and she's ready to be done with all of this, at last. "We have no secrets."

Carey looks at me again. I look at her.

She lifts her eyebrows. *It was your fault we saw it. You say it.*

I give a quick shake of my head. *No, you've been here longer, you say it.*

She juts her chin forward. *This was* your *idea.*

She wouldn't think twice before killing me.

Her eyes narrow, so mine narrow, too.

Pushing out a breath, Carey finally says, "We have an entire season of *Home Sweet Home* in the can. The announcement about the new show is happening next week, on your book tour for *New Life, Old Love* . . ." She pauses. "Your, um, book about successful relationships. The hope is for this announcement to go well, and the book to hit the *New York Times* bestseller list."

Melissa lets out a low growl that makes my balls climb up into my body. "Thank you for the concise summary of all the stressors fueling my insomnia. Did you request a meeting in the middle of the night to go over the totally obvious?"

"No, I requested a meeting because earlier," Carey says, taking a deep, fortifying breath, "James and I, well, we found Rusty and Stephanie . . . together . . . in the editing studio."

Melissa's head turns. It turns so slowly, and on such a level axis, that I have to blink to stave off the mental image of Melissa Tripp's head rotating an entire 360 degrees, spinning faster and faster and eventually dislodging from her neck and flying away, out of this room.

When I open my eyes, I'm relieved to find her simply staring at her husband. But I can't read her expression or her silence. My limited experience with the Tripps is that silence generally means 1) Melissa is not in the room, or 2) Melissa is asleep. This is, frankly, terrifying.

Rusty played football in high school. He's about six foot four and has that sort of dimpled smile, clean shave, and soft floppy hair that makes him seem eternally boyish and therefore harmless. Grown doughier with age, the diet of the wealthy, and a love of American beer, Rusty's face has only become more affable, not less. Right now, he looks happy and placid, like he's not the center of a storm that's about to land directly in his company's headquarters. I've gathered that reading the room isn't his forte.

Carey looks at me. I look back at her. We both brace ourselves.

"Say that again," Melissa says to Carey, but she doesn't take her eyes off her husband.

Carey's expression tenses, and she searches my face for help—I have none—before reluctantly turning back to Melissa. "Um. That we saw Rusty with Stephanie?"

Melissa nods. "Yep. That."

Do we . . . leave the room? Is this when we step out and let them hash out whatever they need to? We don't really have to be here for this, right? Does Melissa need more proof? From the way her blank expression is slowly transitioning to one of homicidal rage, I'm guessing our word was pretty good.

Rusty bows his head and lets out the longest breath imaginable. Finally, he looks across the room at Robyn. "I don't want to do this anymore."

Melissa's sharp laugh could cut through stone. "Oh, *really*?"

"Rusty," Robyn coos as if to a child, "you don't mean that, honey."

"I do. I need a break from all of this madness."

Melissa tilts her head back and lets out a laugh so

maniacal that it could be coming from a sewer drain or a hyena standing on a pile of dead baby lions. "You want to *take a break* two days before our *marital advice book* launches?"

And with this reaction—sarcasm, not rage—I am suddenly very confused. I didn't want to be here before, but right now if I could bolt from this room and leave only a James-shaped cutout in the drywall, I would do it. I want to be anywhere but here. Send me to my aunt Tammy and uncle Jake's house in Poughkeepsie, and I'll listen to them bicker for hours. Send me back to the childhood days of soccer and my utter inability to coordinate running and kicking at the same time. Even send me back to the Worst First Date in the History of Time, with Bekah Newmann, where the Indian food didn't agree with me and I didn't quite make it to her bathroom in time.

Anywhere but here. I'm too new to this job, too unclear on what's really going on behind the facade of a happy marriage, and too eager to stop being a quasi-assistant and start doing the job I was promised: engineering unique, creative pieces for the Tripps' upcoming second season of *Home Sweet Home*.

I stand. "Carey and I can check in with you all tomor—"

"Sit. Down." Melissa's shrill voice is terrifying when she's mad, and she aims a pointed finger at the floor. "No one on this team is leaving until we figure this out."

This . . . team? Granted, given the duration of her tenure with the Tripps, I can see how Carey is a critical part of Melissa's day-to-day life—which may include being privy to certain marital dramas. But Robyn lives in New York and

I . . . well, everyone knows I'm the new guy and essentially useless here.

"You fucked Stephanie?" Melissa explodes. "*Stephanie?*"

Rusty sticks his chin out, like he's being brave by admitting it. "I tried to get you to leave the party!"

"You—?" She stares at him, speechless. "Are you stupid, Russell, or did you have a stroke?"

Inwardly, I groan. *Ugh, Melly.*

"We were hosting a party." She enunciates every word, as if she's teaching him English. "The job always comes first."

"You didn't used to say that," he says quietly.

"Am I understanding you correctly? I wouldn't leave when you wanted to, so you thought you'd just take Stephanie for a ride in the editing room instead?"

He sniffs, shaking his head. "It wasn't like that."

"She doesn't even have believable implants, you imbecile," Melissa growls, and I shift my attention to Carey, who is sinking lower into her seat, like she'd be happy if it swallowed her entirely.

This is not going down the way I expected. It's not that I completely bought into the perfect Tripp image—no marriage is all sunshine—but I would never have guessed at this. No sobbing heartbreak, no wailing demand why, no apologies; only an indifferent man and a shrewd businesswoman.

"You can't keep your dick in your pants? Fine. But to screw her at our own wrap party, where anyone could have found you? Where two of our employees *did* find you?" Melissa shakes her head. "You are so *sloppy.*" She levels this as if it's the most damning of criticisms. I suppose in the world of Melissa Tripp, it is. "I don't understand what the hell is wrong with you! Do you know how hard we've worked to get where we are?"

"I know exactly how hard we've worked," Rusty counters. "I'm telling you, I don't want to do this anymore."

His wife, her expression icy, asks, "Do *what*, exactly?"

"The book tour. The damn *books*. Hell, maybe the show."

Robyn throws up two shaking hands, immediately placating. "Okay. Whoa. Let's take a breath. Deep inhale through the nose, out through the—"

A vein appears on Melissa's otherwise smooth forehead. *"Fuck you and your breathing, Robyn, are you fucking kidding me right now?"*

I purposefully let my vision blur.

Robyn's voice wavers. "I'm going to call Ted."

Ted Cox, producer of *Home Sweet Home*, is not going to appreciate this call from Robyn at—I glance again at the clock—1:30 a.m.

Robyn puts the phone on speaker so we can all hear it ring. Melissa stands and paces the room, looking very much like she would like to pick up one of the football trophies Rusty insists on keeping and throw it at his head.

An incredibly groggy Ted comes on the phone. "Ted Cox."

I close my eyes, wincing against the disgust I feel toward anyone who answers their phone with their own name.

"Ted," Robyn says, "it's Robyn Matsuka. Listen, I have Melissa and Rusty here in a bit of a crisis. I think we need a little pep talk to get us back on track."

"We don't need a fucking *pep talk*, Ted," Melissa cries

out. "We need someone to throttle this idiot." She turns on Rusty, eyes wild. "I don't care who you screw, how much beer you drink, or how many fucking times a day you check your stupid fantasy football team lineup. What pisses me off, Russell, is you got messy. You think the press would ignore a story like this?"

"Sorry," Ted sleepily cuts in. "What's going on?"

Melissa ignores him. "Who paid off the reporter that got wind of TJ trashing a hotel room in Vegas?" She waits for Russell to answer this, and the only sound is Ted, across the line, groaning at what he now realizes he's been dragged into. When the kids get weaponized, the conversation is going nowhere good.

"You did," Rusty concedes, finally.

"That's right," Melissa says, on a roll now. "And who made sure to bury the story of Kelsey getting her stomach pumped after her first frat party?" She doesn't even wait for him to answer this time. "That's right. *Me*. Because both times, you were watching TV, or playing with your tools, and didn't bother to answer the calls. Do you think if word gets out that you're sleeping around—that our *perfect marriage* is a mess—that reporters will hesitate to dig those stories up and throw our kids' lives into the mix? Can you imagine the glee the media will have breaking the story that, not only are we terrible at being married, we're terrible parents?" She stares at him, chin wobbling. "You think if we stop now, you can keep your airplane and your Super Bowl tickets? You think we'll get to keep our four houses and your ridiculous collection of trucks? You think your kids will weather this fine, and we'll live happily ever after, rolling in cash?"

When she shakes her head, her hair comes loose from its bun, the wild strands sticking to her cheeks where tears have tracked. "No, Rusty. We'll lose everything. So, I'm sorry that you got busted sleeping with a washed-up beauty queen who can't even spell 'asbestos,' but this is bigger than anything else you've got going on. We're in too deep. You can just suck it up and keep making millions of dollars by being an idiot on television."

That was brutal, but masterful. I have to actively resist the impulse to let out a low, impressed whistle.

Silence falls, slowly covering the lingering echo of Melissa's tirade.

"That seems to cover it," Ted says groggily over the line. Before he hangs up, he asks, "When does the book tour begin?"

Robyn lets out an incongruously chipper "The day after tomorrow!"

"Robyn," Ted says, "I assume you're traveling with them?"

"Yes," she answers, just as Melissa counters with an emphatic "*No.*"

"No?" Robyn eyes her. "Melly, the plan has always been that I'd—"

"Carey will come with us," Melissa interrupts.

My stomach drops because I have become clairvoyant. I know what's coming next. Melissa's eyes swing to me, and the two words stretch out in slow motion. "And James."

Robyn gives her a tight smile. "I'm your publicist. You'll need me out there."

"No, I need you here with a reliable signal where you can monitor what's happening and put out fires as they arise. I need Carey with me, and Rusty needs James to help keep his dick in his pants."

"Uh." I'm afraid to correct her, but I'm less willing to let this ship go down without a fight. "I don't think—we shouldn't plan, uh, that I go anywhere near Rusty's—He doesn't need me for this."

"Yeah, I do." It's the first thing Rusty has said since Melissa's tirade. He looks at me, oddly determined, like he's scoring a win against his wife by strongly agreeing with her. "I'm not going without James."

Carey and I glance at each other, and I'm sure her pulse skyrockets, too.

I am immediately scrambling. "It was my understanding that, in addition to Robyn, the tour company has a handler in place to coordinate everything, so you'll have a staffer on hand."

Ted sighs, reminding us that he's still there being deeply inconvenienced. "I'm going to ask that you two join the tour. We need you to help manage the public-facing aspect of this, and Robyn can handle things backstage. I'm sure I don't need to remind you that all our best interests lie in keeping this ship sailing true. Get some rest, and I'll see everyone in the morning."

When the silence feels infinite, I know Ted has already hung up.

Robyn turns her face from her phone screen up to the

room. I can see the moment she realizes this is the only way and, to salvage her dignity, she needs to appear Completely On Board with this plan. "Yes," she says, gaining steam. "*Yes*. Absolutely. Ted is right."

I'm already shaking my head. I negotiated this week off when I was hired; it was meant to be my first true vacation in four years. The workload at my previous job in New York at Rooney, Lipton, and Squire was so overwhelming I didn't take a single day off while I was there. And then I was so desperate to find another job after the FBI raided the firm's offices that I applied for fifteen positions the next morning—including director of engineering for Comb+Honey—and was offered the job at the interview a few weeks later. They were the only ones who called me for an interview at all.

Although I've yet to do any actual engineering, I do work nearly fourteen hours a day managing Rusty's schedule, meetings, paperwork, contracts, blueprints, and general poky-puppy bullshit. I haven't had a second to breathe.

"Actually," I say into a room that is so tense the air feels wavy, "I'm headed to Florida to see my sister and her kids." I pause. "We negotiated this when you hired me. I can't go."

Carey meets my eyes, and I think it's fair to say she would bare-hand strangle me if I were closer.

"And I had plans, too," she says, her voice thin.

"I write both your checks," Melissa reminds us, "and if you want to be around to cash the next one, you'll start packing." Striding angrily to the door, she opens it, walks out, and slams it shut.

"Sorry, Jimbo. If I'm stuck, so are you." With an infuriating little *Oops, my bad* shrug, Rusty stands, too, and leaves.

"Robyn," Carey starts with similar desperation in her voice, "we don't need to go. I know them. They'll get it together in the morning. They always do."

"We can't risk it, Carey." Robyn shakes her head, resolute and unsympathetic. "Everything is riding on this, including your jobs. Change your plans and pack up for a weeklong trip. Your only job for the next ten days is to keep the Tripps from falling apart." She attempts a smile, but it is a sad, sad approximation as she glances at her watch. "See you for Netflix in seven and a half hours."

She leaves, and when the door closes, Carey grabs a pillow, bends, and releases a scream into it that is surprisingly primal.

I, too, want to let out an unholy string of curse words. I want to scream to the room, *Why can't I find a job that is somehow both legal and relevant to my graduate degree?* Is that too much to ask? Am I being transitioned into Rusty's full-time errand boy?

If I quit now, the only other position on my résumé is the black stain of RL&S; my former firm is still on the front page of national newspapers for its shocking accounting scandal that, so far, has resulted in fourteen arrests, job loss for nearly two thousand employees, and apparent loss of hundreds of millions of dollars in company retirement benefits. A few brief months at Comb+Honey won't make my résumé look better. I'm backed into a corner, and the Tripps know it.

"This is bullshit," Carey says. "And one hundred percent your fault."

"*My* fault? I wasn't the one having s—" With a full-body

shudder, I press the heels of my hands to my eyes until I see bursts of light. Maybe if I press hard enough I'll never have to see anything again. "I wasn't the one cheating on his wife. This is Rusty's fault, and we're the ones who are paying for it."

"I knew I shouldn't have helped you." She sits back against the couch with a growl. "This is what I get for trying to be nice."

"That was you being *nice*?" I start, stopping short when she turns to glare at me. I drop my head into my hands. "At least you're doing what you've been hired to do. Babysitting adults is not what I went to school for."

It was apparently the wrong thing to say. The last person to storm out of the office is Carey, with an infuriated "Yes, yes, James, we all know you're *brilliant*."

Carey

My roommates, Peyton and Annabeth, pause midconversation when, just over twenty-four hours later, I roll my shitty suitcase into the living room and set it beside theirs. I look back longingly at their enormous leather sectional; it's not pretty—it's old and bulky—but I had really looked forward to making it my home base for the next week. Yet here we are: instead of a staycation at home in my pajamas, I'm facing eight days cooped up in a van with a married couple in the midst of a crisis and Mr. Morality McEngineeringpants.

"Don't worry," I tell my roommates. "I'm not crashing your romantic getaway."

Annabeth looks at the suitcase and then turns bright, inquisitive eyes on me. Her face falls. "Oh, no."

"Oh, yes." I round the counter that separates the kitchen and living room and open the fridge to retrieve a protein shake. "James and I have to join the Tripps on their book tour."

Peyton lets out a sympathetic groan. "He's the new one, right? The hot nerd assistant?"

I swallow down a long drink of the shake—as well as the petty desire to ask her to slowly repeat the word *assistant* while I record it for him. "Yup."

"What happened?" Peyton pulls her thick dark curls into a ponytail. "I thought you had the week off?"

"It's complicated." That's about all I can say. NDAs aside, I've never complained about work—other than my long hours—and never disclosed just how rigid Melly can be, how maddening Rusty can be, and how hard this job is most days. In other words, I've always done what I can to protect the Tripps. I owe them that loyalty.

Because of this, Peyton and Annabeth think my bosses are everything the public believes they are: charismatic, creative, in love. It's such a happy image; I hate to ruin it for anyone, even the two people closest to me in nonwork life.

Is that depressing? That the couple I met through a classified ad when they were looking for someone to rent the second bedroom in their condo, and whom I rarely see, are the closest thing I have to friends? Is it terrible that I haven't made time for my brothers in at least six months, and they only live a half hour away? Am I a monster for not having been home for Christmas in two years?

Obviously the answer to all of these questions is yes. My life is an embarrassment. This is also why I started seeing a therapist. I'd never been to therapy before—never thought it was for me—but sometime last year I realized that I never really *talk* to anyone. I didn't have anyone I could unload on to help me unclutter my brain the way I unclutter Melly's inbox, QuickBooks, and calendar.

Maybe it helps that my therapist's name is Debbie. She's soft and comforting and looks a lot like my aunt Linda. The first thing I saw when I walked into Debbie's office was one of those granny-square afghans that my dad used to keep on the back of his La-Z-Boy. After a few sessions, I felt right at home. We're currently working on my ability to be assertive and brainstorming ways I can take control of my life. As you can see from the suitcase I didn't want to pack for the trip I absolutely don't want to go on, I'm not crushing this assertiveness thing.

I stare at my roommates' luggage—they're bound for Kauai to celebrate their fifth anniversary. I can't even imagine taking a trip to the Hawaiian Islands by myself, let alone with a significant other. It's like I started walking down one road and a day became a week became a month became a year, and here I am, ten years later with no idea if this is the right road or what I'm supposed to do when I'm not walking down it.

Flopping onto the couch, I moan dramatically. "Have fun, but feel sorry for me occasionally."

Annabeth comes and sits near my feet. Her auburn pixie cut perfectly frames her face, and I can already imagine how sun-kissed she'll be when she returns. "We will raise a fruit-decorated drink in your honor."

"Oh my God," I lament, "I was going to lie on this couch for days and drink boxed wine and catch up on like seven hundred different shows."

Peyton leans over the back and puts her hand on my

shoulder. "I know I've said it before, but if you want a job with regular hours, I can always find a spot for you."

Her offer is sweet, but the only thing that sounds worse to me than being Melissa Tripp's assistant is being an assistant to an insurance claims adjustor.

"That's so nice of you—" I begin, and Peyton cuts me off.

"But you want to keep your insurance," she says.

I do. The medical benefits are amazing, and I'm not sure I'd be able to find that in a private plan that won't bankrupt me.

"And even if that wasn't the issue, you'd rather die first, I know," she adds.

I laugh. "The idea of nine to five and three weeks of vacation a year sounds almost mythical, but—"

"But then you wouldn't get to work with Melissa Tripp!"

I look over at Annabeth when she practically sings this, and grin. "Exactly."

She's not being sarcastic. Annabeth is such a sweet, innocent angel baby it would be a shame to burst her image of Melly, who, admittedly, used to be a dream boss. But fame—and then her clawing need to hold on to it—is slowly eroding anything gentle or lighthearted about her. I'd feel sorry for Rusty if he hadn't eroded in opposite but equivalent ways.

Annabeth and Peyton are dressed and ready, which means that they're about to leave to catch their flight, which means it's nearly seven and I need to get a move on, too. I haul myself up from the couch, hug them in turn, and try not to look back at their bright, sunshiny dresses on my way out the door.

Granted, I was never an exceptional student—my crowning achievement in high school was a C in AP Lit and being voted secretary of our Future Farmers of America club—but the short walk from my car to the van has got to be some kind of metaphor for what a college education can do for a person. My shaggy old suitcase chugs along, veering off-path every time it hits a pebble. The fabric is worn out, the lock is broken, and the wheels are barely attached to the case. Up ahead, James McCann is shiny as a penny as he climbs out of his sleek BMW coupe and extracts his glossy aluminum luggage. He sets it down like it weighs nothing and, behind him, it glides across the parking lot like an obedient, high-end robot.

I want to throw something at him, preferably my shitty suitcase.

Plus, he's wearing a neatly pressed navy suit like we're going to another Netflix meeting instead of climbing into a cramped van for a fourteen-hour drive from Jackson to Los Angeles.

Irritation crawls up my spine.

"You're wearing work clothes?" I have to yell to drown out the horrifying screech of my suitcase wheels struggling to stay connected to the bag.

He doesn't turn around. "Are we not headed to work?"

"Not *work* work. We're going to be sitting for a while." *Thanks to you*, I think. "I assumed we should wear something at least fifty percent Lycra with no zipper."

"I left my yoga pants at home." He still doesn't even look at me over his shoulder. "This is how I dress, Carey."

"Even when relaxing?"

"We have an event tonight."

"And we can change at the last stop," I say. "Won't you get wrinkled?"

This time, he looks back at me over the top of his glasses. "I don't wrinkle."

I glare because, as impossible as it seems, if anyone can figure out how to be both stain- and wrinkle-proof, it's James. He keeps walking, and I riffle through my memory. In the couple of months that he's been working for Rusty, I don't think I've ever seen James in casual clothing, or looking anything less than recently pressed. No jeans, certainly no sweats. Now all I can imagine is James McCann washing his silver BMW in his driveway wearing tailored chinos and one of his many Easter egg–hued button-down shirts.

He's definitely never spilled a forty-ounce Super Big Gulp down *his* cleavage.

"Why are you so interested in my clothes?" he asks.

For the record, I'm not—I mean, not really. It's annoying that he's seemingly so perfectly turned out, but if I have to endure a week of this, *I'm* doing it in an elastic waistband.

"Because we're here against our will," I say, "and you and I are about to spend the entire day driving to Los Angeles. I'm wearing what I want."

"I'm sure Melissa won't have anything to say about that," he says dryly.

I glance down at my leggings and faded Dolly Parton T-shirt. Melly doesn't like what I wear even when I'm dressed up, though I do use the term *dressed up* loosely. Fashion is not my forte. But if I have to tolerate her disapproving face anyway, I might as well be comfortable.

We roll our suitcases around the side of a building that houses one of the Comb+Honey warehouses, and James comes to an abrupt stop. My face collides with his shoulder blade.

I'm too busy being annoyed that his back feels wonderfully solid and defined under that dress shirt to immediately realize what caused him to pull up short.

"So I guess they're not going for subtle," he says.

I follow his attention to the giant bus parked at the loading dock.

Wow. "Am I the only one who thought the publisher had booked a van? I mean, a fancy van, but still."

James heaves a sigh of resignation at my side. "No."

"I definitely didn't think we'd be traveling inside Melly's and Rusty's heads."

But why am I surprised? Melly loves flash and she *loves* her brand—the Comb+Honey logo is literally stamped or embroidered on everything from golf shirts to key chains to the staplers in the office. (If she didn't think tattoos were the worst kind of tacky, I'm sure she would have gotten a Comb+Honey tramp stamp years ago.) So obviously I was expecting a logo on the door. At most, I was thinking the book title would be tastefully scripted along the side. I did not expect a mammoth tour bus wrapped in a giant photo of Melissa and Rusty.

Their too-white smiles are stretched in vinyl across forty-five feet of windows and steel. Don't get me wrong, the Tripps are a good-looking couple, but nobody looks their best at that scale, in high definition.

I leave my bag at the curb and take a few steps to the left, and then a few to the right. "The eyes follow you."

James doesn't even crack a smile. Apparently engineers don't enjoy humor as much as assistants do.

A brown head of hair pokes out of the bus door, followed by the rest of a man with broad shoulders and a set of biceps that test the durability of his T-shirt. I've never really been into muscles before, but . . . I mean, I'll admit these are pretty nice.

"Hey there!" Biceps shouts, easily skipping down the three steps from the bus to the ground, landing with an effortless bounce. "You must be the assistants."

Beside me James goes completely still, in what I'm sure is an attempt to not have a toddler-level tantrum in the parking lot. Of course, I am delighted. Roll-dragging my suitcase toward the bus, I smile, make a fist, and shake out my fingers before offering my hand. "Yes. Yes, we are. I'm Carey."

I catch him logging my movements, but he gamely takes my hand to shake. I've never enjoyed a handshake before, but in this case, I'll happily make an exception.

"Joe Perez. I'll be the handler on the bus. Our driver, Gary, is in there getting settled." He jerks his thumb and I wave to a portly older guy already seated behind the steering wheel.

Joe looks over my shoulder to where James has begrudgingly joined us, and smiles, introducing himself again.

"James McCann," Jimbo replies. "Director of engineering."

I look at him, amused, but he doesn't meet my eyes.

The two shake hands and do the requisite guy nod, and

then Joe is showing us the enormous luggage compartment under the bus. "I know this isn't a very extensive tour," he says, unlocking the metal hatch, "but I'll be riding with you guys, making sure everything goes as planned."

It's possible Joe is the best-looking man I've ever seen up close. And he's coming with us? Like, the entire time? Well, well. I do a mental pat-down in search of my lip gloss. Maybe this is a chance to take some of Therapist Debbie's advice and assert myself, step outside of eighteen-hour workdays and no social life. To put my phone on silent and do what I want for a change. Mixing work and pleasure is likely to be the only way it's going to happen for me, and I'd risk the fallout for those biceps.

Joe's hair is dark, cut short on the sides but curly on top. He has a dimple in his cheek when he smiles, and his skin is sun-kissed and golden brown. When he reaches to place my suitcase into the open compartment, his shirt pulls taut across his back, muscles straining. My eyes follow the movement in a way I'm sure resembles our old dog Dusty watching hungrily outside the chicken coop.

"Easy there, Duncan," James says under his breath.

"Shut up, Jim," I quietly fire back.

Straightening, Joe turns to us with an enthusiastic clap of his hands. Of note: he's not wearing a wedding ring. "Okay, who's ready to poke around with me?"

"Holy shit," I say for the fourth time, eyes moving over every surface of the bus. I am sure this divine coach has never carried an object as grubby as my suitcase.

"Amazing, right?" Joe runs a loving hand along the front passenger's seat. May I one day have a man look at me the way Joe is looking at the soft leather of the captain's chair.

I walk slowly down the center aisle and my feet sink into thick carpet that is nicer than the condo's. Strips of purple lights are inlaid into the ceiling; the cabinets and desk are solid wood with marble countertops. This tour bus is an odd combination of luxury villa and party limo.

"There are two lounges." Joe points as he walks. "Seating for nine up front, a wet bar, a full galley kitchen with microwave and espresso machine." He moves toward the back, pointing out various amenities as he goes. "Bathroom with a full stand-up shower, flushing toilet. Room-specific temperature controls, so nobody has to fight over that." Joe grins and the dimple in his left cheek makes a delightful reappearance.

"Two forty-six-inch TVs," he continues, "each with cable and Blu-ray players. Wi-Fi throughout." He opens a door at the end of the hallway and points into what I assume is the rear lounge. U-shaped leather couches and a reclining captain's chair offer seating for at least ten more people, and a giant TV hangs in the center. "Oh, let Mr. Tripp know that MLB Extra Innings and MLB.TV have both been enabled."

James glances at me, expression typically superior. "You can let him know when you're going over the itinerary."

"You're his right-hand man, Jim," I counter. "I'll let you deliver the good news."

Exhaling slowly, James tilts his head up to see his reflection in the mirrored ceiling. Joe and I follow his lead and there's a weird moment of silence when all our eyes meet in the reflection. I'm sure we're all thinking the same thing: we are going to be right on top of each other for *days*.

Joe breaks the awkward quiet. "Anyway." He claps his hands before reaching for a folder tucked into a corner on the kitchen counter. "I've got the itinerary right here . . ." He shuffles through his papers. "You've probably got your own, but I've printed one for each of you."

James nods and takes his, slipping it into his own folder. I fold mine quickly and tuck it in my purse.

"The tour company booked all the hotels that you sent us in the request—I'll double-check both of yours," he adds, referencing my last-minute scramble to secure rooms for James and me. "When we arrive at each stop, I'll take care of everything and bring out the keys. The Tripps can stay in here and relax away from the public eye."

"Probably a good idea to keep the Tripps out of the public eye as much as possible," James says to me, and I elbow him—gently!—in his annoyingly taut stomach. Rule number one of Project Trouble in Paradise is *Trouble, what trouble?*

Joe gives us a brief, puzzled look. "I'll let you guys get settled. I imagine the Tripps will be here shortly, and someone will be coming by to take food orders. We should hit the road in about a half hour."

I watch Joe until he's completely out of sight, then busy myself with peeking in each of the cupboards. When I feel the pressure of James's attention, I turn and catch him looking with distaste at where I've shoved the printed itinerary haphazardly into my purse.

"Is there something you'd like to complain about?"

He blinks away. "Nope."

I eye his collection of color-coded folders; he's even printed labels for each one: ITINERARY. NETFLIX. CRITICAL PRAISE. LOCAL CONTACTS. I am very clearly the Pigpen to his Schroeder. "We can't all be as organized as Jim McCann. It's one of the many reasons you're so good at assisting Rusty."

Under the heat of his answering glare, I open another cupboard and let out a cry of delight when I find a canister full of Jolly Ranchers.

"Listen," I say. "I may not carry a folder of crisp papers, but I have a system and it hasn't failed me yet." My brand of organization would probably drive him nuts. I write everything down in a series of notebooks—usually whichever one I can find—and take them with me. It's not techy, and my handwriting isn't pretty, but it works. James is so organized that he probably has a spreadsheet to keep track of his spreadsheets.

We both straighten at the sound of the Tripps approaching the bus. Dread is a bucket of ice water poured over the top of my head. I feel it seep down into my shoes. James meets my eyes, and I see the parts of each of us that hoped they'd pull out last minute die sad, painful deaths in unison. This is definitely going to be awkward and miserable, and I remain unconvinced they can keep up the lovebird act in public.

"I really wish you'd cut your hair like that again," Melly says, and I can only assume she means the clean-cut style Rusty has on the enormous bus wrap. His current hair is a weird, shaggy style that makes him look like he constantly just rolled out of bed. Dye it black, and he could cosplay as Burly Joan Jett.

"The stylists thought a longer look would appeal to the younger demographic," Rusty says. "You know, like hipster."

"The stylists were wrong."

Side by side, James and I kneel on one of the couches, trying to make out the Tripps through the tiny perforations in the vinyl-coated windows. Our shoulders touch, but neither of us shifts away. It surprises me that I feel more of a sense of comfort and relief at his proximity than aversion; for all our differences in temperament and style, I'm probably lucky to have an ally here.

But then, too loud, he says, "I see they're off to a rollicking start."

I slap a handful of Jolly Ranchers into his palm. "Whenever you feel the temptation to speak, put one of those in your mouth."

Outside, Joe jogs up to join them.

"I see our stars are here." He claps his hands, so sweetly enthusiastic. I'm already sad to see his bubble burst.

"Yes! We're very excited," Melly says. A moment of silence stretches between the three of them, and I know her well enough to look down just as she subtly leans her frighteningly sharp heel on Rusty's toe.

"VERY EXCITED!" he shouts.

"Yikes," James whispers next to me, and then dutifully pops a Jolly Rancher into his mouth.

My stomach clenches. "We just . . . need to work on her delivery." I stand as they approach. "It'll be fine."

Melly is the first on the bus; her sharp blue eyes do a RoboCop scan of the interior, and I swear even the bus holds its breath waiting for the verdict.

"So much marble," she says with a saccharine smile, and then blinks to me. "Carey, I need to go over the Belmont sketches." She brushes past me and drops her bright orange Birkin on the couch before slipping into the booth that surrounds the table. She makes a show of trying to get comfortable before she looks up at Joe. "Can we get a better chair in here?"

I don't think I'm going out on a limb assuming that nobody wants to tell her no.

Joe takes one for the team. "I'm not sure if we can get something before we're set to leave"—he checks his watch again—"but I can certainly try!"

"Great." Melly pulls out her laptop, and only quasi under her breath says, "For what I'm paying for this tour, I'd like something that's not going to leave me hobbling by the time we get to LA."

So we're not even pretending to be nice today. Good to know.

As Joe passes him on his hunt for a chair, Rusty offers a look of commiseration that I'm sure is the dude equivalent of *I know, right?* But then Rusty steps into the back lounge and his misery is, as ever, short-lived: "Baseball all day?" he calls out, gleeful. "All right, my man!"

Melly takes a deep breath and bends her head to rub her temples. I can, oddly, relate.

* * *

We stop at a gas station in Salt Lake City for bathroom breaks, fuel, and junk food. A country song filters from the speakers overhead, and I find James in the Maverik coffee aisle, typing furiously into his phone. Stepping up beside him with arms full of Funyuns, Peanut M&M's, and Red Vines, I bump his shoulder with mine.

"Still glad we told Melly?" I ask, snapping a bite of a Red Vine.

Instead of responding, he slumps. "They just rode Expedition Everest."

I'm definitely missing an important piece of this conversation. "Who did?"

James turns the screen toward me and I see a pretty brunette grinning into the camera and standing just behind two scrappy boys wearing mouse ears. They look exhausted and sweaty and euphoric.

She's got the same luminous brown eyes and narrow nose, but it's the smile that gives it away. The McCann children apparently have great teeth. "Your sister?" I guess.

Nodding, he slips his phone back into his pocket and reaches for a Styrofoam cup from the display.

"Right, your sister in Florida. You were supposed to go with them. That was your vacation." Ugh. I guess I could continue to give him shit about screwing up this week for both of us, but missing a trip to Disney World with his sister and nephews seems like sufficient punishment.

"It's fine." He places his cup under the spigot labeled LIGHT SUMATRAN.

"It's not fine, but I get that it has to be. I'm sorry, James."

He glances at me, surprised. "Thanks."

"When did you last see them?"

James reaches for another cup and places it under the Almond Joy latte spout. See? Getting Rusty's coffee. Assistant.

"I saw them at Christmas a year and a half ago." He glowers at the coffee machine. "Rusty and his stupid dick."

My eyes widen. "It's been that long?" I guess I assumed that everyone around my age was much better about the work-life balance.

"Andrew was three, Carson was six. We had Christmas at my mom's place—which, incidentally, is also the last time I've been home." He drags a distractingly large, strong hand through his hair. "This trip, I promised my nephews we'd ride Everest until we puked." He shoves the top onto Rusty's sugary drink with a little more force than necessary, and it sloshes over the side.

"That's an admirable goal. I can see why you're disappointed."

Drinks wiped off and tucked into a cardboard carrier, he takes a second to study the collection of food in my arms and meets my eyes, brows raised.

I raise mine back. *Yes?*

He scratches his chin. *That's quite a snack pile.*

I grin. *And?*

James grins back and my heart thumps once, hard, at the weight of flirtation in his gaze. Unexpected, but welcome; this trip is already really boring.

"I'm stressed," I explain, looking away and breaking the tension. "When I'm stressed, I eat." Not the healthiest coping mechanism, but it's that or my vibrator, and that would just be awkward for everyone on the bus.

James apparently comes by those teeth and also the muscles genetically and not from a personal ban on junk food—he reaches for a Red Vine and takes a bite. "About the trip or the—" He grimaces at the unintentional pun. "The Tripps?"

I laugh into another bite. "Both, I guess. I'm not used to babysitting them like this," I admit. "Usually I just help with logistics."

We stop at the line that leads to the register, standing behind two women in their midtwenties. The brunette absently scans the front magazine rack; her purple-haired friend scrolls through Instagram on her phone. I follow the first woman's attention to the magazines, and my pulse accelerates as I am reminded there are four different weeklies with various images of the Tripps' euphoric marriage emblazoned on the covers.

"I swear to God these two are everywhere," the brunette says, picking up a copy of *Us Weekly*. The cover features a photo of the Tripps on their farm, leaning casually against an iron gate. Melly's head is thrown back in laughter. Her teeth are so white I'm sure they can be seen from space. Rusty smiles at her adoringly, happy that he can still make his wife laugh like that after all this time.

"They're just salt-of-the-earth types!" the brunette sings sarcastically to her friend. Her voice lowers as she flips to the next page of the feature, and on some instinct to duck or hide or otherwise eavesdrop more subtly, I step closer to James just as he presses against my side, too.

"Seriously," she continues, "I bet she's never actually ridden a horse in her entire life, but look at him. Look how he looks at her. I've gotta find a man like that."

The purple-haired woman looks away from her phone and groans. "I don't know. Whenever I see some celebrity couple on every magazine, my first thought is that they're in damage control mode." Even so, she leans in and starts to read over her friend's shoulder.

James and I exchange another look, and this time we're both making the *Eek* face. On instinct, I lean forward to peek out the window and my breath cuts short. Out there, visible to anyone nearby, Rusty and Melly are clearly arguing.

Melly points a finger at Rusty's chest and leans forward, appearing to lay into him. Rusty has the gall to not even look at her; his attention is focused to the side, bored gaze fixed on the horizon. I remember the days when he'd hang on her every word. I remember, too, when Melly would roll with anything, always the optimist. Now it feels like she'd start an argument in an empty house.

James and I exchange another look.

"This is how shit goes viral," I say under my breath.

"I think this is when we intervene," James replies.

I jerk my chin toward the door. *So go.*

He jerks his in return. *No, you go.*

Instead of being annoyed, I'm oddly on the verge of laughter. Nervous laughter. Nauseated laughter. I have never had to do this before; my job has always allowed me to blend easily into the background. I imagine walking out there and trying to mediate whatever's happening between them. I imagine Melly's hard stare, Rusty's avoidance of eye contact. It makes me feel like I have a worm farm in my stomach. "Don't wanna."

He reaches for a penny in the Give a Penny, Take a Penny tray. "Heads or tails?"

"Heads."

It lands on tails. Damn it. James grins at me. I toss him a ten-dollar bill for my food, but he tosses it back to me, waving the thick silver Comb+Honey expense card. So now I'm going out there, pissed off that I have to deal with the Tripps *and* pissed off that no one ever trusted me with a platinum card.

I step a foot out onto the oil-stained asphalt and absorb the sight of Melly and Rusty standing in front of the giant vinyl funhouse version of their blissed-out marriage.

"Hey, you two!" I call out, a pathetic singsong. My voice is shaking and reedy; my gut is a cauldron of bubbling anxiety. Ever since I applied for another job a few years ago and wasn't hired—and had to eat crow when the potential employer called Melly for a reference—I feel like I'm often walking on eggshells with my boss.

She looks over at me, eyes wide, like she forgot she was out in public. I know her well enough to get that she doesn't like my intrusion, but we're all in this awkwardness together, and there's no one to blame but Rusty. And, to be fair, probably Melly, too.

Her arms are folded across her chest, but she immediately drops them casually to her sides. And, Lord, why does she have to travel like this? Her tailored black pencil skirt and Louboutins are completely out of place in the scrubby parking lot. Salt of the earth, she is not.

Aside from their meltdown in the Jackson store all those years ago—and in their office the other night—I've really only ever seen them bicker, and they're usually careful to do it away from witnesses. This current messiness makes me wonder if Melly is more hurt than she's letting on—whether the affair with Stephanie has been a tipping point in their relationship and she's not able to retreat to her bubbly persona as easily.

"Hey, Carey-girl," Rusty says. It's the first time he's addressed me directly since all this happened.

"Hey. Everything okay out here?" I ask.

Melly glares at Rusty before giving me a smile that's too tight at the edges, and fans her attention across the gas station parking lot, mentally clocking who might have seen them arguing. "Of course, hon!"

"Great!" I call back, matching her enthusiasm. "Just reminding y'all there are eyes everywhere!" I absolutely hate this new role. I feel like I'm wearing wet wool for skin. "Okay, I'm headed back on the bus!"

"We'll be right there!" Melly smiles brightly.

I take the steps two at a time and make a beeline for the back, where I know Melly won't come, because it's where the sportsball games live. I'm terrified that she's going to feel free to chew me out for interfering once we're behind closed doors. Is it going to be like this every public-facing second of the tour? Probably.

Tonight we have a signing at a Barnes & Noble in Los Angeles. Then we're up in Palo Alto. After that, it's San Francisco, Sacramento, Portland, Seattle, Idaho. The events are always the same: We're escorted to a greenroom, where there's a rush to find an actual chair for Melly to sit on, not a stool or—God forbid—a director's chair. There's usually a friendly bookseller, some screaming fans outside, Rusty's dad jokes onstage, and the Tripps answering the same questions at every stop.

How did you get your start?

When did you know you'd done something big?

What's it like working with your spouse?

Do you ever argue?

What can we expect next?

They perform in front of cameras every day. As long as they stick to the script it'll be fine . . . right?

The bus rocks gently as we move down the highway, the hum of the tires a welcome distraction from the speed of James's gunfire typing. Every time I start to like him, he has to turn up the intensity somehow. Is he transcribing over there?

Melly has been on a call for about forty-five minutes. During that time I've managed to polish off my entire bag of Funyuns—a tragedy—and I try to focus on the design program in front of me. The project is an 1,100-square-foot home we'll hopefully incorporate into a future season. It's for a family of five—soon to be seven with a set of adopted twins on the way. Back in the old days, Melly's designs favored a river rock aesthetic—with lots of plants, stones, and water features—but eventually she built her brand on the idea that even small spaces can be adapted to work for everyone.

At first it was "transitionable" furniture. That all started with a window display I'd put together mostly because I was bored in the long afternoons just after the holidays, when no one was redecorating their houses. In the display, along with a beautiful hand-crafted daybed, I put a small table Rusty had built and to which I'd added wheels so I could move it around throughout the day. The space could be a small dining area, a cozy sitting room, and, later, a small bedroom.

Melly got about ten new customers that day. Rusty loved it, too. I showed him some of my sketches, and he got to building. We've all seen a table that can be extended with a wooden leaf, but what about a circular table that holds two hidden crescent shaped leaves? When the main circle is rotated, the leaves fan into place, turning a four-person table into one that can accommodate eight in only seconds. Rusty sold about forty of those tables in just a couple months.

Together, we designed consoles that expanded using the aesthetic and structural aspects of my dad's favorite Leatherman tools, kitchen islands that functioned like Swiss army knives and packed many purposes into the smallest footprint possible. The concept grew to include the buildings themselves: stairs that retracted when not in use, rooms built on platforms that offered hidden beds or storage underneath, walls that opened to reveal entire closets tucked into the space behind an ordinary flat-screen TV.

High-end style and design while utilizing limited space. It was popular even in the larger, more expensive homes in Jackson but when customers in some of the bigger cities heard about it, it became Comb+Honey's, and Melly's, signature.

My hands are bothering me more than usual, and I'm hoping I can nail down the logistics of turning an attic into an office with a half bath and lofted sleeping area before it becomes obvious I'm struggling with the Apple Pencil. I normally do this sort of thing alone, or with Melly, who already knows that my hands cramp when I overuse them, and it's hard to hide with everyone—particularly James—right here.

It's then that I notice the typing has stopped, and I glance up to find him watching me.

"You think we're almost there?" he asks, and if he happened to notice anything out of the ordinary in my movements, he doesn't let on. His blue-light-blocking glasses have slipped down his nose. The lens color makes the entire area around his eyes look like he's suffering from jaundice. I snicker as I reach for my backpack.

"It's a fourteen-hour drive," I remind him. "It's been five."

Closing his laptop, he stands to stretch and the groan he lets out is both sexy and terrible.

I grin up at him. "I thought engineers were really good with numbers . . ."

His dirty look is cut short by a shout from the back of the bus: "Jimbo! C'mere!"

"Sweet Jesus." James drops back into his chair.

Not to be ignored, Rusty calls him again. "Jimbalaya!"

I slide my messy stack of notes into my bag. "He's not going to stop until you acknowledge him."

"Jim Boy!" Rusty shouts, even more insistent. "Come back here!"

Melly covers her free ear and takes her phone into the bathroom, closing the door with a very pointed click. James gives me a pleading look, as if anything I can do will save him from keeping Rusty entertained for the next nine hours.

"Can't you help him?" he asks, offering his closed laptop as evidence. "I'm trying to finish something."

"He probably has a super-important engineering question, and I'm busy here doing assistant-y things. Besides, you're the one he's calling for, *Jimbo*."

"More likely he wants me to cut a hole in the bottom of the bus like he saw in *Speed* and ride the panel back to the gas station for a bag of Doritos." His grumpy expression deepens when he glances at my iPad, still on the table. "That doesn't *look* very assistant-y." He bends to get a closer look. "Are you . . . playing Minecraft?"

Instinct makes me click the side button so he can't see my design program. "Yep."

"Jimmy Dean!"

"Go on, Engineer Boy," I tell him. "I'm sure whatever he needs you for is way above my training."

Resigned, James stands with a groan and passes Melissa as she emerges from the bathroom.

"Is James having some sort of issue I should be aware of?" she asks once he's gone, slipping into the booth across from me at the small table. Her body is so tiny, honed from years with a trainer and a steady diet of cotton balls and water. I'm just kidding—she also stores my tears in a jar. It keeps her hair blond and her crow's-feet at bay.

Rusty's cheer carries above the baseball game when James finally steps into the little back room.

"Just your husband," I say.

"Well then, we have the same issue." Melly wakes up

her computer, and I'm sure she's immediately on all the retail sites, reading reviews of the book, checking its ranking. I'm torn between keeping this quiet moment of peace and wanting to say something about this trip and how it will be so much easier for all of us if they can just set aside what's going on until they get back to the privacy of their own home.

I think of what Debbie would tell me: Make the decision to assert yourself and follow through. Decide what you want and be honest in your communication. Don't sugarcoat, don't apologize, and listen to the response. Stay calm. Use *I* whenever possible. Practice in your head if you have to.

I think of what I want to say, but when I look at her face—tight, controlled, no-nonsense—the words dry up in my throat.

"Show me what you've got," she says, and points to my iPad.

I slide it across the table and she inspects my work.

"This is really good," she says, scrolling through the different computer-generated images. "I'm not sure about that desk."

I glance at the screen. The space allotted is minimal. "How would you change it?"

She purses her lips as she considers. "It's just not working as is. I want it to be more, more . . ."

Silence stretches between us, and I come to her rescue.

"I could make it vertical?" I suggest, clicking through and zooming in on the area. "Two-tiered instead of a single flat surface? Nobody would expect a two-storied workspace like that."

"*Yes*," she says with a firm nod. "That's exactly what I was thinking."

Inside, I'm beaming. Melissa isn't exactly sparing with her compliments, but you have to earn them. She's never apologetic about that, and it's something I've always admired. But outwardly, I just nod once, keeping my smile in check. Melly doesn't like gloating at compliments, either.

"Finish that up and send it to me," she says, sliding it back. "Ted asked for a couple of early schematics they can use in promo shots. I'd like to send them to him before we get back." She stops and looks down at my hands. "Unless you need a break."

I have to be honest when it matters. "Maybe a small one."

With her eyes back on her computer, she asks, "When's your next appointment?"

"A few weeks."

She nods. "It's on my calendar?"

I'm about to answer when a voice rises up from the back of the bus—the unmistakable drawl of Russell Tripp after a couple of beers. "There something going on there with you and Carey-girl?"

I keep my head down, noisily shuffling through my bag like I haven't heard a thing.

"Uh, absolutely not," James says with zero hesitation.

Heeeey. I mean, I'm not interested in James, either, but he didn't have to sound so horrified. I frown down at my Dolly shirt and brush away a few lingering Funyun crumbs.

When I look back up at my iPad, I feel Melissa watching me shrewdly and make the mistake of meeting her gaze.

With a roll of her eyes she goes back to her screen. "As if you and I have time for a personal life, anyway."

Something about the flippant way she dismisses the possibility rubs me the wrong way.

You and I?

It's true; I don't have time for a personal life. But that's because I'm sacrificing everything for the brand. I handle her schedules, her kids' occasional promotional appearances. I answer her emails and deal with Robyn, Ted, and the Tripps' editor. On top of all that, I do most of the designs. I spend more time on Melly's life than on my own.

I glance down to my bag and all the work I just put together for her. I don't have time for a personal life, but because of everything I do for her, Melissa Tripp certainly should.

LA WEEKLY BOOK PICK: THE TRIPPS' *NEW LIFE, OLD LOVE* IS A MUST-READ FOR SUMMER

LA Weekly's *Book Picks is your look at the hottest new releases this week—from biographies, how-tos, and reissued classics to romantic summer blockbusters and new voices garnering buzz. Check here every week before you make your next weekend-read plans.*

New Life, Old Love is an ambitious project for the lighthearted home-renovation power couple Melissa and Rusty Tripp. Their two previous books, *New York Times* bestsellers *The Tripp Guide to Home Décor* and *Small Spaces: DIY Projects to Make Any Size Home the Perfectly Sized Home,* were exactly what fans of their breakout show, *New Spaces,* were hoping to get from the pair. But instead of remaining in the arguably safer world of home renovations, their new book, *New Life, Old Love* (out this week; $24.95), focuses on the couple's twenty-five-year relationship, with honest and poignant looks at how they met, the sacrifices they made to open their home décor storefront in Jackson, Wyoming, and the various hurdles that endangered their relationship while they were building their careers.

Coming out of these obstacles, the couple writes, they always emerge stronger and with more proverbial tools in their belt. They claim they don't fight—they *negotiate.* Their breakneck schedules aren't new—Melly has always written detailed lists of goals she hopes they both achieve each week. And they don't need breaks from each other; instead they've found that spending time together fuels the creative spark they need to keep their business ideas fresh.

But rather than being a book that only applies to their marriage in their circumstances, *New Life, Old Love* is a more powerful guide to what it means to be a partner, how to turn differences into complementary strengths, and when to listen rather than push. It's an optimistic and engrossing read that perfectly ties in their trademark phrase—*Be flexible!*—with genuine advice for how to accomplish just that.

The Tripps have embarked on a West Coast tour to launch the new book, with their first stop at Barnes & Noble at the Grove. The room was packed with bloggers and VIPs, a few of them wearing *Be Flexible!* T-shirts and waiting for up to three hours in line to get their books signed. Playfully teasing throughout, the couple truly appeared to practice what they preach: Melissa laughed with loving exasperation at Rusty's slew of dad jokes. Rusty gazed adoringly at his wife as she fielded questions from the audience. It was everything that megafans of the couple wanted to see, and we were able to cap off the evening with a quick Q&A with the pair.

LAW: For those out there who haven't read your book yet, how did you get your start?
Melissa Tripp: As a couple, we met at a party during our first week of college. Early on we knew we wanted to work

together, in some capacity. So we opened the furniture store in Jackson, Comb+Honey. The name is a play on structure, plus the function inside. The store was set up like a series of rooms—where Rusty built most of the furniture, and I would find amazing pieces to accentuate the design. After we were featured in the local paper, the *LA Times* did a story on our business in the weekend magazine, HGTV found us, and the rest is history.

LAW: When did you first know you'd done something big?

Rusty Tripp: I remember coming back from lunch one day and seeing a whole slew of news vans parked outside the store. I had to work my way past the crowd all standing in front of the display—I remember it so clearly, it was this living room display with silver accents and a sapphire-blue midcentury-style piece I'd built—I'd had this gorgeous walnut from a guy up in Billings, and never knew what to do with it until—

MT: [laughing] Honey. Stay on target.

RT: See? She keeps this train running. Anyway, the room display was breathtaking. Melly had created a waterfall feature on the wall using some river rocks from our trip to Laramie. The blues all shimmered together in this totally otherworldly way, and the people with cameras around their necks all just stood there, staring. Not even taking pictures, just staring like they'd never seen anything like it before. That was when I knew.

MT: We'd already been featured in the *Casper Star-Tribune* by that point—

RT: Right, so this was just before everything exploded. After the *LA Times* feature, everything changed. But that moment was when I knew it would.

LAW: I have to ask: What's it like working with your spouse?

MT: Honestly? It's amazing. I can't imagine another life.

RT: She keeps me grounded, keeps me on task—you've already seen that [they laugh], and it's true: we're two halves of a whole.

LAW: It's amazing how many people want to know: Do you ever argue?

MT: You mean, how often do we *negotiate*? [laughs] We have disagreements, sure, but they're the same kind of mild together-all-the-time moments that every couple has. When it comes to our business, we don't argue. We're in this together, and stronger when we're a team.

LAW: So what can we expect next?

RT: Now, *that* we can't tell you quite yet. But trust me, later this week y'all are in for a doozy.

Well, Rusty, as a fan of all things Tripp, I can't wait.

Submitted by staff writer Leilani Tyler

James

I meet Carey in the hotel lobby at five thirty the next morning, both relieved and a little disappointed that she now seems to be dressing the part on tour. Honestly, I liked the Dolly shirt, especially when she told me about the concert where she got it, and used the phrase *three sheets to the wind* to explain that she was so drunk, buying the shirt is the only part she remembers. Instead she's in a pink skirt and a white tank top . . . which I make an effort to not study too closely.

Pop culture would have us believe that men look at women and immediately imagine them naked. That is not always the case, actually. As far as my job is concerned, I have generally been too busy and frazzled and worried about *keeping* it to think about Carey as a warm-blooded woman with responsive body parts. This morning is an exception. To be fair, though, the hotel does have the air conditioning on pretty high.

Hotel. Incorrect. We are most definitely staying at a *motel*—a Motel 6, to be specific, and I realize I ought to be grateful for the four hours of sleep I managed on the hard, creaky mattress. The pillows were roughly as thick and supportive as construction paper; the blankets as soft and warm as rucksacks.

Carey, holding a leather notebook and a steaming Styrofoam cup, seems to correctly interpret the deep blue circles under my eyes. "Don't blame me," she says by way of greeting. "This trip has been booked for months. The Ritz was full, and I had, like, two hours to find something else."

"One might assume something exists in the space between Motel 6 and the Ritz."

"You'd think so, wouldn't you?" she says with a sarcastically sweet smile. The sarcasm breaks and she hikes a shoulder skyward, admitting, "I was in denial and then full-fledged panic."

"It's Los Angeles," I remind her. "There are approximately one billion hotel rooms."

"*Jim.*" She rubs her eyes with the back of one hand and then takes a sip of coffee. "It's too early to argue. Add me to your 'negotiation' spreadsheet for later."

I repress the temptation to remind her that the early alarm, too, could have been prevented. We are scheduled to meet the Tripps at the tour bus at six thirty outside their hotel. Carey, who clearly has no sense of Los Angeles geography, booked us at the Motel 6 in Hollywood, which is about eight miles away from the Ritz-Carlton on Olympic. On an average LA weekday, this translates to an hour-long drive.

"You're acting like we aren't going to be in a vehicle for seven hours today anyway," she says.

"No, I'm acting like an additional hour of sleep would be preferable to an hour in a car."

"Come on. It wasn't that bad."

I give her an incredulous lift of one eyebrow.

"Seriously, it was clean and the bed was relatively comfortable, considering the price." She reaches out to straighten a framed black-and-white print of some iconic Hollywood landmark. "It's just a little drab and predictable. Nothing some different colors and updated furniture couldn't fix. They could make the simplicity feel like it's intentional. Wouldn't take much money, either."

She scribbles something down in her notebook before turning her attention to me, studying me in playful exasperation. "Again with the suit."

"Have you ever heard the phrase 'Dress for the job you want, not the job you have'?"

"Have you ever heard the word 'highfalutin'?"

I laugh. "People actually say that?"

Ignoring me, she rolls her dilapidated suitcase toward a wall of vending machines, tucks her notebook away, and starts searching through her purse. "I'm familiar with the phrase," she answers, finally, "but it seems like something people only say to girls."

I follow and pick a wayward piece of lint from my sleeve. "My sister says more men should follow the advice women get."

Whatever she'd planned to say next seems to stall in her mouth. She studies me again, open wallet in hand, but this time her eyes don't stray from my face. "What does that mean?"

I shift a bit under the press of her attention, inexplicably unnerved. "Probably that women are always being told to behave in a way that makes everything more harmonious, productive, accessible. They're told how to do everything from how to dress to how to smile. Men are never told to make things easier for people, but maybe they should be."

She's still staring. "Who *are* you?"

"Who am I?"

"Why are you here?" she asks. "Why do you even have this job? Why didn't you quit the second Robyn told you we had to go on tour? Actually, why didn't you quit the first time Rusty asked you to get his coffee or clean his golf balls?"

I wince and press a hand to my stomach. "There's something about that phrasing that really doesn't work for me right now."

She ignores this.

I watch as she carefully coaxes a handful of crinkly dollar bills into one of the vending machines. Her movements are stiff and unnatural, and I'm on the verge of offering to help her when the machine finally takes the cash. I glance away as she presses the button for a granola bar.

"Seriously, though," she prompts, "why are you here?"

For a moment, I briefly consider telling her the truth and then decide evasion is easier. "That's a long story."

"We've got," she starts, looking down at her phone, "eleven minutes until our Lyft is here."

"It's also a depressing story."

"I live for other people's drama." Depositing the bar inside her bag for later, she grins up at me.

I blink away, looking across the lobby to the reception desk, where one employee is on her phone and her male counterpart is asleep in his chair. I don't relish the idea of telling Carey about all of this. It's not that I worry it makes me look bad, but I worry it will make her pity me, and few things are more emasculating than pity. "My last job—the only job I'd had in the four years since I finished my master's—was at Rooney, Lipton, and Squire."

Carey's eyes narrow and then go wide in recognition. Blue-green. Neither blue nor green, but a pretty blend of the two. "Wait. What? Seriously?"

"Seriously."

Thankfully, her expression isn't pity, it's fire. "Isn't that the firm that funneled all that money into—"

"The very one." I reach up, scratch my chin, feeling uneasy in that nauseated way I always do when I remember that the four years of endless workdays and stress-induced sleepless nights were essentially supporting a completely corrupt company. "So, I really need to build my experience and contacts here. I can't just bolt." I reconsider. "Or, I suppose I could, but then I might have a hard time finding something else. Rusty promised me an engineering role. Ted promised me an engineering role. I've been Rusty's de facto assistant so far, but if I can just hold on until season two starts shooting, I think I might actually like what we're doing here. Plus, I admit I'm thrilled that no one here seems to be breaking the law."

She whistles. "Wowza."

Yeah, wowza. There's also the fact that my plan only works if Rusty and Melissa can keep it together. Wanting to change the subject, I ask, "If you don't mind my asking, why do you still work for them?"

Her answer is immediate. "Melly needs me."

I believe that's true, though from what I've seen Melissa also doesn't treat Carey particularly well, so it seems awfully generous of Carey to prioritize Melissa's needs over her own.

But surely she wants my pity even less than I wanted hers. "You don't think she would manage, after a while?"

Carey turns her eyes up to me, and given the freedom to look directly at her, I'm struck by the awareness that not only is she a warm-blooded woman, she's disarmingly pretty. More than pretty—she's beautiful. Her skin is flawless, cheeks always flushed. I like her mouth, the way it curls up on one side before the other when she's amused. The strong angle of her jaw, the hint of dimples in both of her cheeks.

Danger, James. I look away, trying not to stare. It's part of Carey's job to blend into the background, but now that I've seen her—really seen her—something heated turns over in me that I'm not sure I can turn back.

"What else would I do?" she asks. "I feel like I've given everything to the Tripps. I know it doesn't seem like it, but I've helped them build all of this."

"Oh, I'm sure you have."

"I don't really want to start over."

I want to say *You're only twenty-six*, but she takes a deep inhale over her Styrofoam cup, seeming to refocus and possibly even relish the smell of what can't possibly be good coffee. The moment has passed.

"At least they weren't terrible last night," she says, a subtle subject change.

It's true. Melissa and Rusty *weren't* terrible at the meet-and-greet. They charmed the crowd, joked with each other, and generally left me with the hope that this might not be the worst week of my life.

"That was my first book signing, so I don't have anything to compare it to, but . . . they were great. Maybe we've been worried about nothing," I say, trying optimism on for size.

"Yeah . . ." Carey starts, and then offers a thoughtful pause.

"But?"

"They *were* great last night, but that could have just been the adrenaline of a first event. I've never traveled with them across the country mere days after adultery in their *twenty-five-year* marriage. We're in open water here. Anything can happen."

This is the opposite of what I wanted her to say. "Did you have any idea their marriage was so bad?" I ask. "I certainly didn't."

She drains the cup and takes a couple of steps to refill it, lifting it as if offering me one. I decline with a small shake of my head. "I knew things weren't perfect," she admits. "But whose marriage is?" She adds in some nauseating powdered creamer and three packets of sugar. "Believe it or not, they used to be really cute together. I actually miss seeing them like that."

I groan. "Do you ever just wish everyone would do what they're supposed to do?"

"Heck yeah."

"Think about what they've built, how lucky they are. Rusty needs to keep it in his pants. Melissa needs to calm down a little. I could help do some of the engineering work and . . ." I hesitate, awkwardly. "You'd hopefully have fewer messes to clean up."

"Of course." Carey gives me a knowing little wink and drains this second cup of coffee. "But think of all the fun you'd be missing if you were just an engineer! I mean, with all you know about LA hotels, you should have booked the rooms!"

⁂

We help Joe get everything reloaded onto the bus while the Tripps sign autographs for a crowd that has gathered outside the Ritz. I'm constantly vigilant, waiting for the Tripps to explode at each other any minute, but they're both wearing steady, easy smiles.

Likewise, the seven-hour drive to Palo Alto is mostly uneventful: Carey is on her iPad again. Rusty stays pretty much in the back. The two of them used to talk more, but I've noticed a distinct strain on whatever father-daughter vibe they had going on. The sounds of ESPN float through the closed lounge partition door, and Melissa parks herself next to the driver, where her motion sickness is the mildest and she can wait for the Dramamine to kick in. I get the distinct impression that that is usually Joe's seat, so he's awkwardly hanging out near the back.

"Joe," I say, and he looks up from where he's shuffling a bunch of papers around. I motion to the couch across from me.

I watch as he passes Carey, and notice him noticing her. A weird beat of satisfaction hits me when she's so focused on whatever she's doing that she doesn't even look up. She's using the iPad stylus with her right hand—and I know she's left-handed. Even so, her fingers move in small, precise strokes. I'm pretty sure she isn't playing Minecraft; not even my nephews give it that much focus. It looks like she's drawing.

She tilts her head, bites her lip, and the gesture sends a shock of heat through me.

My view of her is blocked by Joe as he sits next to me, startling me back into focus.

"Tired of sports?" I ask. For the day and a half we've been on the road, with Melissa up front, Joe has spent most of his time in the back; as likable as Rusty generally is, I'm sure the prospect of all-day beers and sports on TV has quickly lost some of its appeal.

Joe looks nervously over to where Melissa has dozed off, and then to Carey, who still doesn't seem to register that we're looking at her.

"They're different than they seem on TV," he says confidentially.

Mild dread feels like a tiny weight in my abdomen, sinking. Of course I know what he means, but—as much as I hate the role I've been given, I should probably chase down his meaning a little. "How so?"

Joe shifts, hesitating. "Nothing specific. They're just not as . . . happy as I imagined."

I close my book and set it on the couch. "It's the travel," I explain, leaning back and draping an arm over the back of the seat, going for unconcerned. "The stress of the road. They miss their kids."

"How old are their kids?"

"Twenty and twenty-four." I clear my throat when his brow lifts in surprise. I'm sure he was imagining toddlers or—at most—middle-school-aged children. "But they're all very close."

This . . . may or may not be true. In the short time I've been working for the Tripps, I've heard Rusty talking to TJ once.

"Plus," I say, "everything is happening so fast for them, I think they're both a little overwhelmed."

"Right." Joe's smile looks a little forced. The Tripps have been megastars for a few years now, but he kindly leaves this unsaid. "Sometimes it takes a few days to adjust to the tour. It can make anyone a little tense."

"They'll get into a groove." I pause. "They were great last night."

Joe nods.

I'm trying to get a better read on him. He doesn't seem all that enthusiastic about last night's event. "Nothing they did last night set off alarm bells, right?"

He shrugs, distracted by a small spot on the couch that bears a striking resemblance to the color of Melissa's trademark pink lipstick. "No, they were fine."

"Seemed to really charm the crowd," I press.

But Joe is oblivious. Motioning to the spot like he wants to get something to fix it, he stands and moves to crouch in front of one of the utility cabinets up front.

When I look up, I realize Carey is gazing with amusement at me.

She leans in, whispering, "Bravo, Jim, brav-o. That was a study in espionage."

"What are you talking about?"

She stands, moving to sit where Joe had been, and,

looking around first, quietly asks, "Were you trained in the CIA?" She glances over my shoulder and then back to me. "It's okay. You can tell me."

I give her a lingering, flat look, but inside, I'm fighting a smile. I like her playful like this. "I was just trying to get a read on what he thought about the blogger event."

Carey leans back, pulling her phone out and swiping her screen open. "Everything I've seen has been pretty positive so far." She smiles, turning her phone screen to face me. "In addition to Joe, various social sites on the interweb provide a great window into the impression the Tripps give at events."

"Okay, Duncan." I look back down to my notebook, hoping she hears my deep breath as exasperation and not that I'm taking a deeper hit of her. "I'm happy to leave all sleuthing to you."

Carey laughs, and then startles a little when Melissa stirs awake up front. It's an immediate shift in mood, like a tiger has just entered the arena.

"Where's my phone?" Melissa asks, voice groggy.

"I plugged it in, hold on." Carey jumps up, running to grab the phone from the small kitchen counter. Before she hands it to Melissa, she says, "Just no reviews."

"I'm not going to read reviews," Melissa snaps.

Carey walks back toward me with a roll of her eyes. She does not look convinced.

❀❀❀

As expected, Melissa spends the three hours leading up to our arrival into the Bay Area reading reviews. From what

I've seen, most have been good, but a few are downright nasty. No matter how much Joe tries to lighten the mood and explain that every author he's ever taken on tour finds bad reviews, and how much Carey pipes in that books are subjective and not everyone will love them all, Melissa isn't hearing it. By the time we're pulling into the parking lot of the Palo Alto bookstore, Melissa is in a *mood*.

She's tiny, but her energy isn't. The bus door opens, and she sweeps past us, barely stopping long enough for the smiling event coordinator to lead her into the greenroom.

Maybe it's the pessimist in me, but almost from the get-go I'm worried that the event is doomed. I wonder if, in three hours when we're all done, I'll find that it was just nerves making me feel this way or whether the tension seems as thick as the San Francisco fog to anyone else. Last night seems Smurfs' Village–level utopia compared to this.

Although Rusty walks in right behind her, they head in opposite directions: Rusty to the snack-laden table on one side, and Melissa to a cooler of water on the other. While Rusty—oblivious to or intentionally avoiding his wife's worsening mood—makes small talk with one of the bookstore staff, the event coordinator for the bookstore, Amy, goes over the schedule for the night to no one in particular: fifteen-minute talk, book signing, VIP photos and meet-and-greet to follow. Melissa aggressively opens a bottle of water, nods with tight smiles, and paces the room. She pointedly does not look at her husband.

Carey comes in loaded down with Melissa's purse, a box of T-shirts for giveaway, Melissa's lunch bag with her fresh squeezed juice, and about five other bags. Her skirt hem hits several inches above her knees and her tank top reveals smooth, tanned shoulders that make me think of biting. But her expression reads: *I'm about to drop something*. I rush over to help but once the load is in my arms, I give her a helpless apologetic look.

"Where should I put this?"

Carey laughs. "Do I get to have an assistant now?"

My first instinct is to tell her I have no problem with that at all, and then my brain snags on the echo of it, how desperate it would sound, and I'm quiet long enough that I just leave her comment without reply.

With a wink, she leads me to a table, standing close as she unloads things from my arms. She put her hair up into some kind of twist, but a few strands have come loose and fall prettily along her neck.

"I'll take this." She unhooks Melissa's lunch bag from my finger.

Our eyes catch for a few loaded seconds. I'm thinking about how the first few times I hear a new song—even one from a band I love—I don't like it. I resist the idea that something new could ever be as good as something old, but then slowly the new song works its way into my brain and I forget what it ever felt like to dislike it. Right now I'm looking at Carey's face, thinking it's like a song I've heard a few times now, and every time I hear it again I like it more.

"What?" Her eyes widen in horror and she reaches up to wipe her mouth. "Do I have crumbs on my face?"

"No, I just—" I pause, putting myself together. I'm developing a crush and I'm not sure what to do about it. "Let me know how I can be helpful tonight."

Gratitude washes over her expression. "Oh. I will." She glances across the room. "We need to get her to relax. She looks like a bomb right now."

I follow her eyes across the room and we both take a deep, steadying breath. This is what we're here for, right? Joe may be impossible to keep in the dark because he's going to be with them unguarded on the bus for days on end, but here we have some control.

But I don't know how to fix the tense mood in the room. Let me wrestle with the constantly changing world of city and municipal building codes. Let me navigate the complexities of engineering licensure or give me an impossible element to make possible in a final design. But handling emotions like this? Between two people I hardly know and who, quite frankly, probably shouldn't be married anymore, let alone telling other people how to do it? I feel as useful as a leaf blower in a kitchen.

Thankfully, though, Carey knows how to manage Melissa's proximity to combustion. She carefully makes her way over to the other side of the room. Beside Melissa, Carey looks so tall, but she bends, making herself smaller, speaking in a low, soothing voice.

Jesus, how many times has she had to play this role? For a beat, I'm mad about it—mad that Carey is only in her midtwenties and already having to be an assistant, usher, peacekeeper, travel agent, and who knows what else.

I feel intensely useless. Having no training in this sort of mediation, I am simply a body standing in the middle of a room. Trying to think like Carey, I walk over to Amy and make a show of looking at the schedule. She's more than happy to explain everything again, and I'm able to keep an eye on Melissa and Carey. They're not close enough for me to catch everything they're saying, so I get only a bit of Carey's murmured, ". . . okay? . . . great crowd out there." And then Melissa's soft, ". . . but the reviews. How am I supposed to . . . blood, sweat, and tears and—"

"Does that all make sense?" Amy asks hopefully.

I turn my attention back to her. I have no idea what she's said. "Perfect. Thank you for all your hard work putting everything together." I glance across the room, horrified to see Rusty chatting up a pretty young clerk. "Um, if you'll excuse me for a second." I gesture to my boss. "I'm going to just . . ."

"Oh, of course!"

He doesn't look at me, still smiling winningly at the twentysomething brunette, but is aware of my presence because he reaches out to pat my shoulder and offers a lighthearted "Hey, Jimmy Jams."

I let this one slide and smile at the woman. "Could you excuse us for a second, please?"

Her cheeks warm to a bright pink, and she nods before rushing off. I lean against a stack of shelves.

"Rusty."

This earns me an innocent blink. "What?"

"You *know* what."

"She's a nice kid," he says, waving a hand. "A big fan. I was just indulging her."

Does he do this to drive Melly crazy, or is he genuinely unaware that flirting in front of his wife is always a terrible idea but especially now?

"Well, let's focus our attention elsewhere." I lift my chin. "Looks like Melly is having kind of a rough day."

He gives me an easy shrug and pulls out his phone to check messages. "You get used to it."

"Rusty." I wait until he looks up at me again. "This is where you need to get involved. Her feelings are hurt, and she's having some insecurities. She's *upset*. You need to go help calm her down."

"I doubt I'd be very useful here."

"But at least appear to be engaged with your wife?" I tilt my head over to where Joe has just walked in and is introducing himself to Amy. "For this week, appearances matter. To anyone else in the room, you come off as totally uninterested in whatever's going on with her."

"What do you expect me to do, Jimmy? Pretend like everything is fine and we're"—he has the nerve to motion between us—"not both here completely against our will?"

Against our will? I take a deep breath. Rusty is here so he can continue to live the sweet life and drive around the lake on his custom Jet Ski. I'm here so I can keep my job and not get evicted.

"Do you want people to figure out that you two are in trouble?" I ask him, growing desperate the longer Melissa is panicking by the window and Rusty appears completely unconcerned. Amy and Joe are still here, but another woman has entered the room and is watching Melissa pace and vent to Carey about bad reviews.

"She should know not to look at those!" Rusty hisses to me. "Reviews always get her back up, and they aren't even that bad! She knows better."

"Not helping," I growl.

With an irritated exhale, he makes his way over to his wife. She looks initially like she's going to blow up at him, but a glance over his shoulder clues her in that they've got an audience, which seems to be the one thing that pulls Melissa Tripp back into the right state of mind. She allows herself to be coaxed into the sturdy comfort of Rusty's hug.

Carey looks at me. I look at her. It feels like we both finally let out a long, slow breath. But the calm is shattered by the sound none of us wanted to hear today.

"Hello to my two favorites!" Stephanie Flores has that husky sexpot voice, and when the former Miss America sashays into the room, completely oblivious, a chill swallows us all. Rusty closes his eyes and lets out a groan that seems to lament the inconvenience rather than the depth of his regret. Is it really possible that Rusty didn't bother to give Stephanie the heads-up that Melissa knows about their affair?

She walks over, embraces a board-stiff Melissa first, and then kisses Rusty on both cheeks. Carey and I stare at the three of them like we're watching a grenade with the pin pulled free. The room is filling with people with Instagram and Twitter locked and loaded on their phones, and who'd love to drop that they're *hanging out backstage with the Tripps!*

To her credit and my unending shock, Melissa manages to slap on a gracious smile and let out a thrilled "Stephanie! Oh, my goodness, what are you doing here, silly? What a surprise!"

Carey sidles up next to me, tucking her hands beneath her crossed arms. "Holy shit. This is bonkers."

"It's like watching a car sail off a cliff," I agree.

"I was really hoping the shit wouldn't hit the fan at the *second tour stop*," Carey hisses, glancing to where Melissa and Stephanie chat like they're old friends catching up after months, instead of secret enemies who saw each other less than a week ago. "What is she doing here anyway?"

"She doesn't know that Melissa knows," I remind her. "In Stephanie's mind, she's just one friend popping in on two others. Not a—"

"Backstabbing asshole?"

I glance down to see her already smiling up at me. My blood heats at her proximity and the glint in her eyes that I know comes from being exhausted and stressed but translates as fuck-it-all mischievousness. Holy shit. I like her.

"That nicely sums it up." I turn back to the two women. "So what do we do? Melissa is a mess with or without the backstabbing asshole, and there's a room full of people out there and a lot more of these events to come."

"First," she says, "we have to keep her off the review sites. I'll set up a blacklist of words to mute on Twitter and compile all of our four- and five-star reviews. If I give her a new list every day, it should be enough to keep her ego going."

"And second?" I ask.

"Second?" she says, and then exhales as we both watch Rusty walk back over to the snack table, and catch Stephanie eyeing him like there might be time for a quick round of Hide the Hammer. "Second, we keep those two away from each other and just . . . hope the creek don't rise."

Even though I've never heard that phrase in my life, I know exactly what she's saying.

❖❖❖

It's a tall order, but Carey's intervention and Rusty's hug appear to have scraped together a little team spirit: Melissa seems determined to keep it together. Walking behind Stephanie, Melissa smiles brightly at everyone she passes. It looks like Rusty is doing his part as well, and has a guiding hand pressed against his wife's lower back as he walks beside her. Carey and I bring up the rear, and it's only from this angle that you'd notice Rusty's only touching his wife with his fingertips, like he's rationing out how much physical contact he's going to deliver.

With every step I think, *I could just turn around and walk out of here and not come back. I could start over, work as an entry-level engineer somewhere in Omaha, Topeka, Sioux Falls*. I'd have to live on instant ramen and roll pennies to pay for gas, but would that be worse than this?

I'm ripped from this internal debate when we stop just at the edge of the bookstore floor. There are streamers and balloons, and posters of the *New Life, Old Love* cover everywhere. The crowd erupts in a deafening cheer when the Tripps step inside, and then loses it again when they see the bonus appearance of Stephanie Flores, who gives a humble little wave and indicates she'll be standing in the back, a simple fan just like the rest of them.

"Thank you so much for joining us tonight," Amy says by way of introduction. "This has been quite a ride for you two, hasn't it? I hear you're traveling by bus?"

On cue, Melissa and Rusty share a fond look.

"Yes!" she sings. "A big, beautiful bus." She's careful to

smile and make eye contact with individual members of the audience, and it's easy to see why millions of women feel like they *know* her.

"But even a big bus can feel really small when you're traveling with an entire team of people," she continues with a self-deprecating smile. "Let's just say I'm going to be better about picking up my shoes when I need to."

"I almost went to the emergency room! They'll tell you!" Rusty says, pointing to the back of the room where Carey, Joe, and I—*their team*—stand. We all shrug and play along with this fictional moment. The audience eats it up. *They leave their shoes on the floor! They're just like us!*

The next question comes from a twentysomething woman in the back of the room. "Do you remember the first window display you ever did that made someone come in and say, '*That*. I want that'?" she asks.

And without waiting for his wife to reply, Rusty looks to the back of the room again and says, "What was that first window you did, Carey-girl? The dining room one, right?"

Carey stiffens at my side as the entire room swivels in their seats to look at her. Silence swallows the space, because the way he cut Melissa out of this recollection is palpably awkward. When I take in Carey's horrified expression, I realize that this is definitely more than easy Team Tripp banter: Rusty has just dropped a bomb in the middle of the bookstore.

Vic @aCurlieee_doll • July 8

Ummm did anyone else hear the rumor that Rusty Tripp is banging his costar?

19 replies 39 retweets 194 likes

Show this thread

> **Jesey** @Jeseylovesshoes
>
> @aCurlieee_doll SHUT UPPP I REFUSE
>
> > **Vic** @aCurlieee_doll
> >
> > @Jeseylovesshoes I just spent an hour on a reddit thread written by someone who was at their event. "They were in a back room and not even speaking—and that was before the side piece showed up. They got it together but there was an ~edge"
> >
> > **Jesey** @Jeseylovesshoes
> >
> > @aCurlieee_doll SHE SHOWED UP? Wow wow wow the balls on that one
>
> **Bennifer** @benniferbites
>
> @aCurlieee_doll ok troll. There's no way. Have you seen them together? Relationship goals.
>
> **Tae** @Wide_eyedbitchy91
>
> @aCurlieee_doll holy shit did Melissa lose her mind?

blaze @ablazeaverysmom
@aCurlieee_doll @Wide_eyedbitchy90 I heard that Rusty wants out and melly isn't having it. Why would she? The endorsement deals alone. They make so much money it'd be best for her to look the other way. people would be pissssed if it all turned out to be a sham. Imagine their sponsors

Tae @Wide_eyedbitchy91
@ablazeaverysmom @aCurlieee_doll speaking of their book, aren't they on tour? God I hope they're paying their handlers well

Ella @1967_Disney_bound
@aCurlieee_doll they just finished their show. Anyone know if they've announced anything else? My spidey senses are tingling

booksnbangtan @booksnbangtan
@1967_Disney_bound @aCurlieee_doll FBI should really hire fandom. I heard there's dirt on their kids too. Rich kids are all the same. Can't wait for this one to blow

See more replies

James

Back at the hotel in San Francisco, somewhere between Melissa seething "You have no idea what I've sacrificed for this family—*no idea*!" and Rusty's growled "Our kids think every day is Saturday and every bill in your wallet is for them!" Carey and I give up on trying to get the Tripps to stop shouting at each other. They barely notice that we're standing there, watching their nuclear meltdown from just inside the door of Melissa's hotel room.

Which is another thing I discovered—the Tripps haven't shared a bed in two years, at home or at hotels. Carey tries to book them adjoining rooms under the pretense that they like a lot of space. When connecting rooms aren't available—and, conveniently, they often aren't—the Tripps are happy not even being on the same floor.

"This is a clusterfuck," I mutter, and feel the way Carey turns to look at me. "What?"

"I don't think I've ever heard you swear before," she says in wonder.

"I do. Sometimes."

Something crashes farther in the room, and it sounds like a remote control hitting a wall.

"Yeah," she says, "but in your suit with your combed hair and glasses, it's like hearing a toddler curse."

"You know toddlers in suits and glasses?"

Carey cracks a smile and starts to respond, but our attention is yanked across the room when Melissa opens the drawer of the nightstand and hurls the Gideon's Bible at Rusty, hitting him in the shoulder.

"Melly," Carey says gently, "can I grab you some dinner?"

The air seems to cool as she turns to face Carey. Her chest is heaving, and her face is flushed from yelling.

"Can you get me *dinner*?" she asks, her face contorted in rage. "Dinner? Are you kidding me? You and Russell humiliate the fuck out of me in front of two hundred people and now you want to shut me up with food?"

I hold up a hand. "Sorry, I've got to jump in here. Carey didn't have any part in—"

"I wasn't talking to you, James." Melissa spits out my name. "This is between the three of us. Carey has just tried to take credit for *my fucking life's work*, so maybe you should just go back to your room, read a calculus book, and stay out of this."

I look to Carey to see what she wants, and she gives me a little *It's okay* nod and tilts her head toward the door.

I don't want to abandon her, but I have no idea what protocol is in this type of situation. There's no HR to guide me. We don't even have Robyn's clumsy presence here, worried about the legalities of Melissa speaking to an employee this way. Refusing to leave and continuing to defend Carey might just get me fired, and for the first time, the prospect of being fired doesn't send even a mild pulse of relief through me, because it would mean I'd leave Carey to manage this alone.

She sees my hesitation and opens her mouth to speak, but I see her embarrassed blush. God, this is painful. "Okay," I relent. "Call me later?"

I'm only halfway down the hall to my room when I hear the Tripps' door open again. Turning, I see Carey come out, wiping her face, and jog in the opposite direction down the hall.

It's already eleven, but there's no way I'm sleeping after the madness of the book signing, the fight in the hotel room, and Carey's tearful departure. I haven't seen her since, and she's not answering her phone. I'm guessing Melissa is doing one of her long, indignant soaks in the bathtub, but I'm pretty sure I know where I can find Rusty.

Indeed, he's bellied up at the hotel bar, with a half-empty glass of beer in front of him and his face turned up to the television screen overhead.

"You a . . ." I look at the teams and need a beat to decipher what BOS means on the scoreboard. "A Red Sox fan?"

He shrugs and takes another pull of his beer. "I prefer football, but it's July."

I'm not sure how July relates to football because my closest relationship to sports was being dragged to my sister's softball games. It's easy enough to decide that if I haven't cared about football for twenty-nine years I certainly don't have to start tonight. With a raised brow, I silently ask if it's okay for me to take the barstool next to his, and order a scotch and soda.

"How's Carey-girl doing?" Rusty asks.

My stomach experiences a weird cramp. "Don't know. She left your room after I did and took off in the other direction." I thank the bartender when he puts my drink down in front of me. "She's not answering her phone."

Rusty shakes his head and stares down at the dwindling foam in his glass. "I told Melly to treat her better. It's almost like she can't help herself, she just takes all her stress out on me and Carey."

I take this as a sign that he's willing to be open. "Do I have permission to speak freely?"

He eyes me warily and then his shoulder ticks up in a casual shrug. "Sure."

"You're not exactly helping," I say.

He pauses with his beer midair and pins me with a look. Rusty is usually the nicest guy you'll meet. But right now, as he continues to watch me with an even intensity, I'm a little afraid.

Finally, the air leaves him in a resigned sigh, and he sets his beer back down in front of him.

"I guess that's fair."

I let myself exhale. "Then why do you leave it to Carey to handle?"

"I know I'm a flirt. I've always liked female attention, but now it's like I can't go to a bar without getting a phone number." I almost tell him that the black card in his wallet might have a little something to do with that, but I let him continue instead. "Do you know what it's like to have numbers slipped into your hand left and right, when your own wife won't pay attention to you?"

"I've never been married, so . . ."

"We used to do so much together," he says, "but the more famous we get, the less I actually see her."

"Have you tried talking to Melissa about all this?"

He laughs into his beer. "You've been pretty sheltered from Melly's temper so far, but imagine her reaction if I told her something like that. You saw how she reacted today."

"Why does Carey stay?" I've asked her this myself, of course, but her answer was so odd and unsatisfying—*Melly needs me*.

Rusty's answer is a world away from Carey's: "A few reasons. For one, she needs the insurance, and even though Melly can be pretty terrible a lot of the time, she helps her with that and some of the appointments."

I realize this isn't the first time appointments and insurance have been mentioned, and it triggers my curiosity again. I should let it go. Carey would tell me if she thought it was any of my business.

"And?" I ask, prompting him to continue.

"*And* Melly would ruin her."

I pull back, confused. "What does that mean?"

He turns his face to me, and I gather this isn't his first beer of the night. He's got a ball cap pulled down low over his eyes, but his gaze swims, watery and unfocused. Gin blossoms are beginning to bloom beneath the skin around his nose.

Rusty Tripp gives me a wry smile and finishes the detonation he started earlier tonight: "It's all Carey, always has been. The design, the original brand, the window displays. Carey did all of that. She's the one who came up with the small-spaces designs, and I'd build them. It's still that way. Why do you think you can't do any actual engineering? We can't have someone else knowing how the sausage is made." He hiccups and thumps his chest a couple of times. "Melly would be screwed if Carey ever left, and she hates her for it."

EXCERPT FROM *New Life, Old Love*

Chapter Four: There's No Vacation from Communication

Relationships are a lot like houses: without a good foundation, they'll crumble. When a light bulb goes out, you don't buy a new house, you change the bulb. When the faucet drips, you don't start mopping the floor before you fix the leak. In other words, no matter how much digging it takes, it's important to get to the root of a problem.

Rusty and I met when we were basically kids. We didn't have the store yet—didn't even have the idea for one. In fact, we barely had two nickels to rub together. What we did have was a whole lot of passion, and zero experience communicating.

We didn't know what it looked like to fight in a healthy way. I'd get mad at Rusty for leaving his socks on the floor, and he'd storm out. He'd get upset with me for making a mess in the kitchen, and I'd yell and cry. Whenever we fought, I thought, *This is it. Happy couples don't fight. I guess we aren't happy, so I guess we're breaking up.*

But here's the secret: of course happy couples fight! Two strong minds coming together are never going to agree on everything, and it's healthy to express those feelings. But what we had to learn was that it was the *way* we were expressing our feelings that wasn't healthy. Shouting doesn't make anyone feel better. Storming off doesn't fix any problems.

In some ways, we had to learn this all over again when the Comb+Honey brand took off. Pressure adds stress, and stress breaks down the communication process. Even though I'd long since learned that when I'm hurting I have to tell Russ what I'm feeling, sometimes when we're busy, we forget to prioritize our relationship.

We came back to that, consciously, when we first started writing this book. We talk every night. We write each other letters sometimes. I know I have to tell Russ when something bothers me, or it'll fester. I can't let it build up. And sometimes, that means we have to be vulnerable with each other. It takes a heck of a lot of trust.

Before I'm steaming mad, I simply say, "Russ, I felt dismissed back there," or he can say, "Melly, I'm starting to feel smothered by you," and we know each other well enough to know we wouldn't bring it up if it wasn't going to become a problem down the road.

That trust takes time. But when you love each other, it shouldn't be scary to be vulnerable and it shouldn't be hard to compromise.

I'd like to share with you what we like to call SACRED HEALING. We use it every day of our marriage, and it hasn't failed us yet!

When you have something you need to communicate, those words are SACRED:

1. **S**TOP when you register something's wrong.
2. **A**DMIT that you have an issue to discuss.
3. **C**ALMLY express your feelings.
4. **R**EFLECT on why you're feeling this way.
5. **E**NGAGE with your partner to actively fix the issue.
6. **D**EVOTE time after conflict to returning to a loving state.

And when your partner is saying something SACRED, it's your job to be the leader of the HEALING:

1. **H**EAR your partner's words.
2. **E**NGAGE with questions for clarification and understanding.
3. **A**CKNOWLEDGE that what they're saying is important.
4. **L**OOK BACK on your own role in the conflict.
5. **I**NITIATE discussion without anger or defense.
6. **N**EGOTIATE a solution with pure intentions.
7. **G**ROW as partners and individuals by fixing the problem as a team.

Carey

The pool is mostly empty at this hour. A group of rowdy teenage boys here for some kind of sports competition—judging from their matching duffel bags—are splashing and wrestling down at the other end, but it seems my red face and pathetic sniffling effectively signal they should keep their distance.

I'm not usually happier alone, but I am right now, vacillating between embarrassment over the way Melly talked to me and anger at myself for letting her. As crazy as it sounds, I'm genuinely sad about how tonight went down, because despite everything, I care about Melissa. She's lost her temper with me before but never like that, never in front of other people, and always about the job, or out of frustration about things around her. In all the time I've worked for her, she's never questioned my character or accused me of being disloyal.

I wipe my face again, wishing I were more furious and less hurt. Wishing I had stood up to her instead of letting her see me cry.

You and Russell humiliate the fuck out of me in front of two hundred people and now you want to shut me up with food?

Carey has just tried to take credit for my fucking life's work . . .

I'd been so grateful when she'd finally made James leave, but she wasn't finished.

I have given you so much, and this is how you repay me?

Melly, I would never—

Are you calling me a liar?

No—

Try that again, and I will replace you in a second. Do you understand? You're not special, Carey. Don't forget that.

Not special.

Rusty just stood there; his eyes were soft with pity, but he didn't dare contradict her and risk getting something else thrown at his head.

SACRED HEALING, my ass.

And then there's James. I want to thank him for trying to stand up for me, but I'm still too mortified that he had to witness that debacle to imagine ever talking to him again.

I pull the last Funyun out of the bag and glance over at the boys, envying their carefree youth and fighting the urge to rush over to tell them to study hard, to go to college, to do whatever they can to give themselves options. Make plans, and make backup plans. Network, and meet people, and don't be afraid to try something new and fail at it—experience is everything. I want to tell them, more than anything, not to settle down in the first job they get.

One of the boys runs screaming toward the pool and

does a cannonball so epic he soaks all of his friends and a good portion of the pool deck.

"I had my phone, you motherfucker!" another shouts. This is followed by a chorus of delighted cackling that echoes off the building. The pool area sits in a U-shaped courtyard created by the exterior walls of the hotel, with floors of windows that look down. I expect a set of drapes to slide open, or a parent or chaperone to appear with a stern warning to Behave Yourselves or Else, but it doesn't happen.

Because they are *clearly* unsupervised, some form of boy wrestling ensues, complete with a few of the dirtiest words I've ever heard—and my dad worked construction, so I've heard them all. Splashes turn into waves that ripple to where my bare legs dangle in the water. The boys are slowly morphing from Kids on the Loose to *Lord of the Flies*, but the chaos out here is still preferable to facing whatever is going on inside.

My phone vibrates, and I look, reluctantly. I have a few missed calls from James. Nothing from Melly, but then, I don't expect that until tomorrow. After a few hours to cool off—and with nobody else around to placate her—she'll apologize in the morning, like she always does. I think.

But there is a message in my group chat with Peyton and Annabeth.

Annabeth

Checking in

I think about how to best reply here. Having to actually type the lie that everything is fine will make my head explode, but I can't really describe what's going on, either. Weirdly, the only person I think would truly understand is James.

And I can't confide in him.

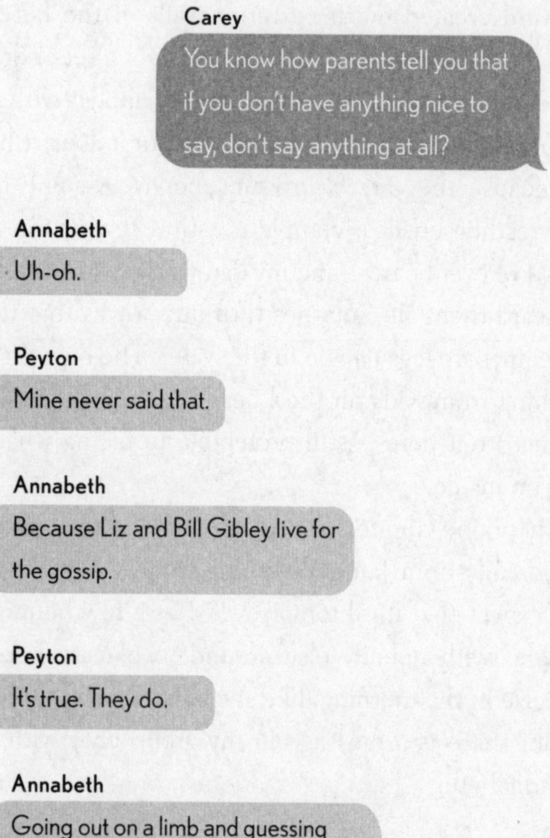

What an understatement.

"Hey."

I'm so startled I nearly drop my phone in the pool, and look up to see James hovering over me. The sleeves of his dress shirt are rolled up, and it accentuates his forearms so nicely it's enough to distract me from my morose mental bender.

"I didn't want to interrupt your Funyunning." He clears his throat, and I blink to focus, eyes scanning down his arms (he really does have very nice arms) to where he's carrying a bag of Funyuns in one hand and a beer in the other. This makes him my current dream man.

With my own bag empty, my mouth waters immediately. From the Funyuns, not the forearms. I think. "Those for me?"

"I thought you might need them after . . ." He jerks his head back toward the hotel. "*That*. But I see you beat me to it."

That.

Embarrassment washes over me again. Muttering a bleak thanks, I take the offered bag and look down; my hair slides forward, mercifully blocking his view of my flushed cheeks.

"Mind if I join you?"

I can think of at least twelve things I'd rather do than talk this out right now, but I motion to the ground next to me anyway. "Knock yourself out."

He takes a moment to toe off his shoes and roll up the legs of his expensive pants before taking a seat next to me and gently lowering his feet into the water. He lets out a quiet, rumbling groan that sends a surge of goose bumps up my legs.

"It's nice out here," he says, surveying the patio and then the balconies overlooking where we sit. "My room has a view of the Hooters across the street."

I laugh. "You're probably the first straight man to ever say that and sound disappointed."

"Never was a huge fan of the color orange." When he grins wolfishly, I am reminded that he has lovely white teeth but very sharp—and oddly seductive—canines. They change his face from nerdy-serious to sexy-devious.

"A shame," I agree.

Reaching into his pocket, he pulls out a bottle opener and pops off the cap of the beer before setting the bottle on the cement between us. I manage to wait all of two seconds before carefully picking it up and taking a long drink.

I watch the boys roughhousing on the opposite end of the pool. For as long as I can with James, I want to ignore the shrill-voiced, platinum-haired elephant in the proverbial room. I open the fresh bag to reach for a Funyun, and my crunch is comically loud in the awkward silence between us.

"Sorry," I say around the bite. James laughs and takes the bag, reaching inside for a few and popping one in his mouth.

"You been out here this whole time?" he asks. *Since you got your head chewed off*, he means.

"I had a really awkward trip to the convenience store on the corner. Who knew sobbing at the checkout while buying junk food would make the cashier so uncomfortable. I'm sure he assumed I was on my period." I pause, adding inexplicably, "—I'm not."

I want to slide into the pool and submerge myself for

eternity. James is understandably silent for a few beats. Finally, he gives a simple "Cool."

One of the older boys finds two pool noodles hidden behind a clump of bushes, and he and another kid start whacking each other. When they team up and hit one of the boys so enthusiastically that he falls into the water like a sack of dirt, James looks nervously back toward the hotel.

"Should we go get an adult?"

But the boy pops back above water, grinning wildly.

"They're just being dumb," I say. "I'd be in there, too, but I'm not paying eighty-five dollars for a fishnet bikini in the gift shop." After another particularly loud thwack from the other end of the pool, I glance at James. "Don't you remember being like that?"

"Like *that*?" he asks, and picks up the bottle as if to ask *Can I?* I nod, and just like that, we're sharing a beer. "Not even a little. Were you?"

"Not *that* specifically, but goofing around at the reservoir. Tubing down the Snake River with my brothers. Skinny-dipping with friends. There was a lot of skinny-dipping."

He coughs, choking. I've never seen him make this face before, but I daresay he's impressed. "Oh yeah?"

"We grew up kind of feral. My parents weren't very attentive. My grandma used to call us 'free-range kids.' Summers meant leaving the house in the morning, and barely making it back before the sun went down. We had a lot of space around us, so it's not like anyone was there to see."

"I always forget you grew up in Wyoming. You've lived there your whole life?"

I reach for the beer and take a sip. "It was different then.

Rural. More farms and houses, fewer multimillion-dollar compounds."

"Did you grow up on a farm?"

"A small one. We'd leave the door open or something and my mom would shout, 'Were y'all raised in a barn?' Then we'd get our asses tanned by shouting back, 'You would know!' My dad did construction and carpentry around town and grew alfalfa. My mom has sold most of their land now, but we used to make forts and go muddin' and cause all kinds of trouble in those fields—most of which my parents never found out about. It's all subdivisions now."

"Skippin' rocks and playin' in the old waterin' hole," he teases with a terrible hillbilly accent.

I give his shoulder a nudge and reach for the bag again. "You're not that far off. I remember someone had a rope swing that hung over the river. It was plenty deep in most places, but some years the water level would be lower, and really shallow along the shore. Some of the more protective parents would cut down that rope every year, but before long someone else would have another one up. I still don't know how nobody managed to kill themselves on it."

"That sounds pretty great, actually. The diving part, not the dying."

"It was. I miss those days. So much room to explore, so much time outside. It was still mostly pre-internet, even though it doesn't feel that long ago." I take another sip, washing a tight band of nostalgia down with it. "What about you?"

"I never had any skinny-dipping, I'll tell you that right now."

"A travesty."

"I'm inclined to agree."

I turn to look right at him. "Come on. You couldn't always have been this buttoned up. Am I supposed to believe you just sprang up somewhere, fully Tom Forded and preloaded with a degree from MIT?"

"My sister can confirm."

I study his profile and notice that he isn't wearing his glasses. Because the universe is never fair about these things, his lashes are long, and dark, and curled. I am immediately envious. He takes a sip of the beer and then swipes a long finger across his upper lip.

James pats my back when I cough, and hands me the beer, careful to make sure I've got it before he lets it go.

Like he knows my grip is sometimes weak.

My stomach swoops low.

"You all right?" he asks.

"Fine," I say, recovering with a sip. "Something didn't go down right." Composed again, I urge him to continue. "She's older than you, right? Your sister?"

He looks surprised that I remembered, or maybe that I'm engaging in real conversation. "By four years. Old enough that I was more of a nuisance than a buddy."

"My brothers are five and six years older, Rand and Kurt. Protective when needed, but if friends were around they were like, 'That kid? Never seen her before.'"

He laughs, and it's this scratchy, honeyed sound. Has he always laughed like that? Have I been in a Melly-induced stress haze this entire time, not noticing laughs and forearms, unaware of lashes, lips, and fingers?

"Jenn could be like that, too," he says. "We'd go to this amusement park in Albuquerque—"

"Wait. You're from New Mexico?" When he nods, I joke, "No one is actually *from* New Mexico."

He laughs this off. "I am, I promise. We moved there when I was three, from Wisconsin. My mom grew up in New Mexico, and after she finished her residency in Madison, she set up her family practice in Albuquerque."

"Sounds like a witness protection cover," I tease.

"I wish my life was that exciting." James's grin is my new addiction. "Listen: My dad is in *finance*. I was the drum major in high school, and president of the chess club—I'm sure you have no problem believing that. We had a house and a dog and everything."

I squint at him. "Sounds believable. I'll allow it. You may continue to tell me about this amusement park."

"It's a big deal in our family," he says, with adorable gravity. "My mom went there when she was growing up, so it's like a rite of passage. It was my favorite place. There were rides and a water park and games—they even did a Food on a Stick Festival every year. I'd beg my parents to take us, and then when my sister was old enough to go with her friends, they'd make her take me with them."

I remember my brothers' whining whenever my mom sent them to drag me home or made them pick me up from school. They were never afraid to remind me how much I cramped their style. "I'm sure she loved that."

"Yeah, I was a pain because I always wanted to go but I was terrified of the roller coasters."

"Then what did you do there?"

"Watch everything, mostly," he says. "Get as close as I could to the rides so I could try to figure out how they worked. I was fascinated by the idea that you could be flying down this track at sixty, seventy, maybe a hundred miles an hour in some cases, and there was no engine powering the car. You're pulled to the top of the hill, but then it's the conversion of potential energy to kinetic energy that gets you through the ride."

"That is the most James McCann thing I think I've ever heard you say, and I've heard you talk for an hour about the principles behind seismic loading." I pop another Funyun into my mouth. "I guess I look at a roller coaster and just see the potential for vomit. Or death. I never thought about how they work. But I can see how it'd be fascinating if you were a super nerd." Pausing, I add, "I mean that as a compliment, by the way. Your brain is pretty great."

James ducks his head and pretends to be interested in a chip in the cement. I take the opportunity to study the sharp line of his jaw. His face is so angular, made up of such extremes of soft lashes and hard features: cheekbones, jaw, the straight line of his nose.

"But wait," I say, suddenly remembering what he was actually going to be doing this week before we were roped into babysitting the Tripps. "What about Florida? You were going to ride Everest with your nephews."

"I'm not afraid of rides anymore. I started figuring out how it all worked, how each part had a specific purpose. Some wheels keep the ride smooth, some keep the coaster on the track, some help with lateral motion, and so on. Once I understood how it all came together, they didn't seem as scary."

"I'd think it'd be even scarier knowing how many things

can go wrong." I laugh. "I guess that explains why you're the engineer and I'm the assistant. You think of things in such mechanical terms. I basically just book us at inconvenient hotels."

He's quiet for a few long breaths. "But that's not actually right, either, is it?"

This catches me off guard, and I glance over at him. "What?"

"Despite what you might think about me, I know how hard your job is. Few people appreciate what it takes to be a great assistant." He tilts his head, grimacing sweetly. "But I know that's not the only thing you're doing here."

For a second, I'm completely lost. "What?"

"Rusty told me," he says quietly.

His meaning slowly sinks in, and it feels like a weight is tied to all the air in my chest, pulling it down inside my lungs. "Rusty told you what?"

"That the designs have been yours. That the whole brand grew out of the work you did early on." He pauses, watching me carefully. "And now."

I'm afraid to try to breathe. "Rusty said that?"

"Yeah."

I turn back to where the kids are packing up to head inside. "I don't know why he'd say that."

"Carey, come on. The concepts and the furniture? The entire brand? That was all you? It's a miracle you're doing literally *everything* and not falling down right now."

My parents weren't perfect, but they valued hard work. My dad routinely put in sixteen-hour days. My mom is a schoolteacher and she's always worked long hours with too little pay and even less appreciation. They taught me that you work until the job is done, and you give it your all. Every time. They also taught me to be humble about it, but right now, hearing those words and the recognition I've secretly craved, a tiny beast flutters to life in my chest, clawing and scratching for more. But it's also terrifying. James has only been here a few months. He isn't as invested in the company's survival. He doesn't have as much to lose if it all comes tumbling down.

"It's not really like that," I say, my heart racing. *What the fuck is Rusty thinking?*

"Isn't it? Because Rusty seemed pretty sure of himself. And that program you were working on? It wasn't Minecraft. You were configuring a layout, weren't you?"

"Just playing around with some floor plan ideas."

"Melissa's reaction at the signing when Rusty asked you about the display . . . and the way you seem to know how all the furniture goes together and how to fix it . . ." He pauses. "I would never tell anyone, if that's why you're not telling me what's going on."

Panic wells up inside me like a tide rolling in. I'm not sure what to say. *Do I deny it completely? Explain it away?*

"Carey—" he starts.

I cut him off. "I mean, yes, the original window displays were mine." I say this quietly, like Melly is standing over us, ready to pounce at any moment. "I did most of them. But I did it all under the Comb+Honey name. If I were a scientist and came up with a new chemical compound, would the formula belong to me or the company I work for?"

"I don't know if that's how something like this works."

"I've worked for them since I was *sixteen*, James," I say, desperate now. "I make good money, especially for someone with my experience—which is none. This is all I've done. I never went to college; I have no training, no degree. I've never had a promotion or a title change because I've never needed a title. I can't go somewhere else and do what I do here, and even if I did it would be because I've worked in *her* store and on *her* jobs and on *her* show."

"You could show someone what you can do, and tell them it's been yours all along."

The sad truth settles over me, and I glance out at the water. "She'd say she taught me everything I know. It would be her word against mine." I look at him. "At least here I get to do what I love. How valuable am I to anyone if I can't even claim what I do as my own?"

He frowns down at the pool, and I can tell he's trying to come up with an argument, but after a few quiet moments, his shoulders fall. "God. That sucks."

I bump his shoulder with mine. "Must be rough for an engineer. So many emotions."

"You called me an engineer, not assistant. Twice, actually."

I laugh.

"What's the difference between an introverted engineer and an extroverted engineer?" he asks.

I look up, and his excitement at getting to tell me this joke makes my heart feel like a wild animal inside me. "What?"

"When the introverted engineer speaks to you," James says, "he looks down at his shoes. When the extroverted engineer speaks to you, he looks down at *your* shoes."

I burst out laughing, and he grins, so sweet and proud that I imagine myself melting on the pool deck.

"What are you doing here?" I gesture around us. "Take that show on the road. There's your escape."

"Yeah, see," he says, sobering. "Not that I want to complain to you, but my work situation isn't much better. Either I put Rooney, Lipton, and Squire down on my résumé and get everything that comes along with it, or I don't and leave a four-year hole in my work history. I have an amazing portfolio, and projects with my name on them, but now all of it is tarnished under this cloud of scandal—me included. I thought this was my way out."

"I'm sorry, James."

Sometime while we've been talking the rowdy boys left, and now the entire patio is empty. Colored LEDs shimmer beneath the water's surface and throw ripples of light on the trees overhead, on the sides of the hotel, even on our skin. I wonder if we could just stay out here all night. Maybe—oops—we could miss the bus in the morning.

"Can I ask you a question?" he says, and I turn at the change in his tone. Serious, almost nervous. "But you don't have to answer."

"Sure."

"Both you and Rusty have mentioned insurance." My breath halts, and he's quick to clarify. "He didn't tell me anything, just mentioned that even though Melissa can be awful, sometimes she helps you with your appointments." He waits for me to pick it up, but I don't, so he adds, "What appointments?"

The words land like stones in my chest. On instinct, I

look down to where my hands lie relaxed and deceptively innocent in my lap. It's weird to be asked about it. With a jolt, I realize I never have. Everyone in my life who ever noticed something was different about me—Peyton, Annabeth, even my brothers, eventually—waited until I explained on my own.

So maybe *weird* isn't the right word. It's *nice* to be asked. "I'm pretty good at hiding it most of the time," I tell him, "but you've probably noticed that my fingers don't always cooperate."

"I did, but—well, we've been together a lot lately. There aren't that many places to look," he says with an apologetic smile. "I chew on my nails when I'm anxious. I just assumed you were a fidgeter."

I laugh, and the tension slowly leaves me. It's nice to be able to tell James what's going on. Means I won't have to sit on my hands quite so much around him. "It's called dystonia. Focal dystonia in my case. Basically, when your brain tells a muscle to move, it's also telling another muscle not to. With dystonia, both muscles around a joint will contract at the same time. It means my hands clench into fists and spasm—mostly my left hand, but occasionally my right. Sometimes my fingers flex and extend, and become generally uncooperative."

"It's worse in your left hand," he says quietly. "That's why I've seen you try to use your right sometimes even though you're a lefty?"

I stare at him for a few seconds. He noticed all of that? I'm not sure if that means he's curious or fascinated, but thankfully his attention feels warm, not clinical. "If I keep dropping my pencil, yeah."

He winces. "Does it hurt?" His voice is so gentle, it's almost painful.

"Sometimes."

"What are the appointments for?"

"Botox," I say, and throw him a dramatic pout. "It keeps the muscles from cramping. But I get it in my hands, obviously, so I don't even get to be wrinkle-free from it."

He lets out a quiet groan. "I'm sorry, Carey."

"Eh," I say, grinning, "I don't have any wrinkles yet anyway."

"I mean about all of it," he says, awkwardly rushing to clarify.

Reflexively pushing past the sympathy, I say, "It's fine. Melly can be terrible, but she's been there for me when I needed it. She lets me design. She lets me make things. I don't know another company that would let me do that with my level of experience." I lie back on the cement and look up at the windows; more of them are dark now than there were before. I imagine looking for another job. Going to interviews. Having to explain to a new boss and coworkers that I won't always be able to keep my hands still, that sometimes I can't grip a phone or a pencil or do something as simple as fasten a button. I've only written a résumé once and I'm sure it was terrible. I laugh when I remember that, the one time I applied for another job, under "Previous Work Experience," I included eleventh grade accounting class.

I put my hands over my face and groan. "Want to hear something crazy?"

"Always."

"I actually started seeing a therapist because I needed

someone to talk to, but then couldn't tell her anything about work because of the way the NDA is worded. How fucked up is that? Okay. I'm going to shut up. I'm depressing both of us."

"No, you're not." I hear James set the empty bottle on the cement. "But come on. Let's do something."

I open my eyes to see him towering over me.

"Like what? It's not like we can go anywhere, and I don't want to go inside. I have to save my money if I'm about to be unemployed."

He slides his hands into his pockets, jiggling some change, and I notice his arms again. Tan, nicely toned, not too veiny. Just a smattering of hair. "Let's swim."

I snap my attention back to his face. "I already told you, I didn't bring a suit."

"When did that ever stop you before?" He starts to unbutton his shirt. His collarbones come into view and—okay, wait, he has my attention now.

I sit up, reaching out to stop him. "I'm not going skinny-dipping at a hotel pool!" I lean forward, hissing, "Are you insane?"

He shrugs out of his button-down to reveal a riveting stretch of bare chest and stomach underneath. I've never imagined James shirtless before.

I was not prepared. He's not at all bulky, but he's defined, with smooth, tan skin and muscles that lengthen and flex as he moves. My mouth waters again, this time not for the Funyuns.

"I'm not talking about getting naked," he says, and I try to ignore the way all my nerve endings sit up and pay attention. He unfastens his belt and nods toward the pool. Have I ever noticed the sound of a belt before? Because right now the slide of leather and click of the buckle are bordering on obscene.

"You can go in wearing what you've got on," he says. "Come on."

"I didn't bring that many clothes," I whine.

He grins down at me. We both know I'm stalling.

With his belt unfastened, he bends and places his hands on his knees, bringing his eyes almost level with mine. He looks pointedly at my clothes. "They'll dry."

He holds out a hand.

Moments pass during which I contemplate all the ways this could end badly, before I think, *But how badly, exactly? Someone sees us having a good time and swimming in our clothes? Is that really so terrible?*

I take his hand—it's really warm—and let him help me to my feet.

"Maybe take this off, though." He points to my denim jacket, buttoned all the way to the top. I know it's ridiculous, but I'm instantly anxious about being able to unfasten the buttons in front of him.

As if reading my mind, he takes a step closer. "Can I help?"

I nod, too flustered to insist that I can do it myself.

First of all, he knows this. Second . . . I just really want him to.

With steady fingers he reaches for the bottom button and coaxes it through the material. It's so quiet I can actually hear the sound of the fabric sliding over metal, the water where it laps against the side of the pool. The way I'm holding my breath.

Breathe, Carey. You will definitely ruin the moment if you pass out, fall, and have to be dragged unconscious from the water.

He moves slowly but surely, from my waist, over my breasts, and to my neck. His eyes never stray from where his hands are working, but even in the dark I can see the way his cheeks are flushed. Does he notice how hard I'm breathing? I'm doing everything I can to not dwell on the fact that he's shirtless and essentially helping undress me.

When he's done, our eyes meet only briefly before he steps back, arms falling loosely at his sides.

"Thanks." I don't think I've ever been this turned on, and he only helped me unbutton a jacket. Lord help me when I see him wet.

Lost in this image, I startle when he finally pulls his belt free with a distracting snap. He sets it with his watch on one of the lounge chairs. I take mine off, too.

"You ready?" he says, recovered and grinning in a way I know I've never seen before, not even when I was teasing him about a tie he wore one day, and then my chair immediately broke in hilarious karmic retribution.

I nod my head. "No."

He laughs and his Adam's apple bobs in his throat and I'm reminded that there is bare skin below—

He unbuttons his pants and steps out of them, leaving him in only a pair of black boxers.

"On the count of three," he says, and I'm rendered momentarily mute, unable to drag my eyes away from his legs and his hip bones and the small stretch of fabric in between. "One. Two—"

He never gets to three. I think of the afternoons on the river, the sun scorching in the sky but the feeling of glacial water on my skin. I remember the rush of gripping the rope and the freedom of letting go, trusting that the water would be deep enough, even though there was every chance in the world that it wouldn't.

I race toward the edge and jump. My heart is in my throat as I'm swallowed by darkness, beating a hundred times a minute when I surface again.

I tread water, using my hands and feet to turn just as James's shout cuts through the air. His cannonball creates a giant splash, and I laugh as he bursts up again.

"Cold!"

"You had your feet in it, this shouldn't be a surprise," I say, cracking up and scooping a handful of water to throw at him.

He chases me around and I swim away, squealing. He dives beneath the surface, his hand gently finding my ankle and skimming up my calf. I kick and flail, the filmy layers of my skirt billowing up around my legs in a pink cloud. I think I kick him in the face. When we finally come up for air we're still laughing.

"I can't believe I agreed to this," I say. "You're a bad influence."

He reaches up to push back his hair. "Me? I'm the goody-goody here. I've never skinny-dipped in my life."

"And you still haven't," I say, splashing him again and then screeching as I try to get away. He dives beneath the water, and it feels like I'm looking into a shimmering funhouse mirror, trying to figure out where he'll pop up again.

I never find out because his arms loop around my waist and I'm pulled under and spun around; a grinning James appears right in front of me. Bubbles escape his mouth as he laughs, but his eyes go wide when I turn the tables and lunge for him. I chase him around the pool, but my hands only skim his legs. And then he stops, surprising me with how close we are, and my palms slide up his stomach and chest.

When we break the surface, I realize we're right at the side of the pool. He spins me so I'm against the wall and his arms gently cage me in. I've never been this close to James McCann before.

I absolutely don't mind.

We're both breathless. Water clings to his lashes in little spikes, his cheeks are pink with exertion—or from my foot—and I have that weird disorienting feeling that we've never really seen each other before tonight.

His eyes are brown and twinkly; his grin is enormous. He licks his lips, and then bites the lower one. A surge of goose bumps slithers along my skin, and it has nothing to do with the temperature of the water.

I know the moment he really notices our position because the giddy smile slips from his mouth and melts into something serious. His eyes flicker across my face and down to my mouth, and he blinks once, twice.

"Sorry," he whispers, and I feel his breath as it mixes with mine; the heat ghosts across my lips. He moves back, and on instinct I reach for his hips.

Seconds tick by, and the water laps against the side of the pool, jostling us together and apart. Together. I look at his mouth, wondering how I never noticed the bow of his top lip, the fullness of his bottom. His boxers sink low on his hips under the weight of the water and my thumbs press against the bare skin there, able to discern bone and muscle. My nipples are hard beneath the fabric of my shirt; my lace bra is useless against the temperature of the water. If I leaned in, even an inch, would he let me kiss him? Would he want me to? Do I?

I lick away a drop of water, and his eyes follow the movement before meeting mine again. He gives me a nod—so imperceptible I'd've missed it if we weren't so close, chest to chest and breathing the same air. I have a room upstairs, a bed. So does he. It would be so simple to kiss him. There are barely inches between us.

But I've been single so long, I'm not sure how this is done anymore. I falter. Did he *really* nod? Is his expression more sympathy, less sexual intent?

My heart pounds inside my ribs, and I don't know which of us decided to move first but then he's there, and his mouth slides over mine, once, then again. He pulls away with a tiny kiss to the corner of my mouth, and we look at each other. We're still at the point where the kiss could be blamed on the movement of the water, maybe. Or, ha ha, such a weird, exhausting night.

But then he leans forward again with a smile, and in the space of a gasp we're kissing like we need to: lips and tongue and the occasional dirty drag of teeth. His hands move down to my waist, holding me to him, and when he presses forward, I lift my legs, weightless, wrapping them around him.

It's been so long, but even still I don't think anything has felt as good as Ja—

"Don't get her pregnant!"

We jump apart, eyes darting upward to see a few of the boys from earlier standing in one of the open windows. I tug my tank top strap back up over my shoulder. James treads water a few feet away, eyes moving from the balcony and slowly back to my face, searching. Nothing sucks more than getting busted, and the tension of the moment has been totally punctured. I'm suddenly aware of how cold the water is, how late it's grown.

But I'm also aware of what we just did, how he felt against me, and how much I liked it.

James gives the pubescent assholes a stiff salute as if to say *Thanks for the tip, you little fuckers,* and I climb out of the pool, grabbing the first towel I see.

Partial transcript of interview with Carey Duncan, July 14

Officer Ali: So you and Mr. McCann were growing close.

Carey Duncan: What makes you say that?

Officer Ali: There seems to be a lot of him in your recollection of what happened.

CD: That's just because we were together nonstop.

Officer Ali: So only as coworkers?

CD: What is this, *The Bachelor*?

Officer Ali: Let me remind you that you can refuse to answer any question, at any time.

CD: I vote for that, then. I don't want to talk about James. Whatever did or didn't happen between us has nothing to do with what happened last night.

Officer Ali: All right.

CD: You're writing that down?

Officer Ali: I'm taking notes, yes. But as I mentioned at the beginning, this interview will all be transcribed and kept on record.

CD: Great. Is it public record?

Officer Ali: Let's switch gears a little. The *Variety* announcement. What was that for?

CD: The new show, *Home Sweet Home*. The Tripps had been filming it in secret while they wrapped up *New Spaces*. It was a lot like what they'd been doing before, but this time there weren't any costars to fall back on. This time the pressure was all on them.

Officer Ali: And how were they handling that?

CD: Will the phrase "hot mess" be clear enough for your transcription?

Officer Ali: Yes.

CD: Then that's my answer.

Officer Ali: So the success or failure of

Home Sweet Home would rest entirely on the Tripps.

CD: Yes.

Officer Ali: Did Mr. McCann like the Tripps?

CD: As much as he could, I guess. I don't think it occurred to me until yesterday, but it's possible Melly knew when she hired him that James had come from a company that had gone down in scandal. Maybe she knew he was desperate and used it against him. She knew he wouldn't fight back when she essentially made him Rusty's assistant. He didn't have any power.

Officer Ali: So you think Mr. McCann took the job because he felt trapped?

CD: I think he took the first job that came along.

Officer Ali: So he would have been glad to have a new situation present itself?

CD: Are you suggesting that James would have a reason to ruin the Tripps?

Officer Ali: Let's take a five-minute break before we continue.

James

If someone had asked me at the beginning of this job—even this tour—whether I could see myself at some point wildly making out with Carey Duncan, I would have given an easy "No." In hindsight, I'm guessing I might have even been a bit of a dick about it. The glaring truth that Carey and I come from two completely different worlds used to seem like a barrier between us: she's a small-town woman who's only ever lived in one place, and I left the Southwest ten or so years ago to live on the East Coast for school, then work. At first blush, we had nothing in common.

But there we were—kissing madly, with a fever I haven't felt in what seems like ages and feelings that seem to grow exponentially with every conversation we have—and now here I am, watching Carey bolt out of the pool and back into the hotel without a backward glance.

I glare up at the balcony just when the kids from earlier duck back inside. They should feel like monsters for breaking up a moment like that, but I'm sure they're oblivious, so there's no convenient outlet for my irritation and disappointment. An electrical storm rages along my skin. I count a slow fifty then climb out, grabbing a towel from a shelf and padding back over toward my clothes.

The concrete is icy beneath my feet. It's jarring to be pulled so immediately back into the most banal of bodily sensations when the feel of Carey's tongue and mouth and skin is right there at the front of my thoughts. Did I know the second I stepped outside tonight that I wanted to act on the quiet longing that's been pulsing in the background of my thoughts? Or was it the way she opened up to me with such unguarded sweetness?

I've never been with anyone like her. My previous relationships have always been with women who seemed to be cut from the same cloth as I am. The last person I was with was a medium-term girlfriend—nine months or so. I knew we were over when we stopped excitedly telling each other every detail of our day, stopped wanting to bring each other along to every outing with friends, and the sex started to feel safe and quiet. I rode it out for another month, but when I realized neither of us was all that invested and she was never going to admit it, I finally put us both out of our misery. The idea of spending the rest of my life in the routine we'd fallen into—of monotonous workdays followed by takeout, polite conversation, and quiet, focused missionary sex—sounded terrible.

But I can already tell there's no chance of that with whoever ends up with Carey. She may take a passive role in her job, but I can't possibly be the only one who sees the passionate woman trying to fight her way out of the mold she's been pressed into. Whenever she manages to figure out what she wants in life, she'll be a force of nature.

I head upstairs for a long, cooling shower. Maybe tomorrow we'll laugh off the abrupt end to the night and the weight between us will still be there. Maybe we'll carefully and quietly shape this into something worth pursuing. Or, maybe Carey regretted the kiss immediately, and tomorrow—an already loaded and stressful day—will be awkward and exhausting. Realistically, the odds of the two of us ending up together are minuscule. A disappointed ache corkscrews through me.

The upside, I guess, is that I don't have to spend much of the next morning worrying about it, because I wake to a flurry of texts and notifications. The *Variety* announcement—that the first season of the Tripps' new show, *Home Sweet Home*, can soon be streamed in its entirety on Netflix—hits all of our socials just after eight a.m. Melissa has texted me to let me know that a stylist is coming to get Rusty ready, and I'm to accompany Carey over to Boulevard restaurant at the Embarcadero to help set up for the party this afternoon. Based on our itinerary, there will be about fifty guests, and Melissa wanted something iconic for the sit-down lunch. By the time guests arrive at noon, we should (according to Ted) have a pretty good idea what the show buzz is, and we'll know in a few days whether it gives the Tripps the expected boost they're looking for in book sales.

I have barely enough time to get myself presentable—let alone spend any of it worrying about how things will be today. By nine thirty, I'm waiting at the curb, ordering a Lyft for us, when there's a tap to my shoulder.

Carey stands there, hair blowing across her cheek in

the San Francisco wind. The woman can't hide a blush, and relief passes through me seeing that she's nervous, too.

"Hey," she says. "I didn't know you'd be coming with me."

"Melissa's instructions." I give a lame little salute.

We stand there for a few awkward beats, and I have to assume we're equally unsure what to say to get the conversation rolling. For the life of me, the only thing that seems to flash across my thoughts is the final second before we kissed last night, that moment of intense anticipation followed by the powerful relief.

"So," she says, wincing sweetly.

"So," I say back, biting down on my grin. Every time I did that last night she'd look at my mouth. Maybe the weight between us *is* still there today.

Carey tilts her head to the side, brows raised. "So is that our car?" She gestures to the curb, to the white sedan that's pulled up, window down, driver leaning impatiently toward us. "James?" he asks.

With a mumbled confirmation, I open the car door for Carey and watch her slide across the seat, giving myself exactly the time it takes for her to adjust her skirt over her legs to appreciate the flash of bare skin.

We pull away from the curb and again, my mind goes blank. "How—um—are you?" I ask.

"I'm glad to get out of the hotel for the day, I'll tell you that." She glances behind us as if to somehow reassure herself that Melissa is well and truly not around.

"I bet."

But is being alone together any more relaxing? I have no idea. It's certainly not relaxing for me. I can close my eyes and remember how intense it was just unbuttoning her jacket, or the way her tank and skirt were soaking wet and clinging to her, or the way she blinked the water out of her eyes and her gaze kept sinking to my mouth as if pulled there by a weight.

"Did you sleep okay?" she asks.

I swallow a laugh. "Not really."

When I look over at her, the blush is back. "Yeah. Me either."

This seems like a fantastic opportunity for us to talk about why we both slept like crap, but of course our phones buzz in unison.

Robyn

Today is the day the Tripps become the most popular home renovation experts in the world!

This is a huge day for all of us. Chin up!

The window to talk about the *us* in the car together closes as the other, bigger Us takes over again. Carey pulls in a deep breath and rubs her face, groaning. This event is probably the most important of the tour. Although the party is small, there will be hugely influential journalists and industry people in the room—from the *Chronicle*, Goodreads, Apple Books, and, of course, Netflix. The Tripps need to be at their very best. So it's probably good if I'm not distracted by the idea of kissing Carey again anyway.

"Tell me how I can help you today," I say quietly.

"I think everything should be ready to go." She opens her notebook. "I have the menu confirmed, seating chart, florist . . ." Trailing off, she drags a finger down the page. "I don't even know that I'll have much to do except make sure things go smoothly."

"Did you and Melissa talk about last night?"

"Um." She closes the notebook in her lap. "Briefly, yeah."

I can tell the abrupt subject change caught her off guard, but I'm invested now in her being more assertive and valued in this job. I don't want her to sweep this under the rug. "I assume she apologized?"

"That's a dangerous assumption to make," she says, laughing a little, "but sort of. She said she was sorry my feelings were hurt, which . . . isn't really an apology, but it's about as good as I'll get, and things are fine now."

She keeps her face forward, and I try to read her expression. Is she nervous? Angry? Or is this type of situation—where Melly blows her lid at Carey and everything moves on as usual the next day—totally normal? Unfortunately, I'm guessing it's the latter. How completely toxic.

For better or for worse, my desire to keep from saying this aloud means I end up addressing the *other* elephant in the room: "It was fun hanging out in the pool last night." I falter a little, adding, "Despite the circumstances."

Carey turns in my direction, and warmth bleeds inside me at the way her eyes light up before her smile appears. "It was. Thanks for getting me out of a bad mood."

Is that all it was? Gentle sarcasm is my instinct: "It's my

go-to move whenever a female coworker is having a rough day. Get them in the pool for some kissing, I guess?"

To my relief, Carey bursts out laughing. "Well, whatever it was, it worked." She looks genuinely grateful. "I know it sucks, but I'm so glad you're here on this crazy trip, Jimbo."

My grin feels too big for the moment . . . where I'm pretty sure we're tacitly agreeing last night was just a way to blow off some steam and nothing more. "I definitely wouldn't want you to have to do this alone."

The quiet returns, but my thoughts are rolling at a wild clip. The kiss didn't feel like it was only about escaping a bad day. But maybe it did to Carey.

We stare out our respective windows, watching the city pass in fits and starts as we wind our way through traffic. There's a small coffee shop, a little hole-in-the-wall bagel place, a bakery. At every one, I want to turn to Carey and suggest that we have time to grab a bite, go sit somewhere anonymous together and pretend we don't have a job to do, don't have to be the young unmarried people propping up one of the country's most beloved marriages.

But I don't. By the time we reach the Embarcadero, I'm amazed how gloomy the sky over the water looks; the city wears the foggy haze like a summertime cloak.

Boulevard is a San Francisco institution, and when we step inside, even I admit the style looks familiar. I watch Carey take it in—the rich wood décor, the whimsical vintage European prints, the warm, muted lighting. In *Home Sweet Home* parlance, the place has "a distinct point of view," and as I follow Carey around the room, looking at the wine storage, the table settings, the open kitchen, the lampshades and art, I know without having to ask that Carey chose this location herself.

"It's beautiful in here," I say.

Carey turns to beam at me. "It's amazing, right? I know minimalism is such a huge thing these days—with mid-century modern, clean lines, simplicity being the trend—but I sometimes wish we could go back to something like this: simple, but ornate." She points overhead. "The ceiling is brick, but with the lighting, the entire space feels warmer. Cozier. We have a lake cabin we're renovating in season two, and something like this would be amazing for it."

I'm supposed to be looking at the ceiling, but I love watching her when she's talking like this. It's fascinating. She's completely in her element right now, and I hope it's a sign of her comfort with me that she's sharing aloud.

I tip my head back and study the way the bricks are arranged in an arc that expands from the corners toward the center. From an engineering standpoint, securing such a heavy material to the ceiling would be fairly straightforward, but from an artisan standpoint, the possibilities for intricate construction are pretty cool.

Carey points to a framed print on the wall. "Like this: The frame is so intricate, but the print isn't. Usually it's the other way around, where the print is the vibrant focus, but here, the frame is the art. I like that." She tilts her head again, studying it before writing something down in a small notebook.

Everything appears to be ready for the lunch—the menu is finalized, the private room has been arranged for our party. There really isn't much for us to do. Or, more accurately, there isn't much for *me* to do. I shuffle around uselessly while Carey confirms that Robyn and Ted have each been picked up at the airport, that the contact at *Variety* is still set to post the announcement at the right time, that we have a gluten-free option for one of the executives, a vegan option for another, and a wheelchair-accessible spot at the table for one of the journalists. Carey ticks things off in her notebook, and when she reaches the bottom, she blows her bangs out of her eyes and then looks up at me with a smile that is so easy and unburdened that I'm suddenly unable to remember why I'm not supposed to be fascinated by her. I know she doesn't need me here to help, but in her expression I see that she *likes* that I'm with her right now, and it makes me feel godlike.

"You do everything," I say, trying to wrap my head around it.

"I do not." She flushes and makes a screwball *that's preposterous* face.

"You do." A strand of hair is stuck to her cheek, and I pull it free. "Don't lie."

Carey bites back a smile. "Well. Thanks."

"I don't mean this as bad as it's going to sound"—I quickly take a glance around to make sure we're alone—"but what does Melissa actually contribute?"

Carey squints at me, her smile flattening. "She's the head designer," she says. "The lead on the redesigns."

Laughing, I say, "Okay, Carey—"

But she shakes her head. "It's not really as bad as it sounded last night. I was just frustrated."

I give myself a second to identify the best response to

this. Who knows what Carey needs to tell herself to do this job? There has to be a certain level of self-deception on her end, and I'm not sure I want to dig too deep there.

"Well, I'm glad," I finally say.

"Melly said she had a surprise for me today." Carey shrugs. "So that's nice, I guess?"

I echo her hopeful smile. Guests begin to arrive at the restaurant, and so far it seems like everyone is pretty thrilled for the show—though it's hard to gauge what the external reaction is, since literally everyone in the lunch party already knew about the upcoming announcement, with many of them standing to make a lot of money if the show does well. Still, Melissa and Rusty seem to be in good shape, and it feels like one more situation where things could have gone so much worse.

Neither Carey nor I get a chance to sit, let alone eat, but the lunch goes by fast. She'd probably murder me if she knew how protective I feel. I try to keep an open eye, watching to see if she seems tired or needs anything. But like always, she's got it under control and makes it look effortless, even though I know now that it isn't. Carey ensures meals get to the right people, that drinks are always filled, that a dropped napkin is replaced, that everyone knows where the bathroom is and where to exit the restaurant if they need to make a call. She is moving a mile a minute, but smiling the entire time even when I think she might be screaming inside. I try to keep up, to make myself useful to her however I can. Funny that I resent being Rusty's assistant but am relishing helping Carey.

During her extensive toast, Melissa takes the time to thank everyone in the room and an additional twenty people for all the blessings in her life, and lucky for us she remembers to thank Rusty just after God.

"Last, but not least . . ." She lifts her glass and looks with melting adoration at Carey, and the room goes quiet again.

Carey straightens and stills, so achingly vigilant, and I realize this must be the moment of Melissa's surprise.

"Of course I would be a scatterbrained mess without my amazing assistant, Carey," she says. "This girl has been with me since the beginning, back when all I had was my marriage, my kids, and a little furniture store in Jackson. She keeps my calendar sane! Carey, here's to another ten years."

The room fills with a few *awwww*s and congratulatory *Hear, hear*s. Glasses clink, but somehow a hush falls in the space around me. To anyone else, this appears to be an amazing honor Melissa Tripp just bestowed on her nobody assistant, but I know the truth. And regardless of what she just told me, so does Carey. I look over at her. Her hair has come out of its bun; her face is flushed from running around nonstop for the past two hours. She even has a smudge of powdered sugar on her cheek. Her left hand is tucked beneath her right arm—a sign that she's tired and struggling with cramping. I watch her hold on to her gracious smile as long as she can, but the moment Melissa turns away, it falters.

I turn to her, nudging her shoulder with mine when she remains as still as a statue. "That was sweet, yeah?"

She stares straight ahead. "I think that was Melly's surprise."

My smile falls. "Carey—"

"I've given her my whole life, and she just thanked me for keeping her calendar organized."

What a punch in the gut. I don't know what to say, so without thinking, I reach down and slide her hand into mine. Although her fingers remain rigid, I hear her breathing ease.

"You know how you can hear someone say a lie so many times that it starts to feel true?" She waits for me to nod and then continues. "I think that's what happened with me and Melly. She calls me her light bulb switch, like I'm just a button she pushes to get ideas. Does she really think that's how this works?"

I open my mouth to answer but don't want to speak without something helpful to say, and right now, nothing helpful is materializing.

"To her I'll always be the teenage girl in cutoffs who wandered into her showroom, probably because that's how I still see myself," she says. "Are we in some sort of sick symbiotic relationship?"

I pause, considering how honest I want to be. "It seems more parasitic to me," I admit. Okay, so pretty honest, then.

Carey looks up at me, and I realize she's about to freak out. Her inhales are coming in fast and shallow; her face has gone a clammy gray.

A quick glance around the room tells me the lunch is winding down. I assume we're expected to stay to settle everything up and make sure every executive gets a cab back to the airport, but Carey isn't going to be very good at her job right now. She's done enough.

Very gently, I tug on her hand in mine.

I expect her to stop once we're out on the sidewalk, maybe take a deep, fortifying breath. But she holds up the hand that's not currently wrapped around my fingers and hails a cab.

We climb in and fall silent once she's given the name of our hotel. Instead of sliding across the seat, she stays close, holding on to my hand.

Carey lets me pay for the cab without argument and follows me out onto the sidewalk, but once there, she turns determined again, taking long strides into the hotel and directly to the elevators.

She turns to me. "Which floor are you on?"

My insides go tight; are we just going to go back to our rooms? It's only three o'clock in the afternoon. I want to help her figure this out, not go sit alone for the rest of the day. "Ninth. Where are you?"

"Seventh."

Inside the elevator, she presses the button for the ninth floor, but doesn't then hit the button for the seventh. Confusion starts to set in, and I open my mouth to respond, but she steps forward with a determination that makes my mind go blank. Instinct brings my hands to her waist.

Her hands twist in my shirt, pulling me down to her, and then her mouth is on mine, hungry and soft. She stretches higher, one hand in my hair, sliding her tongue over me, licking me like candy. It's sweet and gentle until she bites my lip with a quiet growl.

When she pulls back, I suck in a breath like I haven't had oxygen in a week. "Carey?"

She makes a fist in the back of my hair and stares at my mouth.

"Not to interrupt your momentum here," I say, licking my lips. They taste like her lip gloss. "But what's happening?"

When Carey turns her eyes up to mine, she looks a little wild. Her gaze is bright, oddly hyperfocused. She's only a few inches shorter than I am, and I can feel the heat of her breath on my chin. My pulse is going so hard and fast it echoes in my ears.

"I was picking up where we left off last night."

"And I like that idea. Very much." I sweep a strand of her hair away from her cheek. "But I don't want to do this just because you're upset."

"That isn't what this is. This is me doing what *I* want for once."

"Oh. So the plan . . . ?"

"The plan," she says in a gentle, husky voice, "is we are going to go to your room. I'll probably have a drink from the minibar."

"Okay," I say, smiling down at her. Not that she specifically *needs* a drink, but I don't think it would hurt for her to unwind a little. "That sounds like a brilliant idea."

The elevator doors open and she pulls me with her so we both stumble against a wall. I bend, sliding my mouth over hers again, and she guides one of my hands up her waist, over her ribs, stopping just beneath her breast.

"And then," she says, and she stares up at me with wide blue-green eyes that seem just south of completely sane at the moment, "you are going to bend me over your bed and fuck me until I forget my name."

Words fall away. My knees turn rubbery and my mouth immediately dries. I am completely in awe of Demanding Carey, and right now there are few things I want more than exactly what she's just described.

Finally I manage a simple "I can do that."

"I think that will help." She lifts a shaking hand, twists her fingers in my hair again. "I'm working on being more assertive. Does that plan sound good to you, too?"

I bend, dragging my teeth along her jaw. "Yes, it does."

She drops her hand. "If I tell you that it's been a solid two years since I've had sex, does that sound pathetic?"

"No."

"It sounds pathetic to me." She takes a step back and throws her arms out wide and yells at the ceiling. "I'm twenty-six! Good sex should be the foundation of every weekend at my age, but is it?"

"Apparently not?"

She looks back at me and presses a hand to my stomach. "And you have a great body and fucking *fantastic* teeth."

I laugh, delighted by this radiant, emphatic woman.

But then a shadow of doubt crosses over her expression. "Am I being too forward?"

Coming slowly back to my senses, I'm aware that her confidence is new. She may be emphatic, but she's never been given space to be this commanding before. "Absolutely not." I lean in, kissing her once, and staying close even when I pull away. "You're the one who left the pool last night, not me."

This earns me a smile. "I would have totally had sex with you, just so you know. Those stupid kids interrupted us and I freaked out realizing that Melly could have been out on her balcony, too. But right now I don't care who sees us."

I kiss a path from her collarbone to her jaw. "Good."

"So we're going to do it now." Her voice vibrates against my lips. "And I think you're going to blow my mind." I straighten, and her eyes search mine. "Right, James?"

Compassion for her agitation makes me earnest: "I promise to do my best."

"One drink," she says. She slides her hand into mine, but doesn't move from where she leans against the wall.

"One drink sounds perfect," I agree. I'm not going to rush her. We could stand in this hallway talking about it for hours if she wants.

"And then you're going to . . . ?" Her eyebrows rise to prompt me.

I grin and heat fills my chest when she stares hungrily at my mouth. "Rumor has it I'm going to bend you over the bed."

"Correct." Carey smiles, tugs my hand, and leads me down the hall.

EXCERPT FROM *New Life, Old Love*

Chapter Nine: Let's Talk About Sex, Baby

Imagine the scene: Melly hands me the outline for this book to look over. As with most things in our life, she's done the initial legwork and so I know it's solid. I do a quick scan and give her an immediate "Yep, looks good," and she hovers for only a second before letting that sassy smile spread over her face.

"Great," she says. "Glad to hear it."

Two months later, I'm handed the outline again. Nothing's changed. Same exact outline. Except this time, I actually take the time to look at it. And this time, I notice that she's outlined for me to write, among other things, the chapter on s-e-x.

Do I take it as a compliment? Hell yeah. Nothing better than knowing your wife trusts you to handle the important stuff. But is it also intimidating? Another hell yeah. It's one thing to talk about sex in the confines of our marriage—we've been together so long that there are things we know about each other's bodies that we probably don't even know about our own. But it's another thing to get on the computer and try to tell millions of people how and when they should be talking about sex in a relationship.

Look. The first thing I realized with Melly was that if we weren't prepared to talk about it openly, then we probably shouldn't be doing it. I realized that because we started together early, before we really had a language for any of that stuff. Before we knew what to do and what we even really liked. We were idiots, shuffling blindly through sexual exploration.

I guess it's sheer luck that we were able to figure it out together, but that—like any aspect of a good marriage—took a lot of attention, effort, and *talking*. Lord, in those early days we talked all night about what we wanted, who we were, and what turned us on.

If you think this chapter is going to be a salacious tell-all about my sex life with the beautiful Melissa Tripp, you'll be disappointed. Go pick up a different book—maybe one with a sexy cowboy on the cover. Another important piece of taking care of a sexual relationship in marriage is to keep it private. My daddy always said, "The only way to keep a secret is to not tell anyone," so this is me not telling you a single detail about my wife and how damn sexy she is when she wears her hair down, puts on a pair of jeans and boots, and goes outside to ride her beautiful Arabian, Shadow.

Well, I guess that tidbit got away from me, but here's the other thing: a healthy sexual relationship happens when you find your partner sexy at one day, at one year, at ten years, and when you're both old as time and slow as honey in the winter. Those things you think are sexy at first might change over time. People aren't as acrobatic at forty as they are at twenty. These are the facts of life.

But when you're near someone and feel like your knees turned to jelly, and when you can look them square in the eye and tell them exactly what it is you want them to do, well, that's just the start of something beautiful.

Carey

In the handful of steps from the elevator to James's room, my confidence evaporates. It's been years since I've undressed in front of a man. What was I thinking? I'm not even sure who this brazen person is. It's a wonder James didn't gently guide me to my own room and instruct me to sleep it off.

Debbie would probably tell me that burst of madness in the elevator was born of frustration and anger—some need to be in control of my life because it feels like I never have any control at all. I've given ten years to Melissa Tripp. My young years! Ten years of hard work and ideas, hoping one day I might be acknowledged for even a fraction of it.

That is obviously not going to happen.

I rarely let myself think this way. Thoughts like these would make the day-to-day too hard, and any suggestion that I'm more than just an assistant would make Melly's head explode. It's not even that I want credit, exactly, but maybe I just need to know that *she* knows? Does she? Or have we played these parts for so long that she's managed to fool herself right along with everyone else?

Here's to another ten years.

Taking a deep breath, I press my face between James's shoulder blades as he swipes his keycard. Gesturing for me to lead us inside, he follows, dropping his wallet, key, and phone on an entryway table. The door sweeps shut, sealing us into an air-conditioned silence. I clock the way he turns his ringer off. Good idea. But before I can do the same, he reaches up and gently slides the purse strap from my shoulder.

"I'll get it," he says.

I've never met anyone before who so easily and unobtrusively anticipates my needs. "Thanks."

His room is a mirror image of mine, but otherwise identical—if not a whole lot tidier: king-size bed and upholstered headboard, requisite dresser and TV, desk, same framed watercolor prints on taupe walls, velvet couch, damask drapes. But my destination, of course, is the minibar.

While he pulls the sheer drapes closed—affording us both privacy and light—I open the small refrigerator and examine its contents. Soda, water, beer, juice, Red Bull. Tiny bottles of alcohol are neatly lined in the door. Normally the only thing I'd be interested in is the single-serving bottle of wine or maybe a bag of M&M's, but today I reach for the hard stuff, twist off the top, and finish half the tiny bottle of vodka in a single go. It burns in the best way. On top of the fridge in individual weighted compartments is an assortment of chips and candy, along with a small box with a red heart on the front. I feel my face heat as I finger the label and read its contents—condoms, lube, personal wipes. And the label: INTIMACY KIT.

Okay, universe. No need to shout.

With liquid courage still smoldering in my chest and making its way slowly through my veins, I pick up the box and turn to face James.

He's standing by the window, expression unreadable.

"I'm usually a very independent person," I tell him.

I toss the box to the bed and his eyes follow the movement, widening when he realizes what it is. "I got that."

"I don't usually like help and I rarely ask for it, but . . ."

He lifts a brow in question.

"I'd like it if you undid my buttons again."

Only a tiny beat passes—the time it takes for the words to travel across the room, for his brain to interpret them—and then James grins, crossing to me in a few short steps. "I was hoping you'd ask."

Slipping off my shoes, I kick them to the side. "I've never had hotel sex."

Slower than I'd have thought possible, he pulls the front of my shirt free from my skirt. "Never?"

"I did have sex outside once." I watch as he undoes one button, and then a second, his fingers lightly grazing the skin of my stomach.

I have to work to keep my voice steady: "I was a senior and dating this guy named Jesse. There's a trail in the Grand Tetons that takes you to Death Canyon. I'd never been there before, but he really wanted me to see it." James pulls his attention from the buttons to glance at my face. I give him a little grin like, *Yeah, I'm sure that's really what he wanted me to see.*

He laughs, this warm husky sound that makes my blood simmer.

"We stopped to have lunch and spread out a blanket in this gorgeous spot that overlooks the lake and—" I give a meaningful pause. "We never did make it to the canyon. What about you?"

His hands pause on the buttons. "Me?"

"Hotel sex."

"You really want to talk about my exes right now?"

I swallow thickly. "Talking is relaxing me."

He pushes out his bottom lip into this adorable pout as he considers. "Mathletes finals in San Jose. Her name was Allison, we were both seventeen. We spent an hour together in a Sheraton hot tub, and she invited me back to her room."

"And?"

He lifts a shoulder. "I was nervous, but it was good."

"'Good'?"

"I'm not in high school anymore," he says with a smile. "And you could say I'm a lifelong learner."

I clear my throat and glance down at the floor. "Listen, I know I was pretty presumptuous earlier. We don't have t—"

"You're right. We *don't* have to." He takes a single step closer. "But I didn't mind the presumption, and I'm very good at following instructions."

"The qualities of a great assistant-in-training," I whisper, and he laughs into a single, sweet kiss.

The last button is undone and he opens my shirt, fingers carefully pushing the fabric off one shoulder, and then the other. I can barely breathe. My eyes fall to his chest and with a little nod, he seems to understand, making quick work of his own buttons, stopping about halfway before reaching behind his neck and tugging the shirt up and over his head.

I wouldn't have thought it possible, but he looks even better than he did last night by the pool: shadows more defined, bones sharper. The part of my brain that seeks out shapes and symmetry wants to capture this image and wallpaper my room with it. Last night I stared in frustration at these bland walls; now all I want to see is him.

We stand in front of each other in the bright diffuse light, with the enormous bed looming beside us. My hands follow the lines of his chest, down his stomach to where his belt sits low on his hips. With his eyes on me he brings his fingers to the clasp, and the sound of the leather as it slips through metal turns me on even more here, in the quiet room, than it did last night.

He pushes one hand into my hair and leans in, pants still closed but belt open. It's like the pool all over again, our chests touching, his breath ghosting across my lips. With a rush of cold air from the vent overhead, goose bumps bloom across my skin; my nipples harden. His lips meet my cheek, my chin, my jaw, and with a quiet groan, he slides his mouth over mine.

It's a hit of warmth and pressure, that indescribable satisfaction of a kiss that promises more. There's only one kind of touch like that, one sensation that stimulates this kind of relief and hunger. It's the pressing of his lips on mine, the small teasing bite, a shaking exhale, and a hungry moan that I lick off his lower lip. His other hand slides around my back, pulling us flush, and only now do I realize how acutely lonely I've been. How long has it been since I've had that quickening feeling shoving every other thought to the side?

I reach for him, gripping his wrist with one hand like I need an anchor when he comes back at a different angle, kissing me with more purpose, less caution. He licks my tongue, plays with me, smiling as he growls.

"I can't believe we're doing this," he says, tilting his head, tilting mine. His hand slips down to my throat.

"Have you thought about it before last night?" I ask.

"Absolutely," he admits.

"Me too."

This is the same James I see every day, the same one who scowls down at his computer, who dresses for the job he wants, not the job he has. But this James also has hungry hands. He makes quiet noises in the back of his throat when I press against him, when my hands slide up his arms and over his shoulders.

This James sucks in a breath when I open my mouth, letting him in deeper. My hands trail along his skin, down his chest to where his heart pounds beneath my palms. I know he wants to help, but he's patient and holds his breath when I unbutton his pants. The sound of his zipper is hilariously loud in this room full of quiet anticipation. I push his pants down his hips, along with his boxers. We both watch as I wrap my fingers around the hard heat of him.

It's like a tiny bomb goes off in me. I think one goes off in him, too. My nerves are gone, and in their place is this ravenous monster of my former self, wanting to get as much of my skin touching as much of his as we can manage. I make a tight sound of impatience and urgency and he pulls back, searching my eyes.

"Talk to me," he says, pushing my skirt and underwear down my hips. "Is this okay?"

I pull him back down. "It's fine, it just . . ." I struggle to find the right words. "It feels like a fever."

I can tell, from the way he groans and runs a greedy hand up over my chest, that he knows exactly what I mean.

This James is eager but gentle as he unfastens my bra; his mouth is a hot trail from my chin to my neck and down as he kneels. I wonder if I'll ever get this picture out of my head: his eyes are closed, tongue flicking against my nipple and then, a few breaths later, between my legs.

I am nothing but ache and impatience as he stands and walks me backward toward the bed.

But he stops me just before I sit at the edge. "Wait. No."

I experience a brief, sharp stab of disappointment, and suddenly the daylight filtering in makes me feel totally exposed. I cross my arms over my chest. "What?"

James shifts me to the side. "We are not doing this on a nasty hotel comforter."

And I melt. With a sharp tug, he strips the duvet from the bed and then returns to me, kissing my shoulder, my neck, my mouth. James guides me down, pressing my back against the cool relief of the sheets. Our kisses become longer and unfocused. And then he's there, hovering over me, with a condom in his hand. His hair falls forward as he sucks on my shoulder and with a gentle hand on my hip and one on my side, he's rolling me over, onto my stomach, the heat of his front all along my back.

"Is this right?" He carefully pulls me to the foot of the bed.

He listened.

"Yes."

I can hear us both breathing sharply, knowing we're here. The fronts of his legs are warm against the backs of mine, his hand presses gently to my lower back, and then he's closer, he's *there*, pushing against me, with his capable hands moving to my hips and a kiss placed to the skin between my shoulder blades.

"Yeah?" he whispers again.

I nod, and the starting gun is his deep, relieved groan; he does what he's promised. He's moving confidently, hard and fast while he whispers something. Something about being what I want today. Something about how this feels, how he'll need it again now that he's had it. I think the same will be true for me—that I'll need this again tonight, and again tomorrow morning when we have to be quiet and, someday, after work at his place, where there's no need to be quiet at all.

His hand snakes around my body, sliding between my legs.

"Tell me if you need something else," he says between sharp inhales, "to come."

I would, but I don't, and even if I did, my brain isn't forming coherent words, only sounds that seem to be growing louder and sharper. He presses his fingers against me and it's happened so fast—we were frantic after our half-shy disrobing—but the feeling he draws from me is like being poured out of a pitcher, warm and freeing. With a cry muffled by the sheets, I fall to pieces, brilliant color flashing behind my eyes. And with a quiet groan, he shakes and then goes still behind me, breathing heat against the back of my neck.

For a few seconds, we don't speak or move. It takes several breaths for the room to stop spinning. And then James presses a lingering, gasping kiss to my shoulder before shifting back and disappearing into the bathroom. I take the opportunity to clamber up the bed and between the sheets, pulling them up to my chin. I want to scream in giddiness and excitement . . . and a resurgence of nerves. There's no dark room to hide in, no nighttime to fall into.

James steps out of the bathroom, naked. He doesn't seem to mind the walk to the bed, the daylight, or my laser-like focus on his body.

"Cold?" he asks, climbing in beside me.

"Shy."

He scoffs, kissing my forehead. "Please. You are many things. But you are not shy."

"Not all of us can saunter naked across a room, Jimbalaya."

He laughs, squinting over at the clock, and I follow. It's almost five. "What are we going to do for dinner?" he asks, but in his voice I hear the same hesitation I feel. Beneath the sheets with him it's so warm and yummy. The last thing I want to do is go anywhere.

"Room service?" I suggest. "We can do rock-paper-scissors for who has to put on a robe and answer the door."

I think he likes that idea. He pushes up onto an elbow, hovering over me. Brown eyes study my face, and when he translates whatever he sees there his smile straightens. "I'm glad it's still light out. I like being able to see you."

And more than just seen, I feel *visible* for the first time in maybe forever—but it isn't scary. Being with James is like standing in the softest, most flattering spotlight. "I like being seen by you."

"So tell me something."

I snuggle into the crook of his arm. "Something about what?"

"About you." His brows go up in a question. "I don't even know where you live."

"I live in a condo with my adorable landlords, Annabeth and Peyton, off South Jackson." With a dramatic pout, I add, "They're in Hawaii right now on a belated honeymoon."

He squints. "You're renting a single bedroom?"

The vague, familiar shame blows a shadow across my mood, and I nod. "Where do you live?"

"I've got a studio down near where the South Park Loop meets 191."

I map the distance in my head. It would only take about ten minutes for me to get there.

"Is that close to you?" he asks.

"Very."

He growls into a kiss. But with the reminder that he's new to the area, it occurs to me that it probably isn't easy to start over—especially not when he's working such long hours. "Have you made any friends in Jackson?" I ask.

"One of my neighbors is a very loud man who comes

home around midnight and unwinds to the dulcet sounds of death metal."

I wince. "Oof."

"My neighbor on the other side, Edie, is a ninety-year-old woman who knocks on my door with a cane to ask whether I need groceries. So, she's pretty cool."

"You should be getting *her* groceries."

"Right?" He smiles, fidgeting with a strand of my hair. "Most of my friends are back on the East Coast, but even they've scattered throughout New England." Shrugging, he says with relaxed assurance, "I'll find my people at some point. Right now the priority has been getting my work life back on track."

I stare at his mouth, thinking on these words. We're both alone, and for so long I insisted that wasn't the same thing as being lonely. Now I'm not so sure.

"What are you thinking about?" he asks.

"I've lived around Jackson my entire life and you've just moved there, but we both need to find our people."

With a knowing smile, James kisses me again, but this time he lingers, and it deepens, heating. I love the firm press of his lips, the quiet sounds he can't seem to repress.

Against my mouth, he asks, "Is the lady satisfied?"

I run my finger down his chin, throat, chest and reach beneath the sheets, gently scratching his stomach. "The lady *was* satisfied . . ."

He growls, dragging his teeth over my jaw, and climbs back over me. "It appears I have more work to do."

Giggling, I throw the sheets up and over our heads. Room service, rock-paper-scissors, and robes can wait.

Carey

When I wake up, I know it's really early. Bird calls haven't been drowned out by the hum of traffic. The sky still feels like a secret—deep blue-black but illuminated, like a light shining through fabric. Under the covers it's warm, and my entire body has that heavy, weighted feeling where I can get lost in the sensation of being completely still.

I love this feeling, love becoming aware of different parts of my body, not just my hands. The pillowcase is smooth against my cheek. I slip my feet to a cooler section of the sheets and press back into the warm, naked body behind me.

His breathing is even, but his hand on my stomach flexes when I move, pulling me into him. I'm not sure he's awake. On a scale of fine to nonverbal for the rest of the tour, how weird is it going to be between us now that we've had sex?

At the risk of waking up my body and getting my hands twisting and turning, I roll over to face him and find his eyes open, carefully watching me.

"Hi."

He smiles. "Hi."

There's a condom wrapper stuck to his shoulder, and I assume it's the one he tossed onto the bed that first time. There's another in here somewhere from the second time; that one was sweeter, quieter, with my arms and legs wound all around him.

I definitely needed the heat and energy of the first time, but I think James liked the second one better. He looked completely wrecked afterward. We skipped the room service after all, and I think we were asleep by eight—no wonder we're awake at dawn. Now he looks sleep-rumpled and wary, like he's not sure how I'm going to behave this morning.

"We had sex," I say.

He nods. "Twice."

"My first hotel sex. And second."

A twitch of his mouth. "Congratulations."

When he reaches up to push his hair off his forehead, I lean back and take a long look down at his naked body. As expected, instead of covering himself, he rolls to his back and tucks a hand behind his head. It's quite a view.

The silence stretches and, with considerably less bravado, he asks, "Are you okay today?"

Am I?

Two weeks ago, I would have laughed it off and said *Of course*. But I don't know how to answer. I'm okay that we had sex, if that's what he means. More than okay. I'm just not sure if everything else feels as easy as it used to, and I honestly don't know what changed. Melly has always been

Melly. Rusty has always been Rusty. But maybe I'm not that Carey anymore.

"Carey?"

"I'm okay," I tell him. "About this, I mean. Are you?"

"Yes." He has a hickey next to his collarbone. My first thought is how relieved I am that he can cover it up; my second is that I never want him to put clothes on again. "I am extremely okay."

"Good."

"Do you want to talk about it?" He rolls to his side again, pushing himself up onto his elbow, and because it's a struggle not to look down again, I decide not to fight it. After a few wordless seconds, he laughs. "I might put some clothes on if we're going to continue the conversation like this." He motions vaguely to his lower half, still on display. "It's a little drafty."

Laughing, I pull the sheets to our chins and cuddle into the heat of him. He picks up my hand and begins massaging my fingers. Although there isn't much he can do to stop the way my hands start moving as soon as I wake up, it's still soothing; the rest of my body melts against the mattress. I'm happy with comfortable quiet. Talking means bringing up what got us here—or who—and what we're going to do about it. I don't know if I'm mentally prepared to deal with it before the sun is even up.

"We don't have to decide anything now," he says, studying me, "but we'll eventually need to be on the same page about what we do outside this room."

I gnaw on my lip, thinking while he continues to massage my hand. "As much as I want to protect this and keep it just between us for a little while, Melly will know. It's like how dogs can smell fear, except it's me with any hint of a life outside of work."

He laughs.

"We don't have to be anywhere for a few hours." He looks at his watch. "Plenty of time to figure things out. I could go grab us coffee and something to eat and be back in ten minutes?"

"Yes, please." My stomach gives a timely growl. "As you can hear, I am starving."

He leans over me, hair a mess and eyes still sleepy. He kisses me once, not too long because we haven't brushed our teeth yet, and then he's up, sliding his glasses on and searching for his pants.

I lie back against the bed and stretch, content in a way I haven't felt in ages. I listen to him move around the room, finding a shoe by the door, the other under the bed. Dressed, he leans over me again. I reach up, brush his hair back, and smile, relishing that this doesn't feel awkward or weird.

"I want you to keep your glasses on."

He lifts a single brow. He knows exactly what I mean. "We'll do that when I get back." A pause. "Don't answer your phone yet, okay? Knowing Melly I'm sure she'll be calling soon, and I want us to talk things out first."

He peeks back over his shoulder at the clock. I groan. It's five—almost time to get up and moving—but I want to stay in this happy bubble so much longer. "I won't."

Another kiss and then he's up. "I'll be fast. I'll run."

I laugh as the door closes behind him and fall back on the bed, grinning up at the ceiling. The room falls silent, but my booming thoughts easily fill the void. I like him. Not only is he absurdly good-looking when he's naked, he's also intuitive and patient and communicative and seems to get me, like *really* get me. Not because I'm simple, but because he's looking carefully.

My smile falters. If he's looking carefully, once the excitement of this wears off, he'll see that there just isn't all that much to me. Small-town girl, never been anywhere, no hobbies.

I like him, but what do our lives look like once we get back to Jackson? Other than the fact that he lives in a studio and has one loud neighbor and one old one, I know nothing about James's life back home. Is he an early riser or a night owl? Does he cook or order takeout every night? I know he's tidy, but is he fussy? Would my disdain for washing dishes drive him crazy? And what would it be like to work with someone I'm dating? I already don't have time for a relationship—would the reality be that we're ships passing in the night, the way it is with everyone else in my personal life?

Another question barrels past the rest: If we can't keep this a secret, would Melly even be willing to share me?

That thought is enough to fully knock the shine off my afterglow. I roll onto my side and feel the crinkle of plastic beneath me. The other condom wrapper. I pick it up, look at it. He said we should talk, and he's right, but I'd be lying if I didn't say I'd rather stay in the bubble and do other things first.

Practically vibrating, I rush into the bathroom. A towel is laid out smoothly on the right corner of the counter.

Neatly arranged on top are James's toiletries: toothpaste, toothbrush, travel bottles of some salon brand shampoo and conditioner, deodorant, face wash, and a small tub of expensive-looking moisturizer. I think of my own toiletry case, packed so full it will barely zip, toothpaste closed with Saran wrap because I lost the cap, a random assortment of shampoo bottles I took from another hotel, everything still covered in a fine layer of the pressed powder I dropped the night before we left. James would probably break out in hives if he took two steps into my hotel room and saw the wet towel I left in the middle of my bed and that most of my clothes are still lying in my open suitcase.

I wash my hands and rush through the rest of a makeshift routine: splash my face, finger-brush my teeth, and help myself to a dab of his moisturizer. I shake out my hair, smoothing it down and then fluffing it back up again. I take one last look in the mirror—I like the way he looks on me.

The thought cycles back: we still have three cities to go. I imagine telling Melly about this. The prospect is terrifying. Better: I'm able to keep James a secret, get through the rest of the tour, and then we take it one day at a time back home. Just like normal people do, right? Working less, playing more. Actually getting to know him—

There's a noise from the other room, a jiggle on the outside door handle.

I race to the bed, heart pounding. The lock clicks just as I lie back against the stack of pillows, hair fanned out around me and sheet arranged so my leg is bare, my breasts barely covered.

The view of the door is blocked by a little hall, and I grin as I hear the door sweep over the carpet and swiftly close again.

"So about those three hours until we have to be downstairs." I pick up the remaining condoms and dangle them midair. "Whatever will we do to fill the time?"

"What. The *fuck*."

❀❀❀

I stop breathing altogether. Melly.

I jerk the sheet over my chest and throw the condoms like I've just been brandishing a handful of shit. "Oh my God! What—what are you doing here?"

"What am *I* doing here?" She waves what I know without question is a honey-do list. "I was coming to talk to my husband! What the fuck are *you* doing here?"

I am so confused. Beyond confused, I am petrified. In a rush, I am up on my knees, one hand out in front of me while the other clutches the sheet to my chest. "Oh my God, Melly. You can't think that I—that me and Rusty—! I would *never*!"

GROSS.

Melly tilts her head as she looks at me, *really* looks at me. She blinks slowly, her feathery lash extensions fluttering like she has all the time in the world. Outwardly, she seems suddenly calm. Her stillness is terrifying.

Oh God, can she smell fear?

"Would never what, exactly?" she says, too quiet, too serene. "Maybe you could clarify exactly which of your betrayals you are referring to, Carey. Never try to undermine me? Lie to me? Sleep with my husband?"

My heart is pounding in my chest. "Melly. I would never do any of those things. It's not what you're thinking." I glance around the room, at my skirt that practically waves like a floozy from the floor where James threw it. I wasn't even sure I wanted to tell Melly—I certainly didn't want to tell her like this—and now I have to. "This isn't Rusty's room."

"It is, Carey." She holds up her key. "They didn't have adjoining rooms, and Joe gave me the spare."

"There must have been a mix-up when he handed them out." I take a deep breath and let it out as evenly as possible. "This isn't Rusty's room, it's James's."

Her forehead moves only infinitesimally these days—all the muscles kept in place with Botox and sheer will—but there's definitely something displeased happening in her expression: the twitch of a perfectly waxed brow, the narrowing of her eyes.

I swallow; my throat is suddenly dry. With another quick glance, I nod to his shiny aluminum suitcase in the corner. "I spent the night with James."

My admission seems to have taken some of the fire out of her, but she's clearly not convinced. Stepping away from the hallway, she finally takes a look at something other than me and my body barely covered by sheets. She stops in front of the closet and cracks open the door. Instead of finding Rusty's jerseys or custom tailored shirts, a row of neatly spaced button-downs stares back. Melly snorts, shaking her head at the view, and for a brief moment I think she might burst out laughing.

But then she closes the door and slowly turns. I barely breathe as her sharp eyes take in the general disarray around us. Besides my clothes, the garbage can is knocked over, my bra is on the desk lamp, and there's a hastily torn open Intimacy Kit next to the bed.

"Well," she says, and steps over what I think is my underwear. "You and James."

I tread lightly. She might *seem* calm, but something's lurking just below the surface. Right now Melissa reminds me a lot of a spider, and this feels entirely like a trap, luring me in.

"I don't know if I would say *me and James*, exactly." I motion to my sheet. "Could I put something on?"

She gives me a clipped "Of course," and I stand up, sheet wrapped securely around me, and head for the bathroom.

Safely inside, I look at myself in the mirror again. I'm the same Carey from ten minutes ago, but I feel like a totally different person. Or, rather, I feel like the same Carey who got into the elevator yesterday, not the one who woke up this morning refreshed, relaxed, sexed, and wondering if—for once—someone might be completely on my team.

I don't want to look at myself anymore. Shaking my head, I pull on the thick white bathrobe from the back of the door and head out again.

My boss is at the window, her blond hair white in the early light. With a nervous glance toward the door, I wonder when James will come back. A few minutes ago, I wanted him to hurry. Now I want the barista downstairs to take their sweet time. I wouldn't wish this conversation on anyone, and I certainly don't wish Melly's ire on James.

"So how long has this been a thing?"

I turn at the sound of her voice.

I'm not exactly sure what to tell her, because I'm not sure myself. "It's new."

She lets out a small, humorless laugh. "Right. That's why you two are always huddled together. Why he's always looking at you. Why you're always talking. Because it's *new.*"

I think back over the last few days and can't really argue. It might have started as camaraderie, as us against them, but somewhere along the way it changed.

"I don't know what's going on with you, Carey. It's always been you and me, a team. But lately . . ."

"We *are* a team. What's happening between James and me isn't about work." *For once*, I don't add, *I didn't think about you for an entire night.*

But of course Melly would never believe this. She turns around, arms folded tightly across her chest. "Isn't it? I used to be able to depend on you—for everything. You were in my corner, and I was in yours."

"I don't understand where this is coming from. None of that's changed."

"You disappeared yesterday," she says.

"The luncheon was winding down." It's hard to admit it, but I suck it up: "I was totally wiped and needed a break."

"So you left without even telling me? With *James*?" She throws up her hands. "I'd just given you a shout-out in front of some of the most influential people in entertainment and then you made me look like a liar by vanishing and leaving Robyn to wrap up the party."

My heart drops. "Melly—"

She brings a shaking hand to her throat. "I trust you

with details of my livelihood and my family. You know things about me that no one knows. And I help you—"

"I would never talk about any of those things. To anyone."

"Really? Not going to have a rough day and commiserate together about the mean boss?" she says, going for flippant and not quite making it.

She, I realize suddenly, doesn't want me getting close to James because she's worried I'll confide in him, tell him what I do and don't do behind the scenes. She has no idea that her own husband has already done that. Even now, I try to downplay it or change the subject whenever James brings it up. Melly has to know I would never have said anything on my own. She has to know that I'm more trustworthy than that.

I take a step closer. "You've known me since I was sixteen. Do you really think I would do that?"

She blinks several times before her shoulders lose some of the tension. "No," she says. "But lately I feel so out of control of everything, and you know I don't handle that well. Between Russell and Stephanie, the book, the tour, and the announcement—I'm losing track of everything. I'm not ready to lose you, too."

It feels like pushing glue through a straw to get the words out: "You're not gonna lose me, Melly." And it's so easy to fall back into this role; it's as easy as breathing. "Right now life is moving faster than a knife fight in a phone booth. Of course you're stressed."

She reaches for my arms and pulls me down on the small couch. Her eyes are glassy. "That's no excuse for losing my temper with you, for not trusting you. I know that."

She gives my hands a squeeze. "We've worked so hard for this, Carey." I nod. "*You've* worked so hard."

My heart pounces on this tiny crumb. "Thank you."

"I can't do this without you."

"I'm right here," I tell her. "I'm not going anywhere."

Melly wipes her eyes, her smile brighter than I've seen in a long time. "It's us against the world, hon. The two of us, just you and me."

I nod again, my smile not quite as bright as hers. "You and me."

Ella @1967_Disney_bound • July 9
I KNEW IT. Remember when I said my spidey senses were tingling?

> **Variety** @Variety • July 9
> Fresh off the runaway success of New Spaces, @Netflix nabs home decorating duo Melissa and Rusty Tripp and their new show, Home Sweet Home. Exclusive: www.variety.com/2L6Kz8l

46 replies 88 retweets 398 likes

Show this thread

> **booksnbangtan** @booksnbangtan
> @1967_Disney_bound omgggg. I saw a tweet the other day that said they barely talk anymore. If they hated each other with an entire cast of costars to share the load wtf will happen now
>
> > **Vic** @aCurlieee_doll
> > @booksnbangtan @1967_Disney_bound is it bad that knowing they hate each other makes me want to watch the show like ten times more?
>
> **Piddy** @broken_box_mmusik
> @1967_Disney_bound still say this is wild speculation. ITS LIKE WE CAN'T JUST LET PEOPLE BE HAPPY

Samira @_Samira_benty

@broken_box_mmusik @1967_Disney_bound idk if it's really /just/ speculation. I've seen three separate posts suggesting that Rusty is playing around and the mood was weird at their signing. That Melissa is on EDGE lately. Something up

See more replies

James

I realize I'm a somewhat socially awkward guy and will occasionally misread a romantic situation, but I'm usually misreading it in the wrong direction—a phenomenon that my older sister calls my "flypaper tendency." Jenn says I'm unlikely to think a girl is interested in me until she's literally plastered to my side. She's not wrong—and the strategy has generally worked.

Last night with Carey, for example. She was pretty clear about what she wanted, and that she wanted it from me, specifically. In fact, I don't think I've been with a woman who was more precise in her instruction. This morning she seemed to want more of the same—and I was happy to oblige.

So when I come upstairs with coffee and bagels to find my room completely empty—no clothes, no condom wrappers anywhere, even the bed has been hastily made—the only conclusion I can draw is that Carey flipped out, and I misread everything.

I sit at the edge of the mattress, balancing a cardboard tray of coffees on my lap and cycling through what we said and did, trying to find where it fell apart. It doesn't take a lot of emotional intelligence to figure out that Carey needed an outlet last night . . . and that outlet was me.

Am I okay being used for sex? Generally, yes. In this case, though, it's complicated by the reality of our future forced proximity, and the genuine feelings I've developed for her. I like her. I like her laugh, and how competent she is. I like her teasing humor that doesn't mask how much she's always taking care of everyone else. I like her mouth, her body, and her skin, too. I like her vulnerability—as much as I know I shouldn't be drawn to it, I am—and I like what I realize is her complete creative genius.

I put her coffee on the desk and step out onto the balcony to drink mine. Am I really that surprised that she vanished? More easily than imagining her waiting for me, I can picture her in my bed, the stress of ignoring her phone mounting until she finally got up and dressed, heading to her room to shower and wipe the slate clean for the day. We've been friendly for only a matter of days, and yesterday's meltdown aside, I doubt she's ever shirked responsibility for an hour.

In truth, we barely know each other, and what we do know tells me we don't have much in common. She might want to stay in Jackson forever; I live in a tiny studio that I've barely furnished because I don't expect to be there for more than a year or two. Relatedly, I don't let Melissa and Rusty hit me anywhere emotional, because it's just a job. But Carey's life is all tied up in theirs; their circus is her entire world.

And yet, despite these problems, I can't immediately

shake the way being with her felt totally right, even if it was for only twelve hours.

***

We have a late start this morning because we're only going to Sacramento to sign some books for store stock before driving to spend the night in Medford, Oregon. The leisurely start to the day means I have time to shower, pack, and then figure out what to do with myself. Rusty is, as usual, sleeping until the very last minute before we leave. Thankfully I won't sit around thinking about Carey or feeling useless: Melissa texts me a to-do list.

James could you take care of the following:
-Pick up some Alka-Seltzer for Russ
-He also needs a pack of plain white undershirts
-The bus could use a humidifier

The air is bright and sharp; the wind catches me off guard. I knew that San Francisco could be cold, but it's still disorienting to feel the chill on my face with the iconic backdrop of a brilliant blue sky over the Golden Gate Bridge. A stress headache pulses at the edges of my temples.

It's not a terrible thing if this fling with Carey turns into nothing. If I can just keep my head down and focus until the second season is rolling, I'll have a great focal point on my résumé. Rather than citing my duration on the job, I'll be able to say I worked on season five of *New Spaces* and the first season of *Home Sweet Home*. Rusty will give whatever recommendation I need him to give, I know.

From here, I can move on to another position—an actual engineering role. While I don't enjoy the cult of personality in the entertainment world, the pace and variety are so much better than the lifeless humdrum of my cubicle at the old job. If I could someday leverage the connections from Comb+Honey to get a job on a show that actually values science and engineering—something on the Discovery Channel—I would be thrilled.

Halfway up a steep hill, my phone buzzes in my pocket.

A clashing blend of relief and unease bubbles through me: it's Carey.

I lift the phone to my ear, turning my back to the wind. "Hey."

"Where are you?" she asks.

For a breath, I want to laugh. Now she's asking where I am? I look up, searching for a landmark or street sign. "Kearny Street?"

"I don't know why I asked," she says, laughing. "I have no idea where that is."

A small ache presses into my chest as I register the dichotomy of this immediate, easy conversation and the complexity of our present relationship. "I don't really, either," I admit. "I'm just following Google Maps to get to a Walgreens."

"Melly honey-do-listed you?" she asks, teasing.

"Yeah."

For a moment, all I can hear is the wind whipping through my phone. I pull my hand away, peeking at the screen to make sure I haven't lost her call.

Finally, she says, "James. I'm sorry I left."

"It's okay," I tell her. And it is. As much as I'd like to do it again, one and done is more straightforward.

"Melly came in."

It takes me a beat to register her meaning. "Came in . . . to my room? This morning?"

"She had a key. I guess she thought it was Rusty's room."

I think back to check-in. Rusty's name was on one room, mine was on the other, but I didn't think it mattered who ended up where; I handed him one and took the second. But it did matter, because of course Melissa asked Joe for a copy of what was supposed to be Rusty's key.

I groan. "That was my fault."

Carey laughs. "Yeah, I'm gloating a little that you weren't the perfect assistant for once."

So she didn't just bolt. I'm surprised by the power of my relief. I'd so quickly convinced myself that it was fine, that I didn't need to pursue this, and then one word from her about it not being what I thought—she didn't panic and flee—and I'm practically melting into the sidewalk. Maybe we can figure it out after all.

"Was she mad?" I ask, wincing.

Carey barks out an incredulous laugh. "What do you think?"

"I think she flipped out. Where are you right now?"

"I'm back in my room. Once I convinced her that I wasn't lying there naked in Rusty's bed—oh my God, what a horrible sentence—she calmed down. The fact that he wasn't still in bed snoring next to me and that there was a tidy row of your work clothes in the closet helped. I should say she calmed down a *little*."

I think she's going to tell me what Melissa said once she knew Carey had been with me, not Rusty, but the line goes silent again.

Finally, I have to ask. "What did she think about . . . us?"

I hear her shift somehow and can imagine her sitting on her left hand, trying to get it to relax. "She wasn't crazy about it."

"I'm sure she wasn't." I hate having this conversation like this, through the phone, where I'm standing in the middle of a windy sidewalk and she's alone in her hotel room, recovering after another tirade from Melissa. I want to be sitting next to her, talking. Even if we didn't touch, I could read her face.

But maybe I don't need more cues. Right now the silence feels pretty definitive.

Her words barely make it through the line: "I had a really nice time, though, James. I mean it. It was the best sex I've ever had. God, that sounds stupid."

"It doesn't sound stupid. I was thinking the same thing this morning."

She doesn't say anything else.

"So," I say quietly, getting it. "That's it?"

"I think so."

One perfect night, and with a nearly silent exhale, we're done.

She clears her throat. "But, it's just the reality. Things are nuts right now, and—"

"You don't have to explain it to me, Carey." I turn and lean into the side of a building. "You know I understand the situation."

"I know you do."

The ease with which we've both let this go ignites something in me, just a spark, but it's big enough to trip the rest of the realization. Carey is so good at taking care of everyone else, but she is beyond shitty at taking care of herself. I know there's a stronger backbone in there—she showed it to me yesterday. I'm not willing to let her bury it just to avoid conflict.

"Actually, wait." I turn against the wind. "No, I don't."

I can practically hear the way this takes her aback. "What?"

"I *don't* understand. We don't have to pursue this between us if it doesn't feel right to you, but Melissa's opinion, stress levels, or demands shouldn't have anything to do with it."

"James." She says this single syllable as if she's exhausted—which I'm sure she is. But the fire has been lit, and I think it needs to be lit in her, too.

"I know that she pays you well," I say. "I know that you're critical for the designs and worry you won't be able to replicate that somewhere else. I know that you have a long history with them, and I even know that health insurance is a really important consideration for you. But Melissa is—and I'm just being honest here—she is abusive."

"She's not—"

"You said yourself that you can't even be honest with your own therapist. What would she tell you if you could?" I pause. "You know she would say the same thing."

When she doesn't respond to this, I press on. "You can find another job," I say. "One that doesn't demand you have absolutely no life. One that gives you credit for your work, and pays you well, and has health insurance."

She still doesn't say anything, but I know she's listening, so I continue. "What does your life look like five years from now? Even if it's not me, do you have someone? Where are you living? You're making good money, Carey, and you don't even have an apartment to yourself, let alone own your own home—why would you? You'd never be there."

"This is shitty, James! I'm only twenty-six! I'm still figuring things out."

"I'm not trying to be shitty!" I turn in a circle, growing frustrated. "But how long can you use your age as a buffer against making a grown-up decision? I care about you. Not just because we had sex, but because I like you, and we're in this fucked-up situation together. A lot of people are making a shit-ton of money from the Tripps, but this situation isn't the best thing for *any* of us."

She exhales slowly, but doesn't say anything.

"Carey. Say something."

"I do want my own house, okay? I want a house with land where I can have a dog and chickens and go for walks outside and get lost like I used to. And I want to actually be there, to have time to make it my own and not somebody else's."

I stop pacing, surprised by this kind of honesty. "These are all good things to want."

We sit in silence for five, ten seconds. "Carey?"

"I'm thinking."

Another moment of silence passes through the line. The wind picks up; a horn honks somewhere in the distance.

"And I do want a relationship."

I don't know what to say to this. The moment feels too delicate for me to try to make a pitch for this, for *us*.

"But it's good for you if they stay together," she says, finally, and I want to hit myself now for not trying to sway her to give me a chance. "You need this job." She doesn't say it with an edge or bitterness; she's just using my résumé woes to argue her case for the status quo.

"Even if that's true, is it worth both of us being miserable? I'm not sure. I want you to have those things, Carey, and I think we're both resourceful enough to find something else. For you, something that gives you credit for all of your work. For me, something that helps me build my résumé back up."

Before she has a chance to respond to this, my phone vibrates against my ear. I pull it back to see the name on the screen.

My pulse is a stampede. "Carey, Ted is calling me."

"Ted *Cox*?"

The producer for *Home Sweet Home*. Why on earth is he calling me?

"Yeah. I should probably take this?" Did we fuck something up? Have Melissa and Rusty run naked and screaming into the street while Carey and I were negotiating our personal shit on the phone? "I'll meet you back at the hotel in a bit."

We disconnect, and I switch over to Ted's call. My voice sounds high and tight. "Ted. Hi."

"James. How are things going?" He must be in a crowded room because a few nearby voices come through nearly as clearly as his.

I go for vague, but honest: "About as well as could be expected."

Ted lets out a quiet laugh that I barely catch over the hum of background noise. "The response to the announcement was astounding." He pauses, lowering his voice. "I really need to make sure we stay on track here, James."

Pacing, I hold back the words I really want to let out—*Sounds like a conversation you should be having with Melissa and Rusty*—and give him a noncommittal hum instead. He barrels on, "There's some buzz that things aren't great between the Tripps—a Blind Gossip post, a handful of vague tweets from bigger names—and so I think this tour needs to be more of a lovefest than it's been so far."

I . . . don't even know how to respond to that. Is this guy for real? Keeping them from tearing into each other in public is challenge enough, and now he wants us to encourage them to canoodle?

"Let's get a few moments of them being tender," he continues, "maybe holding hands, or embracing where they think no one can see them."

I want to laugh trying to imagine what he's describing. My eyes are squeezed shut, my palm to my forehead when I let out a tight "We can try."

His answering silence tells me that this isn't quite enough of an assurance. I hear a door open and close, and then the background noise disappears. "Listen, I realize this has been a frustrating gig for you," Ted says.

"And for Carey."

He ignores this. "I also realize you were hired to do more of the actual engineering on projects, and I am in a position to make you lead engineer and get you an executive producing credit on season two."

A car blasts past me, startling me from my momentary stupor. He's got my attention.

"We'd just need to make sure we get to season two," he says when I've been quiet a beat too long.

"I understand what's at stake here," I tell him.

He waits for me to say more.

I want to tell him about Carey, about how she's been creating designs for Melissa for years, about how she's the real mastermind behind all of this, and in truth if Carey and I were given freedom to run with the platform, we could do what the Tripps have been letting the world think they're doing for the last decade. They could continue to be the face—but we could do what we both love to do: the work behind the scenes.

"Carey and I will do everything in our power to get them to show some more tender moments at these events," I tell him. "But I want the engineering role and producer promise in writing."

He goes quiet, and then my phone buzzes against my ear. I peek at it and see a text message has arrived from Ted, with a photo attached.

"I just wrote it down on a napkin, okay?" he says. "'James to be hired as lead engineer and EP on season two.'"

Even if he's being cheeky, relief flushes heat through my veins, making me bold: "I also think if we can get more recognition for Carey—"

"Carey?" he repeats. "The one with the hands?"

The roaring in my ears feels like a semitruck passing too close.

The one with the hands.

The heat of confidence dissipates immediately, and I stumble past words for a few shocked seconds. "She has a movement disorder, yeah, but she's brilliant. She's actually the one—"

"We can look into getting her a producer credit, too." He pauses, then adds thoughtfully, "Actually, it would look great for the crew lineup to have her listed as a producer. Being inclusive, and whatnot. Makes the whole operation look like a solid family business—she's been Melly's secretary for years."

His words feel like a punch to my chest. "Right, but she's more than Melly's—"

"Look, James, I've got to get into a meeting, but are we good? I can trust you to handle this?"

His question hangs in the silence that follows. It sounds easy, but I know better. And it feels shitty to be getting this opportunity when Carey has taken more flak and sacrificed more than anyone. A producer credit isn't enough—she deserves a lead designer credit.

But I can't negotiate from the bottom, and maybe if I get some leverage, I can use it to pull Carey up with me. I don't know what to say, other than "Yes. You can trust me."

"Good."

He disconnects the call and I weave a little on my feet as my own words to Carey come echoing back to me: *A lot of people are making a shit-ton of money from the Tripps, but this situation isn't the best thing for* any *of us.*

It's still not clear whether it's the best thing for her, except now, staying with the Tripps is very clearly the best thing for me.

Carey

When Joe ushers us out of the hotel later that morning, we're shocked to see that the bus has been rewrapped overnight. In addition to the Tripps' ginormous faces and book cover stretched along the sides, it now includes promo for the new show, too. Nothing like a forty-five-foot visual reminder that you're trapped inside a giant PR machine that surges full steam ahead, whether you're ready for it or not.

It also says a lot about the Tripps that a guy who regularly deals with entitled, difficult people for a living doesn't seem to be weathering this tour well. In the days since meeting the Tripps, Joe looks like he's aged five years. His swoopy hair has deflated; his eyes are dim and glazed over with a constant air of panic. Even his muscles seem sad.

With a clipboard in one hand and a bottle of Kaopectate in the other, he says, "I wanted to go over the schedule for the next couple of days." Joe checks his watch with a frown. He frowns a lot lately. "We're stopping in Sacramento to sign stock at four different stores. We'll have to be pretty quick at each stop because we need to make it to Medford tonight. The event tomorrow is in Portland, at Powell's. It's a ticketed event and we've sold out both the signing and the Q-and-A . . . which is good." He wipes his forehead. "But both today at the stores and tomorrow at the event there will be a lot of eyes, so . . ." He lets the sentence hang to see if anyone will complete it for him. When there are no takers, he adds, "Let's try to put on a good show."

I startle when Melly leans in, whispering, "Tomorrow we can get ready together." She smiles, and in the stark daylight, I see how much she's aged from the past several months; tiny lines fan from the corners of her eyes, and her mouth has taken on a mild tilt. Instead of softening her appearance overall the way time generously managed for my mother and grandmother, it makes Melly seem slightly unhinged. "We'll get someone to come to my suite and get blowouts before the signing. That way you can relax."

Relax. *Did everyone get that?* Melly gives my hand a little squeeze as if to emphasize that this is about me, not her. The me who has never had a blowout before in her life and who never gets downtime to relax.

We both know she's pointing out how good she is to me. It's her way of keeping me close, but also clearly keeping me away from James.

The elephant in the room doesn't care that we're back in the tight quarters of the bus: the short drive to Sacramento is as awkward as you might expect after having sex with one person and being found naked in bed by another. James clearly wants to talk and is quietly waiting for his chance. Melly is watching him watch me, but also watching to see what I'll do if he dares to try. Rusty is in the back avoiding his own elephant, and once we're on the road, Joe locks himself in the bathroom, wanting to avoid us all.

The sprawling landscape of the East Bay is a blur on the other side of the windows while I stare down at my small leather notebook. Work is usually my escape, and any one of a number of upcoming projects could easily occupy my time, but the weight of James's and Melly's attention is like a physical presence in the air, pressing down. It makes me anxious, and my fingers soon become stiff and uncooperative.

When my pencil falls to the floor, both Melly and James practically nosedive to the carpet to retrieve it. Melly is closer and reaches it first, setting it on the table with a victorious little smirk.

"Thanks, guys." I give them each a *You've just gone overboard* look. I'm sure I've never seen Melly rush to pick up anything in her life—even if she's the one who dropped it.

"So, James." Melly settles back in her seat. "You've been with us for how long now?"

James looks up, surprised at being addressed directly. "Just over two months."

I blink across at her, wondering what she's up to. I've never seen her engage James in conversation before. Someone is just full of surprises today. "Remind me what you did before?"

"I was a structural engineering consultant."

She taps her lips with a graceful finger. "I forget—where did you work?"

A muscle in James's jaw clenches, and color slowly blooms along the tops of his cheekbones as we both realize what she's doing. "Rooney, Lipton, and Squire."

"Ohh," she says, like it's just now come back to her. "Right, right. That was the place with all the embezzlement. They were inflating the books and taking money from employee pensions, right?"

He answers with a clipped "Yes."

She whistles. "I sure hope you didn't lose everything."

My stomach drops. I can tell from his expression that he did.

I catch our driver Gary's eyes in one of the oversize mirrors, and we both wince. I can never tell how much he hears, but the tension is so heavy and the conversation so razor sharp, he'd have to have cotton in his ears to miss the feel of it.

"Aren't they still investigating that?" Melly's saccharine voice is wrapped in a brittle veneer of indifference. "Maybe you'll get some of your retirement money back."

"Melly." I very rarely admonish her, but I'm already tired of whatever this is.

"He's one of my employees and I'm just concerned about him." With a breezy wave, she goes back to her magazine. "I sure hope he isn't in a sticky situation."

Closing his laptop, James stands, meeting my eyes across the bus. "I appreciate your concern."

When he disappears to the back of the bus, I walk to the kitchenette and open the fridge, needing a little distance. The close proximity is starting to make me feel panicky and oddly dissociated from my body, like we've all been put here for something else entirely, and none of this is real. In some ways, that might even be a nice outcome: Ted and Robyn step out at some point, smiling broadly, admitting they're not a producer and a publicist but instead are really collaborators on a psychological study on the effect of forced proximity while attempting a task with absolutely no chance of success.

As I survey Melly's pressed juices and gluten-free, dairy-free, taste-free snacks, my mind drifts back to James. I can still feel what we did last night in the tenderness of my joints, the ache that lingers from the delicious frenzy of our first time. Every move I make today requires the use of some sore or exhausted limb, and the sensations become these mocking little reminders about what life could be like if I decided to be brave.

In truth, our phone call earlier shook something loose inside me. I've never thought of Melly as abusive before. Temperamental, yeah. Manipulative, sure. But abusive? What *would* Debbie say if I was honest with her about what really goes on? Have I held back from describing everything accurately not because of the NDA but because I've always known, deep down, that what James said is true?

He asked where I see myself in the future. If it were up to Melly, I'd be working with her for at least another ten years. *Keeping her calendar organized*. My stomach clenches with dread. I don't want that. Working for Comb+Honey solves one problem but creates another: I have the resources to pay for anything I need—including whatever treatments I might need in the future—but the constant stress of dealing with the show and the Tripps is making my symptoms worse. If I'm struggling to hold a pencil now, what will it be like in five years, let alone ten?

Unfocused but staring into the open refrigerator, I imagine telling Melly that I'm quitting, damn the fallout. It would be unpleasant, but it wouldn't last forever, and then I would be free to think, for the first time in my life, about what I'd really like to do. I'd be broke and it'd be hard, but I might have James. I might have time to get myself a house and a dog and a few hobbies. I might actually have a life.

Just knowing that the possibility is there is like that first gulp of air after kicking toward the surface. Somehow, the elephant doesn't seem so huge.

James tries to talk to me a number of times once we get to Sacramento, but it's just too chaotic. We are off the bus, into one store, signing stock in a flurry, then getting back on the bus to weave through downtown Sacramento to the next store. It doesn't actually seem to be the best plan, because obviously we are not at all inconspicuous inside Melly's and Rusty's heads on wheels, and by the time we pull up at a Barnes & Noble, a few cars have trailed us on the journey, with fans getting out and asking for pictures.

Joe paces in the background, fighting what seems to be a strong urge to check his watch every minute that Melly does what Melly does best: chatting with people and smiling for photos. I'm grateful that Rusty put on a nice shirt, and I realize with a mixture of fondness and surprise that it must've occurred to James to remind his boss that he might be in front of a lot of fans asking him to pose for selfies.

James sidles up to me, and my pulse jumps. I like the smell of his laundry detergent on him. I remember how it lingered on his skin even when his clothes were on the floor.

"I need to talk to you," he says.

I look up, grateful for the distraction of fans so he and I can share one quiet minute. "Me too," I tell him. "I made a decision about something . . ."

He frowns a little and then his expression clears, like he thinks he knows what I'm going to say. "Yeah?" His voice has dropped a few decibels and the volume turns it a little scratchy. "Then you go first."

"I'm going to quit," I say. His face doesn't do what I expected it to; he doesn't immediately smile. "I'm going to tell Melly tonight. I'll give her until they wrap up the tour in Boise."

James frowns. "Are you sure the timing is good?"

"What you said. On the phone?" I wait until he nods, barely. "You're right about all of it. I realized today I don't talk about it with Debbie—my therapist—because I know what she'll say. Working here isn't good for my hands. It's not good for my mental health. I can find something else."

He shifts on his feet, looking back over his shoulder at Melly and Rusty. "Melissa will be a mess without you."

"I know, but this is insane, right?" I search his eyes for the conviction I heard in his voice earlier. "Like you said, what does my life look like in five years?"

James squints past me, into the distance. Something about his demeanor makes my stomach do a weird flip. I expected a grin, maybe a quick, covert hug. Hell, I'd take a thumbs up at this point. I didn't expect him to look so . . . conflicted.

"I thought you'd be a bit more supportive and a bit less . . . I don't know. *Concerned*."

"No," he says quickly, "I'm just thinking." He meets my eyes again, and his are so deep and emotive, I want to pull him into the light and study them more carefully, the way he studied me last night. I feel like that connection has been severed, and I don't know if it's the fact that we aren't alone, or if it's something else.

"I know what I said," he continues, "and I do think you should leave. But we both made a commitment to get them through this, and it won't look good for either of our résumés if they fall apart on this tour. If they become a scandal, it'll just be another Rooney, Lipton, and Squire for me, and an unending stretch of being an assistant to a scandal for you."

My gut turns sour. I can see his point, and hate that my decisions seem to simultaneously be too late and too impulsive. "I don't know how to do this," I admit, my voice thin. "When does it end?"

James seems to have a physical response to the desperation in my voice because something in his demeanor shifts, like it hurts him to ask this of me. "Just wait until the second season is a go, okay? Just a few more weeks, at most."

I think ahead to what we have left: a drive to Oregon tonight and then finishing the trip to Portland tomorrow, where we have a big event. From Portland to Seattle for another event and a stretch of interviews, then Boise before heading back to Jackson. From there, the Tripps are *supposed* to gear up for a tour of the East Coast. If all goes well, I definitely won't be around for that.

I look to where Melly fawns over a woman's pink coat,

and I know she'll climb back on the bus and immediately comment about how ugly it was, and how could someone wear something like that in public? James wants me to hang in there for another couple of weeks—and I know he has my best interests in mind because he's good like that—but I don't even want to be around them for another hour.

But then Joe comes over, hands me his phone, and grimaces.

Looks like someone from the hotel caught a picture of Melly and Rusty fighting as they got into the elevator alone last night. Melly's pointed index finger is spearing Rusty in the chest. Her face is so twisted in anger that she looks like she's spitting. The photo on Twitter has only been up for an hour and already has over four thousand likes.

James

When we arrive in Portland the next afternoon, there are already photographers camped outside the hotel. Because Melissa is still banned from Twitter, she gets excited when she sees them. Carey doesn't have the heart to tell her they're here because they're hoping to catch the couple fighting.

But, for once, I do.

"Before we get off the bus," I begin, and Melissa halts, turning to look at me with overt irritation, "you should know that someone caught you fighting in the hotel lobby."

"We weren't," Melissa says immediately, and looks to her husband for backup. His indifferent shrug doesn't really help her case.

I turn my phone to face her. "I don't think the photos are doctored, Melissa."

Joe shrinks to the back, as if he needs to tidy up, even though all Rusty does back there is sit and watch television. In my peripheral vision, I can see Carey staring at me, surprised.

"So here's how it's going to go," I continue. "You're going to get off this bus and show the world you're in love." I lift my hands, relaxed, like this is the easiest ask they've ever received. "Every married couple fights. Not a big deal. If you didn't fight, it'd mean there's nothing there worth fighting for, right?"

I wonder whether Rusty has even read their book, because clearly only Melissa and Carey recognize the quote. Carey smothers a smile. Melissa's eyes narrow.

"Tonight," I say, "you're going to have dinner in the hotel restaurant and you're going to be *delighted* with each other's company. Sound good?"

Melissa takes a deep, slow breath. I don't have to guess that she's slaughtering me in her head; it's written all over her face. "Sounds good."

Voices filter from the other side of Carey's door, and I double-check the number before reaching up to knock. She calls out to me from inside and then the door opens to reveal a smiling and recently showered Carey. My heart gives my sternum a small punch.

"Come in." She's already on her way back inside.

"I wanted to talk to you abou—"

"I'm just talking to Kurt. Can you shut the door behind you?"

Kurt? Her brother?

The door sweeps closed and I take in the space: her suitcase seems to have exploded on her bed. A wet towel has been tossed onto the sofa near the window. I stop when I see her sitting at the desk, laptop open and projecting a smiling man on the screen.

They look so much alike, even though her hair is long and sandy-brown and his looks dark and curly.

"I can come back . . ." After all, this is her older brother and I'm in her hotel room . . . while she's presumably naked under that robe.

"No, no. We're just wrapping this up." She turns the screen toward me. "Kurt, this is James, *the engineer*. James, my brother, Kurt."

We share an awkward wave, and then I turn my attention back to her. "Seriously, it's not important—"

She's already shushing me and pointing to the bed. "Go sit. I'll just be a minute." Carey tosses a magazine in my direction before turning back to the screen. No doubt I relish diving into the latest issue of *Taste of Home* as much as the next guy, but eavesdropping on Carey's conversation with her brother is hard to resist.

"Okay, so you were updating me on Mom," Carey prompts him.

Kurt pushes a hand through his dusty hair—as in, dust actually clouds around him—and then tugs a faded baseball cap on. The tips of his ears are sunburned, and so is the tip of his nose. He looks tired, the sort of bone-deep tired of a man who spends his day working in the hot sun. I wonder if, like their father had been, Kurt is in construction.

"Mom is Mom." His voice is a deep, raspy growl. "I talked to her for a few minutes, but Ellen down the street had a knee replacement so she was taking them over a casserole. She pitched a fit that I took one the last time I was over, but she still had three disasteroles in the damn garage freezer!"

Carey giggles and it's a sound I've rarely heard. The easy delight does something wild to my pulse.

"How's your truck? Still hassling you?"

Kurt groans and takes his cap off again, uses the bill to scratch the top of his head. "Don't get me started."

I try to turn away from their conversation, but that is also the moment that Carey chooses to cross her legs. The white fabric of her robe parts to reveal the smooth expanse of her calf, thigh . . . and higher.

"I just replaced the injectors," he says, "but I don't think that was it. I think it's the motor. If that's the case I'll probably have to take out a loan to have the whole damn thing rebuilt." Kurt's voice slices through my dirty thoughts, and I immediately immerse myself in a chicken pot pie recipe. The last thing I need in this day is to have him look over her shoulder and catch me ogling his little sister.

"It has over three hundred thousand miles on it," Carey reminds him. "I don't know why you don't just replace it. It's nickel-and-diming you to death."

"Because a new truck would cost more, and by the time I'm done it'll practically be brand-new," he tells her.

I envy him the ability to fix his own car. I learned from my parents, whose motto seemed to be *Why do it yourself when you can hire someone to do it for you?* My dad still leases a new BMW every three years; I'm not sure he or Mom has ever changed a tire.

Sometime in my mental meandering, they finish their call, ending it with promises to drag their other brother, Rand, out with them soon.

"Sorry about that," she says, standing from the desk and closing the laptop.

"I'm sorry I interrupted." She waves me off, and in an effort to keep my attention on her face and not her legs, I add, "He seems nice."

"He's a grumpy old shit, but he's all right." She laughs. "We hardly ever see each other, so this is generally how we keep in touch. You might have guessed he's not much of a texter." She motions to her robe and points to the bathroom. "Just a second."

I give the room another once-over, noticing the row of bras and underwear swinging in the breeze of the air conditioner from where they hang over the headboards of both queen beds.

"Have you been doing laundry in here?"

The door opens, and she steps out in a pair of jeans and her Dolly shirt, her hair tied up in a hasty bun. "Yeah, sorry," she says, crossing the room to retrieve them.

"Don't be sorry. It's resourceful." I recognize the blue bra and it makes my mouth go dry.

"I'm almost out of clothes," she admits, giggling again as she pulls them down one by one. "I'm sure this explains why I'm always wrinkled. Let me just . . ."

She jogs back to the bathroom, so she misses my quiet "You're perfect."

When she returns, she sits at the edge of the bed. She's stripped off the comforter, and I'm reminded of the last time we were in a hotel room together. The memory echoes across my skin in a heated, frantic pulse.

I give myself a few breaths to look at her. I wonder if, when she's watching a show, she mimics every expression the actors make on-screen: happy, sad, confused, delighted. Right now I feel like she's mimicking me, with wide, exploring eyes.

If memory serves, we decided in San Francisco that we aren't kissing anymore, but for the life of me I can't remember why. In fact, I can barely remember why I came up here in the first place, but now that I'm here, I really just want to press her back into the mattress and let her have her way with me again.

She looks away, breaking the tension. "I was impressed today," she says.

I blink back into awareness. "Oh, on the bus?"

"Yes, Señor Bossypants."

This makes me laugh. "There were a few seconds there when I thought Melissa might walk over and punch me in the dick."

Carey falls back on the bed in laugher. "I thought the same thing," she says, pushing up onto her elbows. "But no. It was good. I think we need to be bossier with her. Otherwise she'll get away with everything."

The reason for my visit comes back to me, and it occurs to me now that it might be a terrible idea. Obviously I can barely be around Carey without wanting to be touching—how will I do over candlelight? But Ted's napkin promise looms large in my memory.

"Well, relatedly," I say, "I was thinking that it might be a good idea for us to have dinner at a table near the Tripps tonight. Just to keep an eye on things."

Her eyes gleam with playfulness. "You don't trust them?"

"Not for a second."

When she wrinkles her nose, teasing, my stomach takes a lovesick dive. "So you're asking me out on a fake date?"

"If you're up for it."

Carey chews her lip, eyes narrowed as she takes me in. "Yeah. I think that's probably a good idea."

My skin flushes, and now I am sure that this was a terrible suggestion. She just threw a T-shirt on; she clearly isn't wearing a bra. A drop of water rolls down her long, smooth neck, and I want to lick it off and then fuck her into next week.

But I suppose if the Tripps can spend this meal pretending to be infatuated, I should be able to spend it with Carey, pretending not to be.

Carey

At exactly 6:35 p.m. a waiter at El Gaucho is pouring me a glass of zinfandel while a smiling and camera-ready Melissa and Rusty Tripp sit just a few tables away. The restaurant is perfect: it's connected to the hotel and filled with the kind of Melissa-approved soft-focus candlelight that makes everyone look great. They're even seated next to a window, and if one of the photographers outside just happens to snap a few photos of the intimate dinner? Well, that's even better.

I've eaten plenty of meals with James, but it's rarely just the two of us, and never in a dimly lit restaurant with fancy alcohol, leather-bound menus, and innocuous classical music playing from hidden speakers. I know this isn't a date—I *know*, we made that very clear upstairs—but it feels like it anyway. I'm in the best dress I own—the blue one I save to follow Melly to morning shows and big interviews—and James is sitting across from me, wearing a navy blazer over a crisp white shirt and a smile that makes me wonder if he thinks this is a real date, too.

He picks up a giant shrimp and dunks it in a dish of

cocktail sauce. "This is a really nice hotel. Almost a whole star up from the Motel 6 in Hollywood. Good job."

I kick him under the table.

He coughs as he chews, laughing into his napkin. "I'm being sincere," he says, once he's come up for air, "it's great. I'm not much of a tub guy, but the one in my bathroom is making me question myself."

Not even going to imagine him sinking naked into a giant tub of bubbles. Definitely not going to imagine sinking into a tub with him, leaning back against his chest and feeling his arms come around my waist, his hand sliding—

New topic. "Did you know it's supposed to be haunted?"

His eyes widen playfully. "My tub?"

I narrow my eyes at him, fighting a smile. "The hotel. I walked downstairs to get some toothpaste because I've lost yet another tube, and there was some kind of tour happening."

"Like a ghost tour?"

I pick up a roll and butter it. "The concierge told me the first owner supposedly haunts the hotel. There's a mirror in the lobby where you can see the reflection of a woman in a turquoise dress. Oh!" I point my buttery knife at him. "And someone claimed they sat up in bed one night and there was a little boy playing peekaboo at the foot of her bed." I laugh at his horrified expression. "The front desk will even bring you a companion fish to keep you company. Pretty cute, right?"

When I glance up again, James is still staring at me, second shrimp paused midway to his mouth.

I lift a brow. "You're not scared, are you?"

He sets the shrimp back down on his plate. "I definitely don't want a ghost child playing peekaboo in my bed."

"I know. I would pee my pants, no question. But don't worry, the guide said the twelfth, ninth, and seventh floors are the only ones ever reported for any activity. And the lobby, of course."

He blinks. "I'm on the ninth floor, Carey."

"Oh." I laugh. "Do you want me to order you an emotional support fish?"

Straightening, James waves the waiter over and orders us both another glass of wine. "Yes to the fish," he says, and grins at me over the top of his glass. "But enough of this will help, too."

I smile back at him across the table and ignore the gnawing worry slowly rising in my chest. This feels so good. How am I supposed to be platonic with this guy? The more time I spend with him, the more I genuinely like everything about him. More than like. Tonight, after dinner, I want to take him by the hand and walk him upstairs to bed.

The idea of sleeping with his bare, lanky body pressed all along mine makes me shiver.

"So, Kurt," he asks, and my sexy thoughts trip and fall over the Incompatible Topics Cliff. "What does he do for a living?"

"He frames houses. Started working with my dad when he was fifteen, and then Dad died and Kurt took over. He was twenty-two and has been doing it nearly every day since. I gave it a try before the dystonia started, but even then I complained so much he actually gave me twenty dollars to go away."

James choke-laughs on a sip of wine, and I kick him again. "So when I called Melly to tell them what time we made the reservations for, she said Rusty was up in your room?"

He nods and looks at me like he broke a rule.

The expression is so hilarious, I burst out laughing. "I don't care if he's in your room, James."

"Honestly, I think he was lonely. Well, mostly I think he wanted to watch the game, and since he and Melissa had to share a room on this leg, and she wouldn't let him use the TV, he came down to me. I'd feel bad for him, but he's just as much to blame for their problems as she is."

I pull back, brows furrowed. "Some would even say he's more to blame, seeing as how he decided to stick his penis in a woman who isn't his wife."

James holds up his hands, immediately clarifying, "I don't mean the affair. I mean the terrible marriage." He leans in, lowering his voice. "You've read the most recent book, I take it?"

I groan. "About a thousand times to hunt for typos, yes."

"It's actually pretty good, right?" He sips his wine, and the way his throat looks when he swallows is very distracting. "If they actually followed their own advice, they'd have an amazing relationship."

"I'm hoping for your sake he's not planning a sleepover."

James starts to laugh, and then his smile falters. "God no." He pauses, sipping his wine again and watching me. "I don't share my bed with just anyone, you know."

The air between us vibrates, warm and charged.

I finally manage a lame "Well, I'm glad to hear that."

He continues to study me the way he always does, but

for once the weight of his focus makes me feel awkward and overwhelmed, and I turn back to my plate. "Just a few days more and the show airs."

"I feel like I've been working for the Tripps for a decade. I don't know how you do it."

"Right? And how have I done it for so *long*?" I agree, glancing over to their table.

From here, their fondness looks real enough. She's talking and he's listening in that way he has, like she's his sun and moon and the only woman in the world. They look like the couple you see on TV. It almost makes me wonder if they have a chance. Would counseling help?

"Do you think there's a way they could ever make it work?" I ask.

He lifts a brow.

"They used to love each other so much."

"I think . . ." He trails off. "I think sometimes we see what we want to see." There's an edge of sadness in his voice that catches my attention.

"This sounds . . . personal." I lean in, way more interested in hearing about James than I am in talking about the Tripps over candlelight.

"My parents divorced when I was fifteen," he says. "They sat us down one day and said that just because they didn't love each other anymore, it didn't mean they didn't love us. I was totally blindsided. They'd never stopped being friendly and warm to each other, so I had no idea they were even talking about divorce. It was like being hit by a truck. They said Dad had already rented an apartment but he'd still come by. Nothing would change."

I reach across the table, squeezing his hand. "I'm sorry."

For a beat, the conversation at the table near us—Melly and Rusty's—goes quiet. I don't have to look over to know that Melly is watching us. And apparently neither does James. He carefully pulls his hand out of mine.

"Not to spoil the story," he says, "but everything changed. I remember asking Jenn if she had seen it coming, and she seemed surprised that I hadn't. I told her they seemed so nice and gentle with each other. She said they fought almost every night after we went to bed."

"You were a fifteen-year-old boy," I say. "I bet if I asked my brother what color my eyes are, he'd have a fifty percent chance of getting it right." Blinking, I add with a grin, "And we have the same color eyes."

James laughs at this.

"But I get what you mean," I continue. "I remember when I first told my mom something was going on with my hand, and she was shocked like it was the first she was hearing of it. My handwriting was getting worse, and she'd say it looked the same as it always had. I'd be doing this," I say, and hold up my arm in front of me, "my entire hand visibly shaking, and she'd say I needed more protein in my diet or more sleep. My dad was having some health issues, too, so she had a lot going on, but it wasn't until my doctors sat her down and told her it was real and not going away that she really got it."

"When did you first notice it?"

"I was nineteen. I'd always been able to draw, but around then my hand would get tired and crampy really soon after I'd start a sketch. I didn't think much of it until I had to do something that required both hands—like helping Rusty put together a table or pin some upholstery to a chair—and that's when I realized it wasn't just fatigue from drawing all the time; there was something wrong. I started hiding my hands because they would spasm or clench up, waiting until I was alone to do anything that required small movements. Melly's the one who noticed and insisted I see someone."

James listens intently. "Melissa did?"

I nod. "I was pretty good at hiding it, but she noticed that I wasn't eating in front of her." At his confused expression I explain, "I drop pencils all the time—and that's with regular Botox treatments. Imagine me holding a fork, at my worst."

He winces.

"They've been great about it. I like to think no one else notices, really, because I'm not out in front of that many people. Then you came along and—"

"You didn't want me to see."

I feel my cheeks heat.

He sits back in his chair, going pale. "I teased you about your job."

"We both teased each other," I remind him.

"The first time I saw you in the studio," he says, "I didn't know what to think." He takes off his glasses and rubs his eyes. "I'm used to always knowing where I fit in, but it was pretty clear early on that the job wasn't what I expected and I . . . I was embarrassed. And trapped," he adds. "Resentful. I took it out on you. I'm sorry."

"I don't think either of us was very nice," I admit. "I liked rubbing it in. A lot."

I can tell that he's miserable, can practically hear him going over every one of our early interactions in his head. I'm about to tell him we have plenty of time to work out how he's going to make it up to me and be my grateful servant for life when there's a crash a few tables away. I know who it is without even looking over, and dread settles over me in a chill.

Rusty is pushed back from the table, the front of his clothes soaked from what I can only assume is a full glass of Melly's sparkling water.

"Our son is a good kid," Rusty says loudly. "You've just babied him so much he doesn't know how to stand on his own two feet."

She's looking down at her nails, bored. A few other diners have turned around to see what all the commotion is about, and I'm out of my chair so fast it nearly topples over.

"Hi, friends!" I gush. "How are you?"

I reach for the napkin at Rusty's feet and attempt to clean him up, groaning when I realize I'm aggressively dabbing at his crotch. "Did we have a little spill?"

Straightening, I put my flattened palm on his chest and push him back into his seat, handing him the napkin to sop up more of the water. "Let's remember that there are eyes and ears everywhere," I whisper through a clenched smile.

Melly ignores me to glare at her husband. "Our son can barely string two sentences together and has been in college for six years," she whisper-shouts.

"He's got ambition," Rusty says, chin out. "Just like his dad."

"He's also got a beer belly," she says with icy calm. "Just like his dad."

Oh shit.

A half-empty bottle of Perrier sits near the edge of the table, and on impulse I knock it over, the bubbly liquid rushing across the tablecloth and into Melly's lap. James is here now, too, leading a furious Rusty away from the table before he can reply.

"Oops! Butterfingers," I sing, pulling out Melly's chair and dragging her toward the door. I stop a passing waiter. "Can you put those two tables on our bill? Room 649, guest Carey Duncan. I swear I'll be down to sign it all and leave you a giant tip. Sorry! Thank you!"

He nods dumbly, rightfully confused, and I push Melly out of the restaurant and into the lobby bathroom.

Once inside, I don't even have to peek in the mirror to know that my cheeks are red-hot with anger. I check under all the stalls before turning on her. "What the hell were you thinking?"

She's already pacing. "I can't believe him! He thinks this family got its squeaky image without me running along cleaning up everyone's mess? Including his?"

"What good will getting vocal credit for everything do when there are photos and tweets and videos of you two arguing?" I ask. "Weren't you the one who insisted we keep this whole thing going?"

She waves this away like my point is frivolous. "It's fine."

"Melly, those photographers outside were here specifically to catch you and Rusty fighting, you know that."

She pauses, then shrugs it off. "Come on. Not everyone is on Twitter, Carey."

"Maybe not, but tonight you were eating dinner in a dining room full of people with phones and various other recording devices. Even if two people there posted about what they saw, you know how many people that could reach? These are people who otherwise might want to buy your book. You know, the one on marriage that you're supposed to be signing tonight with the man you want everyone to think you're happily married to?"

My phone vibrates in my hand, and I wish I had a pillow to scream into. I close my eyes, take a deep breath, and count to five before I look. Thankfully, it's a text from James. Unfortunately, it doesn't make me feel any better.

You better get up here. Room 940

I look up to see her reflection in the mirror. "We need to get upstairs. Now."

She steps up to the sink and calmly washes her hands, dries them. She smooths her hair and touches up her lipstick with a tube from her clutch. Aside from the wet spot down the front of her clothes, she looks a little flushed but camera ready, as always.

Luckily, we're not alone in the elevator; I know Melly well enough to know that she would change the subject as quickly as possible and I'm grateful I don't have to answer any questions about James. The people with us either don't know who Melly is or are too polite to mention it, thank the Lord. My phone starts vibrating with increasing frequency by the second floor, and by the time we make it to James's room there are a handful of messages from James, some from Robyn, and shit—one from Ted.

Judging by the look on James's face, his says the same thing:

FIX THIS

Ella @1967_Disney_bound • July 12
HOLY SHIT THEY CANCLED THE TOUR?

> **TMZ** @TMZ • July 12
> Cameras catch lovers' spat as Melissa and Rusty Tripp dine together amidst rumors of infidelity and scandal. Promo tour canceled. www.tmz.com/2L6Kz8l

387 replies   1644 retweets   2639 likes

Show this thread

booksnbangtan @booksnbangtan
@1967_Disney_bound I cannot be reading this right. They lost it in front of an entire restaurant? And what cover up are they talking about in the article?

Ella @1967_Disney_bound
@booksnbangtan Like you couldn't just eat your pasta primavera and be nice?? Not positive on the rumors but it's been a circus the last few months. Remember this doozy?

> **TMZ** @TMZ • April 4
> Melissa Tripp out with friends. Sources say mysterious bruises have team concerned www.HollywoodLife.com/2L6Kz8l

booksnbangtan @booksnbangtan
@1967_Disney_bound WHY ARE THEY SO MESSY THO?

And mysterious bruises? Please, if we going knock down drag out my money is on Melissa. A lot of pent up rage behind all that makeup

Ella @1967_Disney_bound

@booksnbangtan idk take your pick lol. I know people suspected rusty had a drug habit after he lost some weight last year, and don't get me started on their kids

Pitty @Pittypattington7th

@booksnbangtan @1967_Disney_bound I was supposed to go to the Seattle event and they canceled at the last minute.

Jenna @Jennanadamcuthbert04

@Pittypattington7th @booksnbangtan @1967_Disney_bound I have a friend who knows their son from school and said he has a thing for hookers and vegas. Do with that what you will.

Abashed1999OC @Abashed1999OC

@Jennanadamcuthbert04 @Pittypattington7th @booksnbangtan @1967_Disney_bound no shit??

James

Part of me is relieved to see the lights fading away as we leave the Portland city limits. But the other part is anxious about what's ahead: we've essentially been banished until the first season of *Home Sweet Home* airs.

The four of us are on our way to a cabin in the middle of nowhere, meaning the gloves can truly come off. With every mile we move farther from civilization. I'm not one hundred percent sure where we're going, but I know one thing: nobody can hear the screams from this far away.

It's absurd, really, that we're still expected to chaperone this nonsense, but my assumption is that everyone is worried that, left to his own devices, Rusty would rather catch a cab home and leave Melissa behind than stay sequestered with his wife in the woods. Just as I'm about to quietly run this theory past Carey, a crash comes from the back of the bus, and Melissa storms out of the lounge, throwing herself on one of the couches toward the front of the cab. Breathing heavily, she closes her eyes and rubs her temples. They're not even trying to pretend anymore.

"I swear to Jesus, Mary, and Joseph," she hisses. "That man—"

"TJ and Kelsey." Carey calmly reminds her boss of the two most important reasons why Melissa can't murder her husband. "Also, you're building a house in Aspen that is going to be gorgeous. You can't decorate it from a jail cell."

Melissa takes a few deep breaths and then opens her eyes to smile gratefully at Carey. What the hell would Melissa do without her?

My phone lights up with a text sent to me, Carey, and Ted from Robyn. It reads simply:

Everything's set.

Carey grimaces at me and types up exactly what Ted can do with his getaway, before erasing it all.

She slides her phone onto the bus bench between us, gives me a half smile, and leans her head back against the cushion. The metaphorical handcuffs have been clicked into place.

I grew up in the Southwest, and I'm familiar with Jackson, of course—obviously it's where the Tripps are based—but I've never traveled the almost four hundred miles to Laramie. The size of the sky out here blows my mind. Half of the circle of my vision is a clear, startling blue. The other half is an explosion of green: hills, grass, plains that go on forever.

We drop off the tour bus in Laramie and, with as little fanfare as possible, we're done. We say goodbye to Joe and encourage him to schedule a long vacation. He takes a final look at the Tripps and wishes us luck—their mutual silent treatment commenced as soon as we got on the bus, and we're all tired of breathing such pressurized air.

Also ready to be rid of us, driver Gary ushers us from the bus into a sleek black sedan waiting nearby. I'm sure these two are about to get very, very drunk. I don't know what happens to our bags, but the car is pulling away from the curb before I have any sense that things have been moved; it's a Secret Service–level transfer. Ted apparently does not fuck around.

With Rusty in the front, and Carey situated between me and Melissa in the spacious back seat, we leave Laramie proper and drive about a half hour into what can best be described as the middle of nowhere, where houses become spaced farther and farther apart, the soft rolling hills so green it seems impossible that they're real. I'm grateful for the silence, because the view is unbelievable. The Laramie River winds its way through the landscape, glittering in the late-afternoon sun like a trail of jewels.

Our driver turns down a series of increasingly rustic dirt roads before pulling up in front of a sprawling log cabin set only about forty feet back from a wide bend in the river. I peek down at my phone: no cell service. I doubt Wi-Fi is robust here, either. Good news, bad news: Melissa won't be able to see reviews, tweets, or Instagram photos of her from her bad side, but we also won't be able to easily check in with the outside world. We are a good half-hour drive from any stores, and—I note with some degree of trepidation—at least as far from any hospital.

Rusty climbs out and disappears around the back of the

cabin, muttering something about needing some air, and I note that Carey and I both relax a bit when we only have one Tripp to manage at a time. Maybe if they don't speak to each other for an entire week, everything will blow over. One can hope.

Melissa stares up at the hulking cabin and lets out a long-suffering sigh. "I guess it's big enough."

I can't tell if she's trying to be funny, or if the woman who helps families fit into the shoe boxes they can afford has genuinely become that spoiled: the home in front of us is easily big enough for twenty people.

There's a dusty old sedan parked along one side of the house, and I'm hoping the keys are inside. As we approach the front door, I see our bags are waiting for us on the porch.

"I have no idea what kind of magic was involved in them beating us here," Carey says under her breath, "but I'm into it."

There's an envelope taped to the front door, and I pull it off. Opening it, I find a key and a short welcome note from the property manager. Once I have everything unlocked, Melissa sweeps past her luggage and disappears inside.

A glance at Carey's hands tells me she's not having a good day: they're rock solid, curled into fists, and even when she tries to shake them out I know that carrying even the smallest bag inside is going to be a challenge. *How physically exhausting must it be to focus on every movement, to feel like your own muscles are fighting you*, I think. I'm suddenly and blindingly furious with Melissa for being so consistently inconsiderate.

But Carey is Carey, and immediately reaches for the closest suitcase. I wave her off, she gives me a tiny, grateful smile, and guilt drills a hole in my stomach. If it weren't for my encouragement, she would have quit before we got to Portland and would probably be home by now. I remind myself that in a few weeks we'll both be out of this mess and in a better position. "Go figure out where we're all sleeping, and I'll bring these in."

When she disappears inside, I take a moment to appreciate the masterful design of the property. The porch platform, columns, and cornice are constructed from the same beautiful redwood that frames each window; the finial and valleys of the roof are deep, sharp angles that make my blood sing.

Inside, the front door opens to an enormous entryway: The house is two broad stories and the second floor overlooks the foyer, with a knobby cherry railing lining a circular view down onto the gleaming hardwood floor. There is a huge living room straight ahead of me, a fireplace flanked by twin casement windows with lead glass, from floor to ceiling, that overlook the river. An expansive chef's kitchen stretches to the right of the front foyer, and a hall to the left of the entryway leads, I find, to a family room, entertainment suite, and game room.

Carey calls from upstairs: "I have Melly and Rusty each situated, and there are ten bedrooms left. How picky are you feeling?"

"I feel like a room with a bed is fine," I tell her.

She leans over the railing, looking down at me, and I wonder if she feels it, too, that heat that seems to blanket us whenever we're making contact—whether it's physical, verbal, or just eye contact like this across an open space. Do I want my room to be next to hers so that we can sneak into bed together in the middle of the night? Yes, absolutely. Is that the best way to make sure this week doesn't end in disaster? Probably not.

"I'm going to give you the blue room," she says, and grins. "It's a nautical theme, so I expect you to speak like a pirate all week."

"Aye, matey, give me a wee breath and I'll bring yar duffel upstairs."

She laughs, and it's on the tip of my tongue to ask her where her room is, but Melissa comes out of the suite at the end of the hall upstairs and pulls up short, staring at us like we're breaking a rule by speaking while unsupervised. Carey shrinks back into a room down the hall.

Well, at least now I know where she'll be sleeping.

The back door opens, and Rusty comes in, tracking mud across the kitchen tiles. I wave my arms wildly and, once he looks up, point to his boots. He full-body winces, like he knows if his wife sees this, he's a dead man. For the next two minutes, we're silently and hysterically searching for a mop to clean up the mess. Finally I find it, in a small closet down in the cellar, and I'm halfway up the stairs with it and a bucket when I hear her—the silent treatment has officially ended far, far too soon.

"Are you kidding me?" she says. "Not ten minutes we're in this house and you're already tracking in mud?"

"Come on, hon," he says as I step out into the kitchen. "We're cleaning it up. It was an accident."

"You better thank your lucky stars it wasn't carpet because I am not paying for any more of your messes."

His reply is probably ill-advised. "Who even puts carpet in the kitchen?"

While they argue, I quietly mop up the muddy footprints and meet Carey's sympathetic gaze when she comes into the room, probably to find out what they're yelling about this time.

With the floor clean, Carey and I check out the fridge, the pantry, and the cabinets to figure out where everything is. All are fully stocked.

She looks over at me, eyes wide. "Are we supposed to cook for them?"

I shake my head. "Definitely not. They can feed themselves."

"Have you seen Melly try to cook?" she asks me quietly, brows up.

"Maybe Rusty . . . ?"

Carey gives me a look that communicates she can't believe I just asked that, and our attention is pulled away when Rusty opens the fridge and pulls out a beer.

Oh, no.

"*Russell Clarence Tripp*," Melissa barks, starting back up again. "It isn't even two in the afternoon yet, what in God's name are you doing?"

"Relaxing?"

"We are not here to *relax*."

"You gonna make me a fucking honey-do list, Melissa?"

Carey's eyes are drawn over my shoulder, away from the

kitchen, and when she looks back at me, she lifts her chin like, *Nearest escape?*

I nod. *Lead the way.*

We find a cabinet full of board games, dominoes, cards, and dice and decide on cards in the family room. We can still hear Melissa and Rusty going at each other, but out here it's more muted and, after a few minutes, I think we're both able to tune them out. Carey hands me the cards to shuffle, and then makes herself a little shelf to prop her cards against, using some hardcover books and a ruler.

"Clever," I say, grinning as I start to deal our hands.

"I'm the cleverest."

"Well," I say, teasing, "I'm not sure you're the *cleverest*. I had a dog—"

"You don't think it's possible I'm more clever than the cleverest dog?"

I hold up a finger. "—who knew how to open the fridge and get a beer out for my dad."

"Okay," she concedes, picking up a card, "that's pretty clever. But could he open it?"

"*She* could not," I admit, "but she was still the best dog anyway."

"We had a dopey old Rottweiler named Dusty when I was growing up," she says, "and one time we were headed to my granny's house in Billings, and we were in my parents' station wagon. I was only four or so—at that age I think my parents just threw me in the back with the dog. Anyway, there was a cake back there and I was supposed to hold it on my lap for the whole drive, but Dusty and I shared it instead. Surprising no one, we both threw up in the car. I was covered in blue vomit from the frosting, my parents had to stop at a convenience store on the way, and I ended up wearing a too-big Iron Maiden shirt to my granddad's seventieth birthday party."

"I'm not sure what part of this story I like the least," I say, discarding. "That you shared a cake with a dog, or that you both threw up in the back of a station wagon. I do like the Iron Maiden part, though."

"It had that creepy mascot Eddie on the front, so I cried every time I looked down."

This makes me burst out laughing, and it feels so good to be genuinely happy for a few breaths that I lean back in my chair. When I sit up again, I realize Carey has won this game of gin and is carefully laying down her hand.

"Holy shit, how did you win so fast?"

She shrugs, and it's a sweet, blushing gesture that sideswipes me in a tender space near my lungs. "I don't think you shuffled very well," she says. "You dealt me two aces and three jacks."

I look down at my own motley hand of random numbers and suits. "I think you just got a lucky deal."

"Eh. I played a lot with the boys back home," she says, reaching for the cards to shuffle them. "A lucky deal was when you joined Comb+Honey."

"Lucky for who?" I ask, grinning.

She taps the cards on the table. "Me."

I think about her words and her tone and her blush as she carefully cuts the deck in two and lines them up to shuffle them, slowly. It occurs to me, watching her, that she doesn't hide her dystonia from me anymore. I don't think she ever would have done this in front of me before this trip.

I wonder who else she's this comfortable around. Certainly not Melissa, not anymore. Things between her and Rusty are still weird, like a stepfather and stepdaughter who don't interact much. I know she has roommates, but she doesn't talk about them often.

"Are your roommates back from their trip?"

She thinks for a second while she shuffles again. "No, I think they were supposed to be gone essentially as long as we were. I bet their trip feels like it's flying by. Can you imagine?"

I give her a sympathetic wince. "What are they like?"

Smiling, she starts to deal. "They're cool. Peyton is an insurance adjustor, which honestly cracks me up because she's so energetic and athletic but chose a job where she's in an office all day. She plays on like three different rec softball teams and umpires for the local high school league. She teaches yoga and is a really active member of a community garden project. And Annabeth is, like, the total opposite. She's so sweet and gentle, sort of shy until you get to know her. She's a flight attendant so they get to travel everywhere and . . ." She pauses, shrugging. "They're cool," she repeats, finally.

I see the cloud start to sweep in, the droop in her shoulders and downward angle of her mouth, and feel like an asshole for bringing up anyone outside of this crazy situation, anyone we know who has a normal life and a normal job and normal attachments.

But the more I think about what "normal" is, the more

I wonder why I think my feelings for Carey would be any different in another circumstance than they are right here. I don't have feelings for her because we've been forced together, or because I feel sorry for her. I have feelings for her because she's frankly amazing: she's brilliant, humble, beautiful, and resilient.

I open my mouth to speak—honestly, I don't know what I'm going to say, but I need to barrel past this emotion clogging my chest. I'm just hoping some words come out and they make sense—but she shushes me, her eyes wide.

"What is it?" I ask.

"Do you hear that?"

I turn in a panic, listening for what she means. "All I hear is silence."

Carey's smile stretches across her cheeks; her blue-green eyes sparkle like the river outside. "Exactly."

But then her smile fades at the same time the realization hits me, too: silence could mean someone has been murdered.

⁂

We tiptoe into the kitchen—no one is there.

No one is in the backyard near the river. No one is in the game room. But when we peek in the entertainment room, we find Melissa on one giant chair and Rusty on another. No gore or blood in sight, only the sound of two people snoring, with *Joe Versus the Volcano* playing on the enormous screen at the front of the room.

We stare for a second, shocked at the sight. Rusty's mouth hangs open; his beer is perched precariously on his chest. I'd bet, even asleep, Rusty could hold on to that thing in a hurricane. Melissa is curled up in a tight ball, like her defenses are up even in her slumber.

Carefully, we back out of the room.

"I'm amazed they were watching a movie together," Carey whispers, awed.

"*I checked for blood.*" Apparently my threshold for celebration is lower than hers. Her shoulders come up and she laughs, silently, looking at me like I'm kidding, and laughs harder when she realizes I'm serious.

I don't even know what to do with myself. We have a giant house, a river, food and games and movies in the middle of nowhere, basically everyone's dream vacation. But more than anything, I just want more time alone with Carey.

"Want to take the car and go for a drive?" I ask.

Her eyes light up. "Hell yes."

The gravel crunches under our shoes. In my mind, we'll be driving around winding dirt roads, hugging the curve of the tall green grasses that race alongside the river. In my mind, we'll have music playing, windows down. Carey will be singing, eyes closed, her arm out the window, fingers dancing in the wind.

In reality, we don't ever get that far. I've driven a quarter of a mile down the road when I feel her hand on my leg at the same moment I start to brake for a stop sign. The second she touches me, my leg tenses and I hit the brake harder than I planned. We both jerk forward and then back, coming to a silent, abrupt stop.

Turning to look at her, I see that same clarity in her eyes she had after the Boulevard event, but this time it's lacking the panic just beneath the surface. Her expression is open, hungry. This time, she doesn't have to tell me what to do.

I lean in and feel the hit of adrenaline the second her mouth touches mine and she lets out the sweetest moan in relief. It is emotion in sound, the direct translation of what I'm feeling, too. My hands come to her face, her hands land carefully on my biceps, and I'm cursing the hell out of us for starting this a quarter of a mile down the road instead of in close proximity to one of the house's ten spare bedrooms.

I reach to the side, flipping my seat back. With her lower lip trapped in her teeth, she smiles at me, climbing onto my lap. Her smile turns to a growl when she settles over where I'm hard, and I like this version of her. I like how unapologetically greedy she is with me like this. I lean back against the seat, thinking, *Take whatever the hell you want.*

Lifting her soft cotton skirt, I savor the heat of her legs under my hands. I love the little sounds she makes, how impatient she is with her touch and bite. Her hands dig in my hair and up under my shirt. She takes her time and doesn't grow self-conscious when she struggles with the buttons on my jeans, doesn't hide from me when she's exploring my chest with her trembling fingertips.

We undress just enough—for crying out loud, we're in fading daylight, but it's enough—and it seems like we've been here for two minutes and two years, like we've always been here, and she's smiling down at me, holding me and the condom from my wallet in her hand, and then we're moving together with our eyes open, laughing into each other's mouths.

"What are we even doing?" she whispers.

"Sex," I whisper back. "I think people call this sex."

Her laugh is a joyful burst against my lips, and I honestly think I've never felt this kind of lightness in my entire life, this much optimism. Maybe it's a release of stress, or maybe it's the absurdity of what we're doing—making love in a car at a stop sign in the middle of nowhere. Or maybe it's that I'm falling in love with her, and as she moves over me, I know for sure we can find a way out of this, and at the very least we can find a way through it together.

Her skin is soft cream under my hands. I feel the way the blood heats it as she moves, can hear her breaths turn into sound and her sounds turn into tight, hungry silence, and then she's cupping my neck, biting at my lower lip, growing frantic until she's falling into pleasure and dragging me right along with her. I would follow her anywhere.

With her eyes closed, she presses her forehead to mine, catching her breath. "I needed that."

"I needed it, too." I kiss a path up her neck. "But I also really wanted it."

She kisses me for that, and it turns into a smile. "Your answer was better."

"They can both be true."

Carey sits up, pressing her hands to my stomach. "Is it going to be weird when we get home?"

I groan, imagining the obliterating relief of sleeping in my own bed. "I think it's going to be blissful to be home."

She pinches me, lightly. "You know what I mean."

"I do." But with her still over me, and my pulse still

well above baseline, I'm not sure I'm coherent enough to properly have this conversation. There are so many things she and I have to talk about once we get home—what we want in a relationship, what we want from our careers. I still haven't told her about my conversation with Ted. And once she has all the information, she'll need to decide what she wants to do, too. It's all definitely too much for this perfect, quiet moment.

So I simply say the truth again: "Like I said, I think it's going to be blissful to be home."

The air grows cool and dark, and we get dressed as best we can in the front seat of an old car.

I look up at the sound of the door opening and see her step outside, arms above her head and back arched in a delicious, satisfied stretch. Climbing out, I walk around to the front of the car and sit back against the hood, watching her.

"Who was your first love?"

Her question takes me by surprise, but I answer. "Her name was Alicia. We were fourteen."

She walks back to me, smiling like she's tipsy, arms loose at her sides.

"Fourteen?" She pretends to be scandalized.

"Ohhh," I say, taking her hands in mine and pulling her closer. "You mean real love? With, like, wisdom and communication?"

"No, whatever you say first goes."

"Okay, well, then Alicia. I was totally infatuated. She was on the diving team. I think I just really liked seeing her in a bathing suit."

I can't make out much of her face but can see the way her head tilts as she considers me. "Occasionally you have these total Dude Moments, and they delight me."

I tug her closer until her chest is pressed against mine. "What about you? Who was your first love?"

"Dave Figota. I swear to God he fell in love with me when he saw me take my bra off without taking off my shirt. He looked at me like I was some kind of sexy witch."

I tuck her hair behind her ear. It's not curly exactly, but too rebellious to be considered straight. It fits her. "I've always found it fascinating how much of a mystery that maneuver is to men."

"It's not a mystery to you because you're an engineer."

I don't have to see her face to know what she's doing. "Why do I get the sense that you're saying that with an eye roll?"

"I think because I'm . . . aware of the differences in our education." She pulls back a little. "Sometimes I feel a little dumb by comparison. I don't even know what an engineer really does, let alone how a person becomes one. Does it bother you that I never went to college?"

"There are bell-shaped curves everywhere," I say carefully. "Just because someone goes to college doesn't mean they're inherently smarter than someone who doesn't. Plenty of idiots get degrees. Plenty of geniuses never bother."

"Are you suggesting it's possible I'm smarter than you?"

"Oh, I know you are." I run my nose along her neck, taste the salt on her skin. "Plus, think of all the experiences you've had that most people haven't."

"Like skinny-dipping?" I feel her smile.

"Rub it in."

Her fingers move to my hair. "We have time."

I pull her forward, taste her sweet mouth and her tongue, and a single thought lands and sticks for those long, forever seconds: I want to make her life better by being the best thing in it.

Partial transcript of interview with James McCann, July 14

Officer Martin: What was the nature of your relationship with Ms. Duncan?

James McCann: The nature?

Officer Martin: Yes. Of your relationship.

JM: With Carey? We were coworkers.

Officer Martin: Solely colleagues?

JM: I mean, in a situation like ours, you get closer, you know?

Officer Martin: Can you elaborate?

JM: It was just us on the road with the Tripps. And Joe. Sort of. Carey and I got close. She really put up with a lot from Melissa and had for a number of years. She never had anyone who understood what she dealt with, and then I came along, and I understood. I think that was really good for her. And me. It was good for me, too. I grew to really—sorry. This isn't about me and Carey. I mean—okay, yes, there were romantic feelings but—how is this relevant to your investigation?

Officer Martin: I'm just trying to understand the dynamics at play here and how they may have contributed to what happened.

JM: But it's clear what happened, right? I mean, we've all told you.

Officer Martin: Mr. McCann, it helps me to know all the facts going into this investigation. Who was close to whom? What your employers knew, what they didn't know. This kind of thing.

JM: Okay, well. Carey and I got close. I mean, we . . . [gestures vaguely]. A couple of times. Technically three times.

Officer Martin: To clarify, you were sexually intimate with Carey Duncan?

JM: Yes. But things with us aren't the same anymore. I made some mistakes with her, as far as disclosing certain information is concerned.

Officer Martin: And what information would this be?

JM: Ted Cox and I had a deal that if the Netflix show was picked up for a second season, he would give me an executive producing credit and the job of lead engineer.

Officer Martin: And was Ms. Duncan given a similar deal?

[Note: The subject didn't answer]

Officer Martin: Mr. McCann? Was Ms. Duncan offered a similar deal if the show was continued for a second season?

JM: Not to my knowledge. [long pause] It was my hope that—I don't really know what to say. It was complicated.

Officer Martin: Complicated how?

JM: Complicated because my résumé was in the trash, and Carey was in an impossible situation and suddenly I had the chance to help her get out of it but it would mean blowing everything up. I wasn't sure I was prepared to do that.

Officer Martin: Mr. McCann, you don't need to be defensive. No one is accusing you of anything here.

JM: Okay, but I can assure you that Carey and I being sexually intimate had no effect on the incident. None at all. What are you writing down?

Carey

It doesn't happen often, but I do have occasional moments of brilliance. Like taking first place in the seventh grade spelling bee. The final word was *rhythm*. I turned bright red, but spelled it correctly not because I'd been studying for days like I told my mom, but because I'd been babysitting for a neighbor the night before and read their 1972 edition of *The Joy of Sex* cover to cover. Twice.

Another would be not giving Rusty and Melly the Wi-Fi password in Laramie until the last possible second. Their usual cabin—where Melly collected river rock for wall pieces—doesn't have Internet or cell service at all. I knew that as soon as we turned down that wooded drive and Melly saw she had zero signal, she'd assume we'd have no Wi-Fi here, either.

See? Brilliant.

But my plan could only work for so long. Eventually I had to relent so we could plug in and collectively stress over the premiere of *Home Sweet Home* together.

On the night of the premiere, the tension in the house feels like a low electrical hum. I'm on my way to make sure Melly and Rusty are both mentally prepared for tonight but am instead lured to the kitchen by the smell of garlic and onion sautéing in butter, of something chocolate baking in the oven. I find an aproned James at the stove, a kitchen towel over his shoulder and a wooden spoon in his hand.

The sight catches me beneath my heart, near my lungs, sending me into a tight, breathless spiral of imagining this moment in a different context, somewhere far away from this cabin. I stare at the broad line of his shoulders, the way his T-shirt stretches across his back and tapers down to a trim waist, a fantastic ass—

Wait. I lean against the counter, and he glances over at me, raises a questioning brow.

"Are you actually wearing a T-shirt, James McCann?"

"Always so obsessed with my clothes." He grins and turns back to his cooking.

"There's definitely a joke in there about being more obsessed with you *out* of them." Uneasily, I look around the kitchen and out into the living room. "Where are the prisoners?"

He reaches for a pair of tongs. "They were driving me nuts, so I told them to find something to do."

I gape at him. "And they listened?"

"I think they can only be obstinate for the sake of being obstinate for so long before even they have to find some way to fill their time."

"Do I ask or want plausible deniability here . . . ?"

James smiles down at the stove, sliding some chopped tomatoes from a cutting board into the pan. He adds some browned ground turkey to the mix. It smells incredible. "They're outside. Rusty found some woodworking stuff in one of the sheds and needed help dragging it out. I told him I could help or I could make dinner—wisely, he chose dinner. And since he didn't dare ask you—"

"*No*," I say. "You mean—?"

Amused, he lifts his chin toward the window, and I follow his gaze. Rusty and Melly are arguing over the top of a dirty old table saw they must have brought outside, a serpent of extension cords coiled on the ground at their feet. Melly is in one of her velvet sweat suits, her bright blond hair piled in a bun on top of her head. Instead of heels, she's in a rare pair of sneakers and looks almost comically small next to her giant of a husband.

"Should we be concerned?" I ask, watching as Melly throws something across the table. "Aren't there like, power tools and rusty nails out there? Aren't you worried someone might use an ax?"

He considers this before pulling down plates from the cupboard. "Worst-case scenario: Someone dies. Easiest to explain is that they were maimed during a tragic woodworking accident that cut short some quality couple time. As far as I'm concerned, either of those options can only improve their image at this point. At least there aren't any witnesses here to tweet it."

With Melly and Rusty occupied, I do what I've wanted to since walking into the kitchen. Pushing off the counter,

I step up behind him, resting my cheek between his shoulders and wrapping my arms around his waist. He makes a low, vibrating sound of contentment, and places his hand over mine to keep me there.

"This is nice, isn't it?" he says, and I nod against him, breathing him in and letting myself enjoy every second. I've never really let myself want someone this way. Never let them know the parts of me that I spend so much time hating or trying to hide. It's nice to just be me. Everything lately feels so hard, but being with James isn't.

When he laughs, I feel it move through him in a deep rumble. "They look like a couple of actors in a really weird silent movie."

I hook my chin over his shoulder to look outside again. It's really just an excuse to get closer. He's right. We can see them shouting but can't hear anything they say. It's oddly relieving.

Rusty has a set of safety goggles sitting atop his head. Melly is holding a giant hammer, waving it in the air. I'm not sure if I'm more worried she'll hurt herself or him with it, but I find I have very little energy to go out there and intervene.

With a click of the stove, James shuts off a burner and lifts a pot from the back, full of noodles, transferring it to a colander in the sink. My grip around his waist is clearly making it harder for him to maneuver around the kitchen, but I don't want to let go until I have to.

"Dinner's ready." With one hand keeping me close, he smiles at me over his shoulder. "Should we tell them they're allowed to come back inside?"

I groan into his shirt. "Do we have to?"

"We don't *have* to do anything," he says, and turns in my arms. "They don't know it, but that door is locked, so . . ."

I only mean to kiss him once, but the crazy thing about not being able to kiss when and where you want is that you never get used to it. Each kiss feels like something we're stealing.

I've been naked with James, had sex half-clothed with James, but the feeling of his hands on my hips and his fingers grazing that tiny slice of skin at my waist sends electricity from my chest to my toes and everywhere in between. *I don't want this to end*, I think. I feel like I don't know what to do with my job or anything else in my life, but I know he's the most sarcastic, funny, thoughtful man I've ever met, and I want him. I know that much.

He moves to kiss my cheek and my jaw, then sucks at the spot just below my ear. It sends another jolt of awareness up my spine and tingles along my scalp.

"As much as I want to keep doing this," he says, the backs of his fingers sliding along my skin to my ribs and just below my breasts, "the show is going live in fifteen minutes. Once we get through this, we'll get numbers from Ted and know if season two is a go. After that, we can head home, and I can take you to my bed without anyone walking in to say a single fucking thing."

My heart pounds in my chest as I consider my options: a quickie in the kitchen pantry, or being thoroughly ravaged in James's bed. "Okay. I'll try to be patient."

He grins, kissing me once more. "Is everything ready to go?"

It takes a moment for my brain to come completely back online, but I eventually get there. The show. "Yeah," I say, taking a step away for a little breathing room. "I've got the router booted up and the big TV connected, and my phone is logged in to Skype so I can hear Ted and Robyn yell at me rather than just read it."

I watch as he walks over to the refrigerator and pulls out a green salad.

"Can I say how much I love that you made dinner and *I* hooked up the electronics?" I ask.

"Sometimes we have to play to our strengths." He sets the bowl on the counter. "Do you want to call the kids and tell them dinner is ready or should I?"

I grin at him as I move to open the door. "Do you want the real answer or the nice one?"

But I never get that far. Rusty and Melly are already walking toward the house, sweaty and grumpy and elbowing each other off the path as they walk. My first instinct is to tell them to knock it off, but then Melly meets my eyes and I don't have to say anything; she knows. It's show time.

❀❀❀

It turns out that James would make one hell of a stay-at-home spouse. I say that with only the utmost respect because 1) I would not, and 2) a single bite of the dinner he made and I'm ready to marry him.

By six o'clock the food is out, Melly hasn't looked away from her phone since I gave her the Wi-Fi password, and the Netflix logo fills the screen.

With Rusty already two beers deep in the La-Z-Boy, and

Melly sitting ramrod straight at the edge of the sofa, James and I hover toward the back of the room. A vibrating, anticipatory silence fills the space and then their new upbeat theme music bursts free, opening credits run, and glossy, bright images of Rusty and Melly flutter happily across the seventy-five-inch TV.

We all hold our breaths.

But the editing is brilliant. It's so surreal to see this thing that we worked so hard for come to life. The premiere episode is with the Larsen family, and even knowing what was going on behind the scenes, I'm still genuinely impressed. The camera follows Melly and Erin Larsen into the Larsens' former dining room, and over cups of tea Melly asks all the right questions and listens attentively to the answers. Erin grew up an army brat who never lived in the same place for more than a few years. Now an adult with children of her own, Erin knows they've outgrown the small two-bedroom house but doesn't want to leave. From there, we watch Melly present a design plan (which I drew up), and Rusty and the crew begin putting it all together.

And then the renovations start. This is exactly what Melly and Rusty do best: Melly appears to hunt for one-of-a-kind antiques that can be repurposed for unique design in the home. Rusty appears to dive into the carpentry and cuts himself within the first five minutes. Suddenly, Melly is there with the Band-Aids and a long-suffering sigh that dissolves into laughter, and you can't help but like them.

"I really loved the way you did the girls' rooms," James whispers.

"Thanks," I say with a smile. "I'd have liked a little more time, but I'm really happy with the way it came out." He lifts a brow, and I explain, "Most of the furniture was built custom to fit the space, so I had to sketch it all. Takes me a little longer some days."

"I was thinking about that. What if I could come up with something to help? Something you'd wear, with a place for your fingers to slip through like a glove, and a mechanism for the pencil? That way you can focus on the movements themselves, rather than having to think so much about the grip." He pulls a folded piece of paper from his wallet, opens it, and lays it flat for me to see.

It's a rough sketch of what he's just described, with all sorts of equations and notes written to the side. "It would be more complicated than this," he adds, reaching up to scratch the back of his neck. "I'd need to account for different weights—like whether it's a stylus you're using or a piece of charcoal, or whatever, and be able to make adjustments—but it's doable."

I blink at him, stunned into silence.

"Could something like that work?" he starts, and begins folding it back up. "We don't—"

I put my hand on his arm to stop him. "Yes, the idea makes sense. I can see how it might work." I bite the inside of my cheek to contain my smile, and feel the tight burn across the surface of my eyes, the rare sensation of tears forming. I wish we were anywhere but here, somewhere I could really thank him. "I—"

My phone vibrates on the table, and I have to restrain myself from throwing it through the TV. It's from Robyn.

Check twitter

Home Sweet Home is trending at #6!

I open the app and swipe to the trending tab and we're not at number six, we're at number two.

"You're trending," I say, and turn to look at Melly where she's now pacing the front of the room, her phone to her ear.

"We're what?" she asks.

I turn my phone to show her and she rounds the couch. "Hashtag Home Sweet Home is at number two in the US!"

Melly drops into one of the chairs. "I can't believe it."

I scroll through both their accounts. Even the tweets that aren't pure unadulterated love are resigned haters. "Look for yourself."

@melissaEllenTripp @The_Rusty_Tripp The show is amazing! Congrats you two! #HomeSweetHome

@melissaEllenTripp melly you are so cute! I need to know where you got the jacket in episode 4! #HomeSweetHome

@melissaEllenTripp @The_Rusty_Tripp I cant with this show. DO ME NEXT #HomeSweetHome

I can't believe these assholes own my Netflix queue AGAIN. When will I be free?? @melissaEllenTripp @The_Rusty_Tripp #HomeSweetHome

Melly scrolls through the tweets. "I was so worried they'd hate it."

"How can you even say that?" I say. "You guys killed it. This is what you do! You listened to what they wanted and made sure that's what they got. That was you. There are a hundred other decorating shows out there, but all of those?" I point to my phone. "Those guys are there for you."

Melly gives me a teary smile and then looks over at her husband. "Did you hear that?" she asks him. "*We* did that."

Rusty rubs a giant hand over his face and puts the footrest down on the recliner. "I need another beer," he says, and walks into the kitchen.

Unfazed, Melly hands me my phone. "I need to call Ted," she says. "Thank you, Carey."

She walks away, phone already up to her ear again. Next to me, James leans forward. "That was really nice of you."

"I didn't say anything that isn't true." I shrug, absently checking my phone when it vibrates again. "Melly is great on camera and with the clients. It's everywhere else that she's a mess."

We sit down on the love seat and let the next few episodes play, continuing to get updates from Robyn.

ET tweet!

Hypable is livetweeting!

EW has their first article up. They love

The FugGirls are watching and tweeting about Melissa's hair!

FYI I agree with them. She does look like a Walmart Reese Witherspoon

Carey, make an appt to get that fixed

People, Just Jared, and Pop Sugar tweeted about the show!

By episode six, I'm full as a tick and already regret the three pieces of cake I wolfed down. Stress eating is not my friend. It's also not escaped my notice that Rusty—back in the La-Z-Boy—is being very quiet, and James seems to be growing more restless with every episode.

"Can I get you anything?" he asks me, standing from the love seat.

"No, thanks," I say, then look closer. "Hey, you okay? It's going great. I have a good feeling."

He runs a hand through his hair. "Yeah, of course."

"Okay." I watch him disappear into the kitchen.

"We're the top trend!" Melly shouts, dropping into James's vacant seat. "Take that, Joanna Gaines."

My phone, Melly's phone, Rusty's phone, and I'm assuming James's phone by the way he rushes out of the kitchen, vibrate at once. Nobody dares to breathe.

The offer for a second season is in. It's official, we're a hit.

If I were an outsider looking in, I'd find the mixture of reactions hilarious. Melly jumps off the couch, screaming with joy. She bends to kiss her husband and immediately Skypes Robyn for details. James practically sags with exhausted relief before looking directly at me with an intensity that reads both *I'm so relieved I could cry* and *I'm gonna sex you so hard* later. Honestly, I love both translations. Rusty doesn't even look at his phone and, with a sigh, flips down the footrest of the recliner again and stands.

"I'm gonna go for a walk," he says.

"Okay. Just—" I pause because what do you say to a six-foot-four adult man? *Be careful?* "Stay close, okay? It'll be dark soon."

"Yes, Mom," he says, and disappears into the kitchen again.

"I can't believe we did it," I say. "Holy shit." I turn to James, surprised to find him already next to me.

"Yeah, holy shit," he says, and then he's kissing me, right here in the middle of the giant family room, with Melly just next door. He's kissing me like he might never kiss me again. And then he stops.

"We need to decide what we're going to do."

"Do about what?" I ask, momentarily confused.

"The show." He cups my face, smiling as he kisses me again. "Listen. I want you to have all the information before—"

His attention is suddenly snagged away, eyes searching the windows.

"James?"

"Wait—shh. Do you hear that?"

I turn my head where he's looking and strain to make out exactly what that sound is. "I think it's a car?"

It takes all of two seconds for both of us to realize what that means. We run to the kitchen and out the back door, feet pounding on the ground to the other side of the house. The car is gone, and so is Rusty.

Thirty minutes. It takes thirty minutes to find a cab, and another forty to get to the nearest bar. Neon signs cover most of the small windows, and a tiny marquee that simply reads HOTSY TOTSY hangs above the door.

It's dark inside, but I'm glad. The cramped space smells like stale beer, dusty peanut shells, and cigarettes. I would not want to know what this place looks like when brightly lit. The bottoms of my shoes stick to the linoleum as we make our way across the room and spot Rusty surrounded by a few men playing pool.

"This doesn't seem so bad," I say. "A little depressing, but he looks okay. Maybe he just needed to blow off some steam. Rusty's a happy drunk. He hugs everyone, promises to help them redo their roofs, then is down for the count."

James seems to consider this. "Okay, new plan. We'll let him get shitfaced, steal the keys, and then roll him back to the car. I'm worried he'd be more trouble if we try to get him to leave."

James takes my hand and tugs me toward the bar.

"This looks exactly like the kind of place my dad used

to hang out," I say, sliding onto a stool and waving to the bartender. I motion to a giant mounted fish hanging above shelves of colored liquor bottles. "I think we had that fish in our basement."

James gives the fish an appraising look as he sits down next to me but still doesn't let go of my hand. Instead he tugs it into his lap, toying absently with my fingers. "My dad was more of a beer-on-the-patio guy. I know," he says, waving away my laughter. "He also wears socks with his sandals, so you should know what the future holds."

The future?

James clears his throat as the bartender stops in front of us, and we each order a drink, thanking him when he steps away.

The silence is heavy for a moment, and just when I think he's going to let it go, he speaks. "Actually, no." He spins on his barstool to face me. "There are enough people dicking us around. I don't want to do that. I think you were right before: we should talk about what it will be like back home."

"Okay . . ." I say, waiting for him to elaborate.

"I don't want this to end."

I suck in a breath. The music playing seems to pulse and fade with my racing heartbeat.

"I don't want it to, either." I swear I have never smiled this much in my entire life. Is this what love feels like? Like your chest is a hot air balloon, and you have to just hold on and go where it takes you?

"Good." A grin spreads across his face. "I'm glad we're on the same page."

The bartender sets our drinks down on the coasters in front of us.

"But I know who you are." We both whip around at the sound of a woman's raised voice near the back of the bar. "I literally just watched you on TV. You're married to the designer. The blond one!"

Rusty drops onto a stool, a tumbler of clear liquid and ice cubes in one hand and a pool cue in the other.

"The designer." Rusty snorts. "Let me tell you a little story. Melissa Tripp couldn't design her own pizza, let alone an entire house."

Oh *shit*.

"Oh shit," James says aloud, launching out of his seat to intervene. With a sigh, I toss back my drink before reluctantly getting up to follow. I do not get paid enough for this.

"What? I love her stuff!" the woman responds. "You were on that other show, too. The one with Miss America."

"Stephanie?" Rusty asks, and my stomach drops.

A crusty-bearded man on the barstool near Rusty joins the conversation with a leer. "Heard she was your girlfriend."

Rusty nods. "I've had more sex with Stephanie Flores in the last six months than I've had with my wife in the last six years. He'll tell you," Rusty adds, pointing to James.

By now people have started paying attention. I catch a couple in a booth listening intently. I see someone else with their phone out.

"Why don't we get you out of here?" I ask, voice low.

"It's been a big day." James lays a hand on Rusty's back to encourage him to stand.

Rusty shrugs him away. "I can't do it, Jimmy. I won't. Did

you read Robyn's text? Another season? Another season of watching Carey do all the work and Melly take credit for it? Of playing the bumbling sidekick to the woman I married?" His eyes meet mine and his are watery, desperate. "They're going to want another book, you know. Another tour, and another show, and the lie will never end."

"Rusty—" James starts.

"I can't even remember the last piece of furniture I built. The last reno Melly actually had something to do with. We had a store and a life, and I was happy with it. I'm done, James." He looks around at the bar full of customers who have now gone completely silent to watch him in shock. Rusty tilts his tumbler to his lips and drains the drink before telling the room, "I'm done, y'all, and I'm sorry, but I don't care anymore. I don't care who the fuck knows."

James

It's a surprise to all of us, I'm sure, when I step over to Rusty and lift him from his barstool and shove him from behind until we are out on the sidewalk squinting in the bright Wyoming sunset. It takes my eyes a few seconds to adapt to the change in light, and it takes my brain a bit longer to realize what I've managed to do: lift a man who easily has fifty pounds on me, bodily escort him from a bar, and pickpocket his keys without him even knowing. I'm not typically a very physically forceful person, but panic makes us do weird things, I guess.

Carey trips after us, eyes wide and breath coming out in these short, squeaky bursts. She gapes at Rusty. "What the hell was that? Do you realize people in there were getting all of that on video?"

If he could produce a yawn right now it wouldn't render his expression more disinterested. "I'm over it," he says simply.

"*Rusty*," Carey says, with as much calm as she can muster, "you don't get to just be over it. You do get that, right?"

His gaze swims as he looks from her to me and then

back again. "Why aren't you two together? But not just together, like *together*," he slurs. "Did Melly tell you not to?"

Carey looks at me in abject horror, and I groan, officially done with this conversation. "Come on, Russ, you can't ask us shit like that. We're your employees."

"Well, if that's the only problem, then you're both fired." He turns to James, but a hiccup interrupts his laugh. "I'll be damned if my wife is going to keep you from getting laid, too." He pauses, scoffing at our stiff silence. "Oh, please. I see the way you two look at each other."

Carey visibly shudders. "Rusty, oh my God please don't talk about this."

With a deep breath, I walk over to the car at the curb, open the door, and shove Rusty into the back seat. I meet Carey's eyes and tilt my head for her to get in. "Let's go."

It's a quiet drive back to the cabin, but I'm sure none of our thoughts are quiet. We're in Laramie, and most people here seem to want to mind their own business, but this could still be bad. I try to remember how many camera phones I saw aimed at Rusty; there had to be at least three. And a couple of people in the booths toward the back were more than likely able to hear him ranting—they could easily have posted his diatribe to Twitter, Reddit, anywhere.

Although I'm glad that the truth about Carey's skills will get out there, I'm not sure this is the way it should have happened.

"We should call Robyn," Carey says quietly.

Rusty makes a drunken sound of protest, but Carey

turns and glares at him so effectively that he immediately lowers his voice to under-his-breath muttering.

"Yeah," I agree. "Call her."

Carey holds the phone to her ear, curling low so she can hear the call over Rusty's back-seat babble. "Hi, Robyn?" she says. "Yeah, it's Carey. Look. I need you to do a social media check. We just picked up Rusty from a bar where he was—"

"Telling the truth!" Rusty shouts, and Carey shoos at him.

"—going on a bit of a rant," she says delicately. "There were some folks there who got video, and I'm sure at least one person in the bar got on— Yeah. Yes." She stares straight ahead, glum. "We *were* there. He snuck out of the house after hearing about the numbers."

"Because my wife is a bitch," he spits.

"You're not exactly a great catch yourself, asshole," Carey says, and I stare at her for a beat before turning my eyes back to the road. Warpath Carey is a novel delight.

"Okay," she says, returning to the call. "Yes, I think that's a good idea." Her voice gets heated. "Yeah, no. I get that you've sent us on this impossible mission—believe me, I'm aware what has been asked of us, Robyn—but I'm not owning this one. Melly and Rusty are making their own mess right now."

She ends the call without saying goodbye, and I give her a few seconds of deep breathing before asking, "So, what'd she say?"

I glance over at her, catching the tightness in her jaw, the tendons rising in her neck. "She said there are some tweets, but she is going to contact the user to get them taken down. She said she's coming out here tonight."

In the back, Rusty groans irritably. I'm not Robyn's biggest fan, either, but I'm glad she's coming to take care of this. Let someone else babysit.

"She started to tell me she was disappointed in us," Carey says, "but I'm sorry, I'm *not* having that." Her hand shakes as she lifts it to tuck her hair behind her ear, and she lowers it, slipping it under her thigh. "I'm not fucking having this anymore."

❖❖❖

Any hope we have that Robyn quickly contained the Twitter problem, or that Melissa had logged off and decided to enjoy the rest of her night unplugged, is shattered when we pull down the long gravelly driveway and see Melissa taking the front steps two at a time. She marches over, already pointing and yelling at Rusty before he can even get the door open.

"What were you thinking?" she screams.

Without a word, he walks right past her and into the house. She follows, calling his name, and—with some trepidation—Carey and I step in behind them.

To no one's surprise, Rusty is already heading to the bar cart to make himself a cocktail.

"Russ," Melissa says, attempting calm. "Did you really go to a bar and start telling everyone that Carey does all my work?"

He burps into his fist, then gives a rumbling "Yup."

Melissa picks up a glass from a side table and takes

a long drink. If I didn't know better, I would think there was booze in there from the way she inhales, trying to draw strength from the liquid. She sets it down carefully. "Why—*why* would you do that?"

"Because it's true."

Melissa's face turns a bright, terrifying red. "It is *not* true."

Rusty bursts out laughing.

I can feel my mouth pulling back in the *Yiiiikes* face, and beside me, Carey shifts awkwardly, waiting for Melissa to blow. I think Rusty is going to continue to give these short, off-the-cuff answers, but instead of pouring the scotch he's holding into a tumbler, he recorks the bottle and sets it down again. "Isn't it time we stop lying to each other?" he asks with sudden, calm clarity.

"What on earth are you talking about?"

"For the past—how long now? Five years? Carey does all the design work, and everyone else gets credit." He takes a step closer to Melissa. "We go on TV and talk about all of our ideas, but they aren't even ours anymore."

"Russell, that isn't true," Melissa says, glancing at me, voice thin and tight. I wonder how this conversation would be going down if I weren't here. Would Melissa admit to what he's saying? Is her denial a show for me?

"Sure it is," Rusty says. "I used to build things based on my own designs—they were basic, but they were solid. And then she came along and I was building things based on *her* designs." He pauses, staring at his wife like he's waiting for her to say something. But she just stands there, red-faced, shaking. "Never yours, Melly. It wasn't even like you pretended to be doing them. Why didn't we ever talk about this?" He reaches up, rubs his forehead like he's coming out of a fugue.

Melissa looks so angry she can't speak.

"I didn't mind," he admits, "because at least I was still building. Maybe we were stealing her ideas, but at least I was having fun."

Wow. I glance over at Carey and see that her discomfort over this conversation has started to shift into fury. She extends and curls her trembling fingers in front of her, and then wraps one hand around the other fist. I move closer to her and brush the back of her hand with mine, offering. She takes it, squeezing tightly; her tremors shake her hand in my grip.

"But now," Rusty says, gesturing to Carey, "she's still doing it all, and we're just pretending. We're not even sleeping in the same room. I flirted with Stephanie for months, and you had no idea because you were so damn busy with the show and the endorsements and writing a book on *marriage*, of all things." He laughs. "I let things go too far, but I just wanted you to *notice* me."

I want to point out that this seems like a very strange time for him to be drawing the line on all of this, but I think it's probably better for me to keep my mouth firmly shut.

Melissa shifts on her feet, looking at me and then back to her husband. "We're in a rough spot, but that doesn't mean we're over, Russ. Every marriage—"

Rusty cuts her off with a deafening bellow: "Have you been listening to me, Melly? It's too late. *I. Want. A. Fucking. Divorce.*"

I don't have a good handle on Melissa or her reactions, but I think it surprises everyone when she lets out a simple, quiet "No."

"Honey," Rusty says, in the most sugary, condescending voice possible, "it ain't up to you."

"*Enough*," Carey says with tight, quiet rage. She looks at Melissa, at Rusty, and then shouts, "Can you even hear yourselves? How is this my job?" She looks at me, eyes on fire. "How are they okay having this kind of conversation in front of us?"

I give her a helpless shrug. "No idea."

"Carey, honey—" Melissa begins, but Carey cuts her off.

"What happened to the down-to-earth couple I met?" she asks. "What happened to the two people who worked hard for a living, personally greeted everyone who came into their store, and took pride in their business?" She looks at them, but they only stare back; I'm sure neither of them has ever heard Carey speak this forcefully and they aren't quite sure how to handle her. If I hadn't had sex with the woman, I might be surprised, too, by this display of fire, but instead I'm just standing here holding her hand and feeling proud as hell.

"Rusty, you're wrong," Carey says. "Melly used to do her own work." He starts to protest, but she shushes him. "She did. She decorated. It's not the same, but she did. She loved putting together a room with your pieces, and you know it. Don't trivialize that."

Melissa starts to say something victorious, but Carey interrupts her again. "No, wait. I'm not done." Carey turns to her. "Yes, you used to decorate, but you never designed, and you know it. You know I came in and designed the daybed and the coffee table. You know I designed the collapsible stairs, and the desks, and the tables, and everything else that came after it. You know the entire *Small Spaces* book is my work. You *know* it's always been me, and you were happy to let the world think it was you, that paying me a lot of money meant that your conscience could be clear, but it's not true. You took advantage of my need for insurance, for a job. You took advantage of my insecurity about growing up poor and not going to college or being good enough. You know you've been doing this, Melly, and it's terrible."

Melissa stares at Carey, and the color slowly drains from her face.

Rusty leans his arm against the fireplace mantel and reaches for a poker to stab at the burning logs. Carey walks over, takes the poker from his drunk hand, and gently shoves him away from the fire. "Russ, go sit down." She sounds so tired.

"You quitting?" he asks, obstinately leaning an elbow against the mantel.

Carey nods. "Yeah. I'm quitting."

Rusty lets out a long, slow whistle. "Isn't that something? All this work. We get a TV show, we get books." He points at me. "He gets a big promotion, and you end up quitting."

My stomach drops out, and a hush falls over the room. Slowly, Carey's eyes move from Rusty—who looks only now like he's said something wrong—and then over to me. "A promotion?"

In all honesty, I haven't thought about the promotion in hours and was going to tell her as soon as we got back home. What had once been the most important part of my life—the trajectory of my career—has slid down the ladder of priorities. I open my mouth to tell Carey that I'll explain it later, but Rusty speaks first.

"Ted told me," Rusty says, grimacing in my direction. There's guilt in his expression, but if I'm not mistaken, I catch a subtly evil gleam in his eye, too. Maybe if he can't get his way, no one can. The good ol' boy has a darkness.

"What are you talking about?" Carey asks.

"Jimmy here negotiated an executive producer credit and the title of lead engineer if we made it to season two."

"You didn't tell me that," Carey says to me quietly.

Russell reaches up, picking at his teeth. "I figured you knew. What with you two being so close."

I open my mouth and close it. I don't want to lie to Carey and tell her that it wasn't a big deal, and telling her that I tried to bring it up earlier just feels like a cop-out. My mistake feels so obvious. "Shit—Carey. This isn't how I want to have this conversation. I wasn't trying to keep it from you. When Ted called—"

"In *San Francisco*?" she says, floored. "The morning—?" Her eyes fill as she puts the timeline together. The morning after we had sex.

I nod again. "I was about to throw in the towel," I tell her. "I wanted you to quit, too, but—"

Melissa cuts in. "*Excuse* me?"

Both Carey and I give her "Shut up, Melly" in unison.

"But you didn't want to," I remind Carey. "You weren't

sure you were ready. When Ted called, I had it in my head that you weren't going to leave, that Melly wasn't going to be cool with us being together, and so when Ted offered it, it was the way that I came to terms with staying to help you with them but getting something out of it, too. We made a deal and then when I got back to the hotel, you'd started to change your mind but I'd already made a commitment."

"You didn't tell me," she says again, and the simplicity of that betrayal feels totally gutting. "You should have told me. I tell you everything and you—what? Did you think I wouldn't understand? I would have been happy for you. It would have made sense why you did a one-eighty and told me to stay. If you'd have just let me in on it, I would have understood."

This feels like a punch to the gut. She did tell me everything; I've become her person, her safe space, and I kept this from her. Why did I do that? She's been quietly doing all the work for a decade, and after one grueling week, I get the promotion of a lifetime and she gets nothing.

"Is there anyone in this house who isn't out to ruin me?"

We all turn to look at Melly when she shrieks this. With wild, furious eyes, she stares at each of us in turn before tilting her head back and letting out a scream so feral and enraged it sounds like it tears up her throat.

"Melly," Carey says with trembling incredulity, "did we dare forget for two minutes that everything is about you?"

"Rusty's asking for a divorce," Melly yells back at her. "You're quitting just like he's been trying to get you to do since you started fucking and—what? I'm the only one who cares about the business anymore?"

Rusty wipes a slow hand down his face and looks at me. "I need the keys, Jimbo."

"Not happening, Russ."

He shrugs and turns to leave the room. There's movement in my peripheral vision, but Carey must comprehend what's happening before I do because she's moving with lightning speed to try to stop Melissa's glass just as it leaves her hand to go hurtling toward Rusty and the roaring fireplace. Rusty ducks in shock, and the heavy crystal tumbler jets past him, barely missing his temple and crashing with a frighteningly shrill blast against the stone hearth.

We gape in the echoing silence, stunned by the violence of it. The glass would have knocked him unconscious, at best, but as close as Melissa is to him? It could just as easily have killed him. For a few tense moments, Rusty just stares at her.

And in those seconds, I watch his heart finally break.

An odd whoosh, like a gust of wind, passes through the room. Carey and I look at each other, some shared instinct making us suspicious. With a start, Rusty stumbles back and we all look down at his muttered "*Holy shit*"—the carpet at his feet is on fire, flames licking at the hem of his jeans.

"Rusty!" I yell, shoving him.

Cursing in shock, he falls back onto the silver bar cart, which topples over. Rusty scrambles quickly away as crystal decanters of alcohol crash to the floor. After an eerie beat of silence, the fire turns from a small trail of flames into a blinding explosion bursting from the fireplace.

Without thinking, I tackle Carey, rolling us to the side.

A huge crash booms, and then we hear the rising hiss of the fire coming to life behind us, fed by a river of strong spirits and a room full of wood and fabric. A chair is on fire . . . *on fire* . . . flames grow instantly, licking higher beside us. I drag Carey over to the wall, clutching her as we take it in, trying to piece together what the hell we're supposed to do now.

Melissa is screaming, and Rusty is throwing ice and yelling, and I realize that Melissa's glass was full of booze, for once in her goddamn life it had to be *only* booze, but I can't think about any of it because the rug is burning now, the couch, the fire is tearing through the room almost like it's been waiting to climb out of the fireplace and take over this house for decades.

The room is a square, and we are on the far side, away from the exit, where we could dart into the hallway toward the entryway or the kitchen. Carey and I scramble along the walls, crouch-walking to stay low. The entire time she is whispering "Oh my God. Oh my God" in this high, terrified voice and I want to tell her that everything is going to be fine, that I'm sorry, that we'll fix this and make it better for her but the only thing we need to do right now is *not die*. In the middle of the room, the flames are giddily swallowing every bit of furniture and fabric, and just to the side, near the windows, Rusty and Melissa are still ineffectually trying to put the fire out with the ice bucket, with bottles of soda. It's a delusion; this fire is too big.

I yell at them to go call 911 and get the hell out of there.

Reaching the door to the hallway, Carey and I stand and make a run toward the kitchen. Rusty is already there, shouting the address into the phone, and then he drops the receiver. It slams against the wall and hangs there, swinging limply. He meets my eyes; his are wide and terrified. Without saying a word, Rusty sprints out the back door, saving himself.

"Melly!" Carey shouts, pulling her shirt up over her mouth before turning back toward the living room. Even in crisis, even after everything that happened back there, she's still taking care of Melissa.

I follow, calling for her, but the house is filling with smoke and soon all I can hear is Carey shouting Melly's name. Through the fog, I see their two figures come together, and behind them, the fire seems to barrel closer in a wave. Without thinking, I run back to the kitchen, grabbing the fire extinguisher and returning to spray with minimal efficacy at the wall of fire closing in on the foyer and climbing the log walls. But it's enough to give us time to break free from the heavy fog. Carey grabs Melissa and pulls the front door open, letting in a burst of cold fresh air that is immediately swallowed by the smoke. Ducking, I follow them out into the clear, darkening sky.

The lawn is wet and chilly; it's such a stark contrast to the inferno inside that for a minute, it seems impossible that I haven't imagined all of it: the fight, the crash of a glass, the explosion of flames. But we turn and look: the living room burns brightly, lighting up the house in a display of sparks and fire now greedily lapping at the connected garage, the huge covered porch, the second story. Against the backdrop of stars, the blaze is strangely beautiful.

The four of us stand, not touching, staring at the disaster of it. I imagine after escaping a fire, some people might huddle together, might hold each other for comfort. I feel the distance between the four of us in the cold air against my arms. We all feel like strangers to each other in the sharp, quiet tension.

When I look at Carey, she doesn't look back at me, even though I know she can feel the heat of my attention. *I love you*, I think. *I'm sorry*. But I'm sure the only thing she's thinking is: *What happens next?* The growing flames are reflected in her eyes, and when she looks over at the Tripps, they fill with tears.

Melissa nearly killed Rusty but instead, she set what has to be at least a ten-million-dollar house on fire. Their careers are ruined, their marriage is over, but the only person I care about is Carey. I don't want her career to be over before it's even started. It wasn't just Melissa and Rusty who built this empire, it was Carey, too, and I know what it's like to be attached to a scandal like this. She's watching her life's work vanish, the Comb+Honey reputation going up in flames, and—after tonight—probably feeling like there's truly never been anyone in her corner. Regret is a tight, aching ball in my chest. I fucked up. We all fucked up so big, and I'm in love with her. The weight of guilt presses down so heavily that I find it hard to breathe.

PEOPLE MAGAZINE EXCLUSIVE

Melissa Tripp Is Ready to Pass the Torch

Melissa Tripp knew that her life was becoming overloaded, but she never expected to find herself standing in front of a burning house on the night of her show premiere, with very little memory of what happened.

The 44-year-old *New Spaces* star and bestselling author opens up to PEOPLE about getting sober after the fire, finding a new place for herself outside of the home renovation world, and realizing she "had to take responsibility for where I was, and what my life had become."

"Rusty has made mistakes—and he owns those," the petite blonde says, looking even smaller where she is engulfed in the pillows of a white couch in the Jackson Hole home she shares with her husband of more than 25 years, Russell Tripp, 45. "But my mistakes, although maybe harder to see with the naked eye, are just as numerous—if not more so.

"Our business took off, and I got real intense," she says, laughing, and her native Tennessee accent curls around her words. "Anyone who knows me can easily imagine it. Russ isn't an intense guy. He wants a simple life, with a solid marriage. He never wanted this wife in stilettos, dragging fancy suitcases around on a book tour. He wants a hammer in his hand, a Rockies cap on his head, and a wife teasing him and loving him in equal measure. I lost track of the girl he fell in love with somewhere. I need to remember who she is."

Tripp acknowledges that the marriage, once believed from the outside to be perfect, is as real and flawed as any other. "We're working through a lot, but I hope we'll make it out the other side intact."

These real flaws, she insists, are why she and Russell were the perfect people to write their recent #1 *New York Times* bestseller, an ironically timed book on marital advice entitled *New Life, Old Love*. "You don't want to hear advice from someone who's never been through it. Russ and I have been through it, and through it . . . and through it," she says with a laugh. "We don't get to choose when things fall apart. If we did, we sure would have chosen a different week."

The home décor guru, recently out of a three-week hospital stay for what her publicist describes as "debilitating stress," says she sees life with much clearer eyes now. "When you work so hard to get to the top, the only thing that starts to matter is staying there. You stop seeing your loved ones as loved ones. They become either leverage or barriers, and to me there stopped being anything in between."

Tripp plans to detail what she calls her "total breakdown" in an upcoming memoir. Writing, she tells PEOPLE, "has become my safe space. Putting words down—my words, just mine—has become the only creative place inside my head I can still trust myself to go."

To fans of her signature décor, the idea that Melissa Tripp is throwing in the towel on the home renovation game may come as a shock. But Tripp encourages everyone to rest easy, saying, "There will always be brilliant, creative women rising to the top in this world. There will be the next Melly Tripp any day now. It just can't be me anymore. Trying to be that person every day was eating me alive."

In fact, the next creative genius rising to the top may very well be someone close to the Tripps. In a jaw-dropping revelation, Melissa admitted recently to *Entertainment Weekly* that the Comb+Honey creative inspiration these past few years came more and more from her gifted assistant, Carey Duncan, 26, who worked tirelessly behind the scenes of *New Spaces* as well as the single-season ratings darling *Home Sweet Home.*

"Carey has been with Russ and me since the beginning," Tripp tells PEOPLE. "She only ever worked for us. When things got busier, I didn't have as much time for the designing aspect of the business, and Carey easily stepped in. But because [Duncan] is a beautiful artist and designer in her own right, her aesthetic became a huge part of the brand, and it grew more and more difficult to figure out where her ideas ended and mine began. That worked fine for a while, but at some point we all registered that Carey wasn't getting creative credit for the work she was doing."

Melissa becomes emotional when she discusses her relationship with Duncan, who Tripp says is "more daughter than employee," and admits the two "talk almost every day, trying to work through what happened, who we are, and what her future can and should be. She needs to get out into the world and find herself, and I want to be the loudest voice in the stands, cheering her on.

"Life went from calm to chaos so fast. I think none of us fully realized what her contribution had become." Melissa Tripp wipes a tear away and nods, resolute. "I had my turn. Now I want the entire world for Carey."

Carey

"She didn't come out and say it was all you from the start," Kurt says, reading over my shoulder.

I close the magazine and tuck it under a stack of papers on the kitchen counter so that Melly's photo—soft makeup, contrite smile, down-home plaid flannel—doesn't just sit there, making me wonder how much of that was real and how much was Melly being a brilliant, calculating businesswoman. My throat feels tight, like something is lodged there high up, making it hard to breathe or swallow.

I realize the situation was totally messed up, but even after everything, I didn't think I would take Melly's disgrace quite this hard.

"This is enough," I tell him. Frankly, she gave me more credit than I ever let myself imagine. "This is good."

Now I want the entire world for Carey.

Whether she means it or not, the words are there in stark black and white. The baton, being so cleanly passed, makes me feel both empowered and overwhelmed. On the one hand, I could call Ted, send him some of my sketches, and see if he knows anyone who wants to see this particular phoenix rising from these ashes. But on the other hand, although I love designing, I don't want to be the next Melissa Tripp. Of all of us, Melly was the only one who ever wanted the world. The rest of us just want our small share of contentment.

And I'm slowly working on mine. It's been six weeks since the fire, and my life doesn't look anything like it did that night.

For one, I got the hell out of Wyoming for a while: the first thing I did when the police dismissed me was take my own trip to Hawaii . . . the following day. I left the police station, took a cab to a hotel in Laramie, booked my trip, and then slept for almost fifteen hours straight. When I woke up, I had four missed calls from James, two from Melly, and one from Rusty. I sent Melly a text letting her know I would send a formal resignation soon, and then left for the airport.

Five days and four nights in Kauai, and after arriving and sleeping for ten solid hours, I had no idea what to do with myself. I only read half a book. I took a lot of naps. I went for long walks, and then came back to the resort and was generally bored out of my mind. I realized I have no idea how to unwind because I hadn't had two consecutive days off in a decade.

You'd think with all that time on my hands, I'd spend some of it thinking about Melly and Rusty. You'd assume I'd take some time to process everything that happened with James. But it was like a brick wall went up, and every time I tried to bring forward the chaos of the previous week, some protective instinct would kick in and I'd literally fall asleep.

On the chaise by the pool. In the chair on my balcony. Once even at the table in the hotel restaurant.

When I got home, I immediately wanted to turn around and head back to the airport. I didn't know if I was stressed about returning to Jackson, stressed because the emotional untangling was still ahead of me, or stressed about facing the blank page of my professional future, but all of those thoughts made me want to vomit. I upped my therapy schedule to twice a week.

Debbie told me to make a list of all the things I want—to focus on making plans rather than beating myself up about the past—and to start finding a way to make each of them happen. Some would be easier than others, she said. Some would take more time. The goal, of course, is to just keep working on making my life what I want it to be.

So, a week later, with a "bonus" from my work on *New Spaces*, I bought a house.

It's better than anything I ever pictured myself living in, let alone owning—a beautiful wooden three-bedroom house in Alpine, just outside Jackson. It has green shutters, a sharp A-frame structure, and a long gravel driveway off a small country road. My closest neighbor is a quarter mile away. Out back there's a wide porch, and a creek big enough to swim in is only fifty feet down a steep grade. I love it more than I think I've ever loved anything in my life.

Debbie did her best to congratulate my impulsive purchase and not look like she was questioning every bit of advice she'd ever given.

Contentment comes in a trickle, though. It's like a faucet dripping; slowly, my bucket is filling. I talk about Melly and Rusty a lot in therapy. I've started a tradition of Sunday dinners with Kurt, Peyton, and Annabeth. Sometimes Rand comes, if he can peel his backside from the bar and come drink beer at my house instead. Sometimes Kurt's best friend, Mike, comes, too. I'm no James in the kitchen: I make spaghetti or tacos, and no one ever complains that we eat my shitty cooking on folding chairs in an empty dining room. The irony of my life at the moment is my complete inability to decorate my own home.

I've met with a financial planner who told me I have enough saved for private insurance premiums and treatment and can take a year to figure things out and still be fine. I don't want to take a year to figure things out, but I don't know what I want to do, either. I'm slowly building those personal connections I've been missing—and although I don't want to date Mike like I think Kurt hopes I will, I can actually imagine a life where dating would be possible. Meaning, I have time to myself. Turns out I like to sleep in, stay up late, exercise midday, and sketch over my morning coffee. Turns out my hands do much better on this schedule, too.

But every time I start to think about a career, I get that drowning feeling of stress rising inside my chest, so I push it aside. My first instinct is to call James to talk it out, but for obvious reasons I haven't. Instead, I call Kurt, or Peyton, or Annabeth, and we go for a hike, or they come over and we sit on the floor in my living room and do nothing but look out at the view of the thick, craggy trees and jagged mountains.

I might not be ready to think about work, but after three

weeks of doubled-up sessions with Debbie, I sure think about James all the time. I think about his voice, and the way his eyes clocked nearly every one of my movements—with interest and, later, adoration. I think about his ambition and his brain and wonder what he's doing now that Comb+Honey has effectively dissolved. I think about how easy he was to talk to, and how I wish I had that with someone else.

Sometimes I think maybe I'll find it if I just keep looking, but part of me knows that what we had was a once-in-a-lifetime thing and I'm lucky to have had it at all. I think about his laugh, and his sounds, and yeah, I think a lot about his body, especially at night. But I also think about what happened at the very end, what sort of bullshit nontrust we had if he could listen to all of my truths but couldn't tell me that he'd found a stairway to the top and was happy to leave me on the ground floor.

He left the police station at some point that day, I'm sure, but I don't know if it was before or after me, because I didn't see him after my interview. I didn't see any of them. No one was charged with a crime. I assume the Tripps paid for the enormous damages the fire had caused, and the whole thing was swept under the rug.

By now, my brother correctly interprets my lost-in-space expression. "Is James coming tonight?"

I stall. "What?"

Kurt looks across the dining room. Though I have them over regularly, I'm attempting an actual cocktail party and have managed quite a spread: cheese plates, veggie trays, and assorted drinks. They're arranged on the lone piece of furniture there—an enormous handmade table delivered by Rusty himself two days ago. He brought it to the door unannounced, with two burly examples of Wyoming's finest behind him holding the mammoth piece. There was a novel's worth of words to share—about the fire, how were they doing, was Melly really searching for the girl she used to be, were they staying married—but our interaction was characteristically simple:

"Hey, Russ."

"Hey, kiddo."

They set the table by the giant window in the dining room, the one that overlooks the downslope of a hill carpeted in green conifers. With a kiss to my forehead and a simple "Been thinkin' 'bout you," he left, and my heart seemed too big for my body.

The walnut gleams in the late-afternoon sun; the top is the most beautiful cross-section of wood I've ever seen, with vibrant striations in golds, reds, and deep browns. I was with him when he found it at a lumberyard in Casper, nearly five years ago. I remember standing there with him, staring at the slab of lumber, wondering if we were trying to create the same thing in our head—a piece worthy of it.

He's had so many chances to transform it into something breathtaking for the entire world to see on television, but that's Rusty, I guess: waiting for the perfect reason to use it. Never rushing and never caring about impressing anyone. Because I know he used to love to hide messages, I knew to look: on the underside, the words *We love you, Carey-girl* are inscribed in Rusty's unmistakable carving style.

Kurt rephrases the question to bring my attention back: "Was James invited?"

"No—what? *No*." I chew my lip, ignoring my brother's

pressing gaze. I'd much rather let my mind wander than discuss the party I somehow decided I was ready to host.

I've planned a lot of cocktail hours. You'd think I'd have this down to a science, but my stomach is a rolling boil of nerves. I wonder if it's a good sign that my first reaction to the thought of having James here is a pulse of relief because I know he would step up without question and help. But the truth is . . . "I'm not even sure he's around here anymore."

With these words, my relief is doused with a flush of dread. What if I'm right? After all this work I've done to process things in sessions with Debbie, have I missed the real window to talk to James about what happened?

I think my brother might be setting up to drop some wisdom, but he just lets out a "Huh," scratches his belly, and heads to the kitchen.

Peyton and Annabeth arrive at six exactly—I get the feeling they were sitting in their car, excitedly waiting for the hour to turn over. *I'm a lucky woman*, I think. Then immediately: *At twenty-six, that might be the first time I thought of myself as a woman.*

Annabeth bursts inside, pulling me into a hug. Peyton waits a few beats for Annabeth to let go and finally just makes do with putting her arms around both of us. I notice they've brought gifts: flowers, a set of wineglasses, and a tablecloth—none of which they bothered to wrap. And now I feel both lucky and tragic, because my two friends just saw me two days ago and here they are, embracing me with a tight, lingering warmth that tells me they weren't sure I'd ever be in my own place, throwing a party.

"Okay, everyone," I say into Annabeth's shoulder, "I'm getting the sense that you were starting to worry about me."

With a laugh that doesn't dispute this, they step back and look around expectantly. I'm grateful they don't point out that I have made very little progress on the décor, even for the sake of a party.

Kurt emerges from the kitchen and hands them their preferred drinks: a gin and tonic for Peyton, and a pilsner for Annabeth. With mumbled thanks, they each take a sip and silence swallows us.

For a tiny beat, I miss Melly's exuberant hostessing skills.

"It occurs to me that I have more liquor bottles than furniture," I say to no one in particular.

"And you're not even really a drinker," Peyton says.

"You'd think for someone with a design background, decorating your own house would be the fun part." Annabeth looks at me. "And yet."

"And yet," I agree.

"Why do I get the sense that you're dreading it?"

I shrug, even though the answer isn't really a mystery. "I only ever had a bedroom to furnish and was never there to enjoy it anyway. This feels . . . bigger."

"It is big, but it's so bright," Peyton says. "This would be my dream home."

Because I don't want to start the party off with an admission that, until recently, I didn't really have dreams of my own, I say, "I have to figure out what's next, I guess.

Design-wise. Life-wise." I move closer to the window and feel them follow. The four of us look out over the steep grade of the mountain. I love the craggy rocks and the way the trees struggle up through the unforgiving earth. There's something creative in there, pushing itself into formation; the rich woods and modern lines that used to inspire me no longer get my brain buzzing. But these rocks do.

"Do I want it to look the way all my stuff has looked for the past ten years?" I ask the view. "Or is there a new style waiting to come out of my brain?"

"In case anyone is wondering," Kurt says pointedly to my friends, "James isn't coming."

I turn to stare at him. "Well, that was random. Thanks."

Annabeth's dark eyes turn to me. "You didn't invite James?"

"I don't even know if he's around anymore," I say.

"He is." Peyton sips her drink.

I gape at her. "How do you know that?"

"Saw him," she says. Her casual shrug is totally maddening.

"How do you even know what he looks like?"

"Adorable lanky guy wearing glasses and a tailored suit? Yeah, he's pretty easy to spot around here."

I wait for more, but it's like maneuvering a boulder up a hill with these assholes. "*Where* did you see him?"

She swallows another sip. "Grocery store."

Their silence is the stony judgment of Mount Rushmore, and their faces are the expression equivalent of *whistling innocently*. I have no trouble at all imagining James doing his grocery shopping in a suit.

My pulse picks up, heavy and annoyed in my throat. "Why would I invite him?" I ask.

Peyton and Annabeth exchange a look with Kurt, who just shrugs and tilts his beer to his lips. I want to punch him for the first time since I was thirteen.

"Seriously, tell me why I should have invited him."

"Because you like him." Kurt's voice echoes inside the bottle.

"I liked him, yeah." I look between the three of them. "But did y'all miss the part where he—"

"Where he fucked up and tried to explain to you what happened, and you wouldn't answer his calls?" Kurt asks, meeting my eyes.

"Oh, I'm sorry," I say sharply, "is my newfound self-preservation making you uncomfortable?"

He looks immediately remorseful. "I didn't mean it like that. I just mean you gave Melly a decade of bad behavior, and I hear you talking to her almost every day, but James doesn't even get a text message?"

This feels like a shove, and I know he can tell because his face does that pinched thing he does when he's trying to look casual, like he's squinting out to the horizon, but the horizon here is the bare living room wall five feet away, and there's nothing there to study.

"You think I should have invited James?" I ask quietly.

I get three *Yeah*s in unison.

I feel a little like the way I used to when I'd dump out a bin full of Lincoln Logs, both overwhelmed and excited—except this is my life, with all these pieces to choose from, and I'm not sure what shape I even want to build.

"Okay, well, I didn't." I turn back from the window and point to the spread of food on the other side of the room. "Eat something and stop judging me."

This party already sucks and it just started. Maybe some music will help.

My stereo sits in the dining room on a low, plain coffee table I found at a yard sale. I've taken two steps toward it when the doorbell rings.

"Someone go let Mike in," I say. "I'm gonna put on some music."

"I'll pick the music," Annabeth says, jogging over. "You go get the door."

I stare at her for a beat, on the verge of asking what the hell is up with all of them, but Kurt raises his beer across the room, eyebrows up like, *Go*.

"It's Mike, Kurt. He can let himself in."

He throws the next words at me with a grin. "Or, maybe it's James."

"Why on earth would it be—"

"Because Peyton invited him," Annabeth says, and chases this bombshell with an evil giggle.

My stomach falls, and I look over at Peyton. "You didn't."

This makes my jerk friend laugh. "No, *you* didn't." She lifts her chin to the door. "But I sure as hell did."

My feet are bricks. It takes me a week to get to the door, and another two days to open it.

The sun is behind him, casting his long shadow across the tiles of my entryway. Because he's backlit, I can't see his face. But then he shifts, blocking the sun from my face, and comes into focus. Glasses. No dress shirt here; a T-shirt stretches across his chest. Jeans hang low on his hips. My eyes sink lower. Sneakers.

"Hi," he says, and I realize how long I just spent taking him in.

"Hi," I say.

He blinks, looking at my mouth for only a second, but the movement is obvious enough to give me the idea, too. And then I'm staring—at that full bottom lip, the one I want to pull into my own mouth and suck on like candy.

"Your place is really nice," the mouth says. "At least from the outside."

I pull my attention back to his eyes. "Do you want to come in?"

He's holding a bouquet of irises. "Sure."

I stand back, letting him walk in ahead of me. Conveniently, everyone else has disappeared into the kitchen. I'm sure James can hear their excited whispering, too.

"Wow," he says, taking it all in, but only for a few seconds before his eyes are back on me. "These are for you."

He presses the flowers into my palm, and then holds on for a couple of seconds, squeezing. He's so warm. His hand falls back to his side, and he looks around again. Good thing, too, because it means he won't see the goose bumps all down my arms.

"You actually bought a house," he says, eyebrows raised.

"It was a weird day," I admit. "I jogged past it, called the Realtor, and then just made an offer on the spot."

"Wow," he says again, and I can't really blame him because I'm not sure what else he can say, other than *Have you completely lost your mind?* My answer would be *Maybe*. But having him here gives me the sense of my feet gently hitting the ground.

"It's empty," I say self-consciously.

"Still figuring it out?"

"Yeah." I hear how emotion pushes its way into the single word, making it wobble. His was a simple question, but filled with enormous understanding. Classic James. "Taking some time."

He nods and sinks one of those perfect teeth into his lip, biting back a smile.

"Actually," I say, "I made a list."

"A list?" James leaves the rest unsaid: *After working for Melly, how can you ever want to see a list again?*

"I made it in therapy. It's for me. It's a good list."

And his expression clears in understanding. He knows I've been seeing Debbie for a while now, but I wonder how the reminder feels here, knowing that I've been talking it all out with someone else while he's gotten nothing but silence. "It's a list of the things I want my life to have."

His eyebrows remain raised in interest, so I barrel on. "A house, believe it or not, seemed the easiest to obtain."

I can tell he doesn't like this answer. "What else was on it?"

I dodge this one. "What are you up to?"

He shrugs, sliding a hand into the front pocket of his jeans. The waistband dips, exposing a brief flash of skin, and it makes my mouth water. "Rusty got me connected to a few guys down at city hall."

"In Jackson?"

James nods.

"In civic engineering?"

He nods again, blinks to my mouth, and quickly looks away.

I want to feel the sweet warmth of his hands on me. I want to admit to him that at the top of my list was a relationship that felt like the perfect combination of safe haven and dirty fun.

"Do you like it?" I ask when he seems unable to produce words on his own.

"It's okay. It's not the most exciting job, but I guess I'm still figuring things out, too." A beat of quiet and then, "I wasn't ready to leave town yet."

"Jackson is growing on you, then?" I grin.

"I guess." He pauses, taking a deep, shaky breath. "I think it's more that I love you, and I don't want to be far away from where you are."

The floor falls away. Voices in the kitchen peter out to nothing.

It takes enormous effort to swallow before asking, "What?"

James shifts on his feet, unsure. "Do you need me to say it again, or are you just surprised?"

"Both," I croak.

This makes him smile. "Okay, well, I'll say it again then: I wasn't ready to give up on this. When it came to finding another job, I wanted something local. Rusty helped." He takes a step closer. "Is that okay?"

I'm staring at his mouth again. I nod, stunned by how fast this is happening, how easy it still is.

Slowly, he bends, and his smile comes closer to mine. "You don't mind that I'm still in Jackson?"

I shake my head. "The other thing you said, though . . ."

He laughs, and his warm breath touches my mouth. "Oh, the 'I love you' part?"

"Yeah. That part."

"You like that part?"

A wave of longing fills me, so gigantic that I feel dizzy again. "Yes."

The smile disappears and his lips part, mesmerizing. "Carey?"

"Yes?"

"I'm sorry I didn't tell you about the deal I had with Ted."

I blink back into focus, remembering that, no matter how edible his lips look, this issue is still a barricade to tasting them. It *is* moving too fast. "Yeah, that wasn't great."

Kurt was right: I did forgive Melly over and over. But I'm trying to take better care of myself now.

James straightens. "It sounds like an excuse, but I do want you to know that I'd always planned to tell you. I advocated for you with him, too."

"But how weird is that?" I ask. "That I'm there for a decade, you're there for two months and can put in a good word for me with Ted? It doesn't just feel sexist and classist, it reminds me how small Melly kept me all those years. And you went and did the same thing."

I see the impact of my words, because his shoulders pitch forward, chest shifts back, like he's been physically pushed. "Yeah. I know." He takes a few deep breaths to put himself together and finally takes another determined step closer. He's only inches away from me again. Kissing distance. When he reaches down, the warmth of his hand engulfs mine.

"It's no excuse, but I was desperate and caught off guard when he called," he says. "You'd disappeared from my bed, then essentially told me we were over. I know we were both in self-preservation mode—the whole situation was a mess." He absently massages my fingers when he feels them begin to cramp. "But I regret how I handled it. And, for what it's worth, I think you're brilliant. I don't care if you want to stay in this town the rest of your life. I don't care what you decide you want to do. The only thing that matters to me is that I have a chance with you."

My stupid attention has snagged on those stupid lips again.

"Carey?" the lips say. They go still, and then they twist into a tiny, knowing smile, and James waits until I look up again. "Do I have a chance with you?"

Ideally I'd make him work a little more for it. Realistically, I give him the most unequivocal nod of my lifetime.

He lets out a relieved laugh. "Holy shit, can I kiss you now?"

I don't answer aloud. Instead I stretch, sliding a hand around the back of his neck, pulling him down to me. Beneath my palm, his skin is warm. When his smile touches mine, it's achingly sweet, but for only a breath, because relief is a consuming thing, and mine sends me down this razor-sharp line between sobbing that I nearly lost him and crying out in joy that he's here.

To think I forgot the precise feel of this, the perfect mechanics of his kiss. The memories I cherished were such a sad, pale rendering of the reality. He's so assured this way, pulling me tight to him, bending to come back to me from a better angle, right here in the foyer of my new house.

My hand holding the bouquet clenches tight and, in a stiff spasm, releases. The irises tumble to the floor and for a second I dread that it's going to break the moment—that he'll bend to pick them up and suggest we find somewhere to put them. Then we'd be interrupted by introductions and having to carry on with this totally lame party I've planned. But James just smiles at me and kisses me again. We both know I'll be dropping things for the rest of my life, and those flowers are just fine where they are.

"I love you, too," I say.

This yanks a surprised breath from him and he pulls me into a hug, spreading a big hand across the back of my head and one across my lower back, and he just holds me there for not nearly long enough. A week like this would barely suffice.

But we only get a few more minutes because then Peyton is there picking up the bouquet, and Annabeth takes it to put the flowers in water, and Kurt is awkwardly clearing his throat because no one likes to catch their sibling in a sexy embrace.

Introductions are made, Annabeth returns, and Kurt tries to make himself taller as he inspects James. I guess he approves, because he offers to grab him a drink from the kitchen; I want to burst out laughing at Kurt's expression when James asks for a glass of wine.

But the party isn't so terrible, I guess. Conversation

takes off. James is a goddamn charmer and apparently his sister, Jenn, is a former college softball superstar, so Peyton immediately loves him. Kurt hands him the wine and gives me a look that says, *If you say so*. I give him a look that says, *In fact, I do say so, you cretin.*

In the midst of all the softball talk and James winning over everyone but Kurt, Mike steps into the house and hands me a six-pack of Coors before groaning out loud.

"When the hell are you going to get some furniture, Carey?"

"When I fucking feel like it, Mikey."

He grins and then looks over my shoulder. Long arms slide around my waist from behind, and James rests his chin on the crown of my head. Sweetly claiming.

"This is James," I tell Mike.

He reaches to shake one of James's outstretched hands. "Hey, James. Mike." He gives me an approving little smile. "I've heard a lot about you."

I scowl at him. "You have not."

"There are volumes in silence, Carey. I could tell how much you liked him based on how quickly you'd change the subject every time you accidentally dropped his name."

"Well, whatever," I say. "You can be right for once. Turns out, he was higher up on the list than furniture was. So you're all going to have to deal with sitting on the floor while I cross things off one at a time, at my own pace."

James is the only one who gets it, but I can tell he likes that answer, because his kiss to my temple feels like a safe haven and his body pressed all along my back promises dirty, dirty fun.

"Speaking of lists," he says quietly, "I made one of my own, and skinny-dipping is right at the top."

I turn back to face him, grinning. "As it damn well should be."

"I might have noticed you have a creek out back." He jerks his chin toward the window. "All you need is some stairs down that steep hill."

Happiness feels like a sweet, frolicking beast inside my chest. "If only I knew someone who could build such a thing," I quietly tease.

He kisses the tip of my nose and raises a hand. "James McCann: assistant, engineer, and infatuated boyfriend, at your service."

Before I can verbalize the incoherent giddiness these words trigger, the infatuated boyfriend bends, brushing his lips against mine. He's careful not to deepen the kiss too much, but in his restraint, I sense how he wants to pull me right up against him and hold me tight.

"I'll build anything you need," he whispers, kissing my jaw. "I'd do anything for you."

What a sweet relief, because I would do anything for him, too. So this is what it feels like to be with someone who wants to give simply for the pleasure of it.

I pull James in close, holding him as tight as I think he needs, and he nearly squeezes the air out of me, letting out the happiest little groan. It is like falling onto a soft bed, the relief of being in his arms. The house seems brighter, the air inside fresher. I look over his shoulder and out the window at the view. My view. My home. My life, finally coming together by my own hands, one piece at a time.

Acknowledgments

We outlined this book together in Salt Lake City on a giant whiteboard and with about seven thousand Post-it notes. It was amazing! It was exciting! It was the best weekend ever!

Sometimes the idea is shinier than the first draft, and this was definitely the case with *The Honey-Don't List*. The idea was so clear in our heads; when we outlined, we were cracking each other up. And then we sat down to write and it was like making a huge mess in the kitchen and then pulling a very deflated cake out of the oven. It just didn't come out the way we'd imagined it.

But that's our process lately, we realized—draft fast, edit later—and after twenty-plus books together, we'd finally hit a point where we didn't panic if it wasn't perfect from the start. We dove back into edits a few times, and each time the book got a little closer to the one you're holding right now. By the time we handed in the copy edits to our editor, we had made the book everything we wanted it to be when we sat in Christina's kitchen, surrounded by a rainbow of Post-its.

The bottom line is that we are lucky to do this together, and have created a friendship and partnership that is truly meaningful, both creatively and personally. We love working together, we love that we get to do this career as a team, and we love you all for picking up and reading our books.

We also love our agent, Holly Root. Quite frankly, anyone who's ever met Holly knows she is the most *together* person in publishing. So wise, so calm, so supportive, and such a badass.

We love, too, our editor, Kate Dresser, who sees the deflated cake come into her inbox and says, "I see what ingredient you left out!" . . . and then finds five hundred more ingredients we left out in the first draft. Sometimes the book she gets probably feels more like a bowl of batter than a fully baked cake, but with her big, amazing brain, we're able to draw out every flavor we'd planned. And then our brilliant and adorable PR rep Kristin Dwyer comes in and makes everyone taste the cake and shout publicly that it is tHe bEsT cAKe EvER!!

Are we diving too deep into this baking metaphor? Perhaps.

Moving on.

Did you know that dystonia is a very real and—in this case—very personal motor disorder? My (Lauren's) family has an as-yet unidentified genetic variant of this disease, which is one that affects the central nervous system, specifically the parts of the brain that control movement. While my father eventually succumbed to secondary effects of dystonia, my sister is living quite capably and with only minor symptoms thanks to regular botulinum toxin treatment of her oromandibular dystonia. Many readers may not realize that Botox isn't just for wrinkles; in fact, a majority of Botox use is for the treatment of movement disorders—such as dystonia—but also spasticity caused by multiple sclerosis, stroke, and various other neurological conditions. An organization that works tirelessly to advocate for patients afflicted with dystonia is the Dystonia Medical Research Foundation. My family—and many others—are very grateful for their work. They can be found online at https://dystonia-foundation.org.

So an enormous debt of gratitude goes out to Erin Service, for reading this book with a particularly sensitive eye to the daily life and internal thoughts of a woman living with dystonia. Although Carey's condition presents differently than yours does, we hope you see a bit of your bright, optimistic, and brave spirit in her. Anyplace where we've messed up or been insensitive is completely on us. Thank you for always reading our books early, but especially this one.

We are very lucky to get to work with all of the spectacular people at Simon & Schuster in the Gallery Books imprint. This is the hardest-working team in book business, y'all! Thank you to Carolyn Reidy, Jen Bergstrom, Kate Dresser, Aimée Bell, Jen Long, Rachel Brenner, Molly Gregory, Abby Zidle, Anne Jaconette, Anabel Jimenez, Sally Marvin, Mackenzie Hickey, Lisa Litwack, John Vairo, the entire Gallery sales force and subrights groups—we adore you all!

Thank you to every bookseller who hands our book to a new or longtime romance fan. Thank you to all the librarians for scraping that budget to get our books stocked—we know what a balancing act it is, and that you take it on for the sheer love of books. Thank you to the reviewers, Bookstagrammers, BookTubers, and all our loves on Twitter and Facebook—we love seeing your enthusiasm!

Thanks, Mr. and Mr. Christina Lauren, for being proud of your wives for doing the thing.

Thank you to my adorable Christina for being the *zing* in this amazing writing partnership. A decade of writing together and we're still having a hella good time! I heart you very, very much.

To my wonderful Lo, I'm writing this on your birthday (September 10! My little Ravenclaw Virgo), and I've spent a lot of time today going through photos and thinking about what a huge impact you've had on so many different parts of my life. I'm a better writer because of you, a better friend and mom and wife and person. I have no idea what I did in a past life to deserve you, but I hope I'm smart enough to do it again. I love you so much. Meet you at the Tower of Terror turnstile!

Can't get enough of
CHRISTINA LAUREN's
romances for the twenty-first century"?
"Witty and downright hilarious."
—Helen Hoang, author of The Bride Test
THE UNHONEYMOONERS
NEW YORK TIMES BESTSELLING AUTHOR OF MY FAVORITE HALF-NIGHT STAND
CHRISTINA LAUREN
my
favorite
half-night
stand
"Truly a romance for the twenty-first century."
—KIRKUS REVIEWS on DATING YOU / HATING YOU
CHRISTINA LAUREN
NEW YORK TIMES BESTSELLING AUTHOR OF ROOMIES
Josh + Hazel's Guide to Not Dating
CHRISTINA LAUREN
NEW YORK TIMES BESTSELLING AUTHOR OF ROOMIES
CHRISTINA LAUREN
NEW YORK TIMES BESTSELLING AUTHOR
Love
and
Other
Words
NEW YORK TIMES BESTSELLING AUTHOR
CHRISTINA LAUREN
ROOMIES
NEW YORK TIMES BESTSELLING AUTHOR
CHRISTINA LAUREN
DATING YOU HATING YOU
NEW YORK TIMES BESTSELLING AUTHOR
CHRISTINA LAUREN
TWICE IN A BLUE MOON
Available wherever books are sold
or at SimonandSchuster.com

GALLERY BOOKS
An Imprint of Simon & Schuster
A CBS COMPANY